**Praise for the Novels
of Lucy Finn**

If Wishing Made It So

"Lucy Finn is a delight. *If Wishing Made It So* is a charming book with a genie to die for and plenty of fun!"
—Maureen Child, author of *Bedeviled*

"A wonderful cast of interesting and colorful characters make this a fast-moving and fun-to-read adventure.... The ending is very entertaining and satisfying."
—*Romantic Times* (4 stars)

"[A] delightful, absolutely funny story...loved this book!" —The Romance Readers Connection

"An adventure brimming with nonstop action and the magic of discovering true love.... This fast-moving read has danger, humor, and a fairy-tale romance that's sure to entertain." —Darque Reviews

Careful What You Wish For

"Finn displays promise and personality to spare in her debut novel.... Fans of high concept, multilayered fantasy romance populated with quirky, comical characters will find this novel a charmer and Finn an author worth watching." —*Publishers Weekly*

continued ...

Also by Lucy Finn

Careful What You Wish For
If Wishing Made It So

Best Wishes Always

Lucy Finn

A SIGNET ECLIPSE BOOK

SIGNET ECLIPSE
Published by New American Library, a division of
Penguin Group (USA) Inc., 375 Hudson Street,
New York, New York 10014, USA
Penguin Group (Canada), 90 Eglinton Avenue East, Suite 700, Toronto,
Ontario M4P 2Y3, Canada (a division of Pearson Penguin Canada Inc.)
Penguin Books Ltd., 80 Strand, London WC2R 0RL, England
Penguin Ireland, 25 St. Stephen's Green, Dublin 2,
Ireland (a division of Penguin Books Ltd.)
Penguin Group (Australia), 250 Camberwell Road, Camberwell, Victoria 3124,
Australia (a division of Pearson Australia Group Pty. Ltd.)
Penguin Books India Pvt. Ltd., 11 Community Centre, Panchsheel Park,
New Delhi - 110 017, India
Penguin Group (NZ), 67 Apollo Drive, Rosedale, North Shore 0632,
New Zealand (a division of Pearson New Zealand Ltd.)
Penguin Books (South Africa) (Pty.) Ltd., 24 Sturdee Avenue,
Rosebank, Johannesburg 2196, South Africa

Penguin Books Ltd., Registered Offices:
80 Strand, London WC2R 0RL, England

First published by Signet Eclipse, an imprint of New American Library,
a division of Penguin Group (USA) Inc.

First Printing, July 2009
10   9   8   7   6   5   4   3   2   1

Copyright © Charlee Trantino, 2009
All rights reserved

SIGNET ECLIPSE and logo are trademarks of Penguin Group (USA) Inc.

Printed in the United States of America

PUBLISHER'S NOTE
This is a work of fiction. Names, characters, places, and incidents either are the
product of the author's imagination or are used fictitiously, and any resemblance
to actual persons, living or dead, business establishments, events, or locales is
entirely coincidental.
   The recipe contained in this book is to be followed exactly as written. The
publisher is not responsible for your specific health or allergy needs that may
require medical supervision. The publisher is not responsible for any adverse
reactions to the recipe contained in this book.
   The publisher does not have any control over and does not assume any responsibility for author or third-party Web sites or their content.

To Heather Lloyd
and
In memory of Melanie McMaster

Chapter 1

"Why is that girl wearing two wristwatches?"

Larissa Smith, called Larrie by her friends, overheard the words whispered somewhere to her left. Her body tensed. She halted midstep. A feeling of total devastation engulfed her, draining the blood from her face and giving her a ghostlike, haunted appearance. The black abyss that had threatened to swallow her for the past year cracked open inside her.

"What's the clunky one on her right wrist? A man's watch? It's *so* unattractive." The twentysomething who was speaking had a nose that was turned up so far, it was a wonder she didn't drown when it rained.

Larrie whipped her head in the direction of the voice. She opened her pale lips to speak—but her mother's fingers gripped her upper arm and propelled her forward. "Ignore that little twit," her mother hissed as she escorted Larrie through the open door of the Amore Italian Restaurant in downtown Pittston, where her cousin's bridal shower was about to start.

Larrie hadn't wanted to come here at all. When the invitations had arrived a month earlier, her mother had telephoned and gently suggested they go. "It's time you get back into the world," she said.

"I am in the world—every damned day," Larrie

snapped into the phone. "It's not the world I want, but I'm sure as hell here."

"You know what I mean, sweetheart," her mother sighed. "You're clinging to the past."

"I am not clinging; I'm exercising a preference. And I'm not going to the shower. End of story." Larrie's voice sounded harsh and shrill. Its abrasiveness almost covered up the quiver that with the slightest loosening of control would morph into a sob.

"I see." Her mother hesitated a moment, then continued. "You know, Larrie, I was in the attic this morning, opening the windows up there, like I do every year once the warm weather is here. I spotted that photo album—you know, the blue one with all your baby pictures in it? Do you remember the cute photo of you sitting naked on the potty seat? You were such a chubby child, but we thought fat babies meant healthy babies back then." She made a noise that sounded like a stifled laugh. "Do you remember the one where you grabbed Zell Shelby around the neck to kiss him and he's screaming his head off? I think I'll just take them along to the bridal shower to show everyone."

"That's blackmail, Mother." The snapshot of Larrie on the potty—her face beet red and her eyes squeezed shut—left nothing to the imagination. It should have been ripped into a thousand pieces years ago. And the one with Zell Shelby! He had grown up to have the worst case of acne and the biggest beer belly in the county. Plus, the man lived in his bib overalls and smelled of cow manure. Mortification flooded Larrie at the thought of her toddler crush.

When her mother spoke again, she said exactly what Larrie didn't want to hear. "Ryan is gone, sweetheart. But you're still here. Life is for the living. He wouldn't want you to be sitting home alone."

Larrie's eyes, light gray like silver moons, flashed with

anger. "I am *not* alone. Aunt Lolly lives in the apartment over the garage, just two hundred feet away. And Ticky Blackstone shows up every weekday to work for eight hours, even when I wish he wouldn't, because he drives me crazy. And—and I have my animals . . ." Her voice trailed away.

"You know what I mean."

Larrie did know. In truth she was alone, a SWWC, single woman with cat (along with three dogs and an occasional rescued wild creature). In the end she had agreed to go to Mackenzie Buffalino's bridal shower. Her mother's threats hadn't been the deciding factor. No one had ever made Larrie do anything she chose not to do. She had ventured forth because her head knew what her heart didn't want to admit.

The turning point happened a few days after the phone call. Her friend Melanie O'Casey had dropped by. She had walked into the house without knocking, the same way she had since Larrie and she had been ten years old, and followed Larrie's voice into the kitchen.

Larrie was rattling on merrily as if talking with a child. "What's the matter with you, little guy? Why so glum today? Dust on your nose? Oh, you don't want to sit on the counter? You're afraid of getting knocked off. I don't blame you a bit. Where do you want to go?"

"Who's that you're talking to, Larrie?" Melanie looked around the huge farm kitchen with its beamed ceiling and slate floor. A perplexed look came over her round face. She and Larrie were the only people in the room.

Color crept up Larrie's neck and turned her cheeks rosy. "Just thinking out loud," she muttered. In truth, she had been having a conversation with a vintage Metlox Teddy Bear cookie jar. The ceramic brown bear wearing a blue sweater had been designed by Helen McIntosh, a Disney artist, and was Metlox's oldest character. To Larrie, this Teddy Bear, with his cocked head, cute turtleneck sweater, and cookie in hand, had the kindest eyes and sweetest smile of them all. The little animal almost seemed alive to Larrie, but it was just a cookie jar, after all.

Talking to an inanimate object can't be healthy, she thought later, especially since it had seemed perfectly normal while she was doing it. She realized that as the months passed she had been withdrawing into a world confined to her loving pets and her antiques business. Lately, the antiques had become not just her business but a way to escape to a less painful world, one that seemed simpler and safer than the present, filled with wonderful objects from long ago like Teddy Bear cookie jars.

But getting lost in the past had blurred the line between fantasy and reality for Larrie. Surrounded by furniture and household goods from a century ago, Larrie could almost believe she was living at the beginning of the 1900s—not now, not here, not in this world of loss and sorrow. And she had begun to enjoy that illusion, perhaps too much.

Then came the cookie jar epiphany. With a knifelike pain that drove the air from her lungs, Larrie realized that if she were to remain sane and whole, she had to accept living in the present and go on without Ryan. It was symbolic, perhaps, to declare this to herself and the outside world by attending a bridal shower. Her own shower, at a halcyon time when she never guessed she could be anything but happy, had been the harbinger of tragedy, not joy. Showing up at Mackenzie's big event would be like jumping into Toby's Creek, its water icy even in July.

Yet jumping into cold water, instead of wading back into life gradually, was Larrie's style: She took off running, leaping before she looked, pedal to the metal, fire the torpedoes and full speed ahead.

She had displayed the same impetuosity when it

came to love. She had loved Ryan almost at first sight and adored him with every fiber of her being. Now he was dead, killed in the Middle East, and his body lay in the cold, hard ground of Perrin's Marsh Cemetery.

His sudden death had shifted Larrie's perceptions about life like an earthquake beneath her feet. It had taught her at twenty-five what everyone learns eventually: The world is a rough antagonist that yanks you by the arms and kicks you hard in the gut. Happiness, if ever found at all, is temporary. And love? Larrie could barely breathe when she thought about what love could do to a person. It fills one's brain with marvelous dreams; then, in the space of a heartbeat, the dreams become a nightmare from which there might be no waking.

But Larrie had survived it all. With a sniff and a toss of her head, she acknowledged she had become old before her time and wise beyond her years. As the empty months after Ryan's death rolled by, her heart had turned hard, brittle, and as filled with cracks as the Depression-era crackle glass she sometimes found when she bought old "stuff." Or as her ad in the Yellow Pages read, "Sparrow's Nest Antiques and Fabulous Junque. We buy one item or many: entire estates, contents of attics and basements, anything old and interesting (no appliances, please)."

Now, on the day of Mackenzie's bridal shower, Larrie told herself she was strong enough to do this. *I can do this. I can do this. I can do this,* she silently chanted like a mantra. Nevertheless, as she walked into the banquet room of the Amore, she felt the meandering current of grief within her quicken. It leapt up, swelled in might, and crashed against the adamantine rock which was her heart.

The feelings inside that had broken jabbed her with their sharp edges. She wasn't ready for this world, and maybe she never would be. She didn't want to be here at all. Ryan's death had left her forever damaged—cracked, splintered, and irreparable.

But Larrie was determined not to fail this self-imposed test. Her backbone stiffened, her chin lifted, and her jaw tightened. Despite her misery, she wouldn't leave. And she couldn't ignore the Amore. The facility demanded attention if not admiration. It assaulted her senses from the outside while her sorrow battered her from within.

Decorated in the ornate, heavily gilded Italianate style of the wannabe *riche*, the banquet hall was lit by massive crystal chandeliers that hung from its high ceilings. Down the center of the room, two lines of white faux columns holding urns of pink roses, white calla lilies, and graceful tendrils of ivy created an aisle fit for an emperor's procession. Beyond the aisle a sea of tables spread out across the gleaming wood floor. Place cards printed on opalescent paper glowed like pearls against pink damask tablecloths. Yards of white tulle, fit for a fairy princess, draped everything else in the room.

Clearly no expense had been spared for Mackenzie's grand affair. According to Larrie's mother—who got it directly from Aunt Josie—Uncle Stash, the father of the bride, a plumbing contractor, had seen the wedding as a business investment. His only daughter had hooked the scion of a wealthy construction magnate currently building condos in the Poconos—with two and a half baths in every unit. Dollar signs should have been printed on the shower invitations instead of cooing cherubs. That the moonstruck bridegroom would also remove the high-maintenance Mackenzie from Uncle Stash's care was a signing bonus.

And there, in the center of the room, stood the princess herself. Mackenzie Buffalino was a vision of loveliness in an off-the-shoulder dress of seafoam green studded with seed pearls. Mackenzie's blond hair had been teased and moussed into an elaborate updo. Her

French-tipped nails accentuated the large diamond on the third finger of her left hand. Her shoes, her bag, the gold bangles on her slender wrist—all were perfect.

Only the expression on Mackenzie's face was not. The sharp features of the bride-to-be formed a petulant scowl. She peered through her false eyelashes like a prisoner through the bars of his cell. She glared angrily at a tight group of workmen surrounding a tall object that sat on the long table across the front of the room. Her hands went to her hips. She swiveled her head and shrieked in the direction of a woman with a large bosom and even larger hips.

"Mother! Mother! Make them do something! We're about to start!"

Turning away from the drama unfolding before her, Larrie glanced down at her own plain white slacks and red-striped sailor shirt. She felt underdressed, but she no longer had any party clothes that fit. She had lost so much weight that her prettiest dress drooped shapelessly from her bony shoulders like a hospital gown. She shrugged. What did it matter anyway?

"Looks like there's a problem with the chocolate fountain," Larrie's mother announced. "If it's a plumbing situation, they better call Stash."

"A chocolate fountain? The thing must be seven feet high." Larrie looked with renewed interest toward the front of the room, where some of the workmen now knelt on the floor. They extracted tools and hoses from a black box; then they hunkered down and squirmed their way under the table beneath the contraption.

A crowd of beautifully dressed young ladies gathered around the defunct fountain, chattering like sparrows. Just then Larrie heard a woman's voice whispering behind her.

"Do you think she cut it herself? Her long red hair was her best feature, remember?"

Another voice, arch and unkind, responded, "If she paid someone to do *that*, she better get her money back. It's hideous. She's really let herself go since . . . well, you know, since her fiancé got blown up in the war. But really, she could wear some makeup. She looks like a dried-up old spinster. I bet she's twenty-six already."

Larrie felt a lump growing in her throat. She blinked away a tear. She refused to let her emotions escape among the tulle and roses, among the hopes and dreams of a bride such as she had once hoped to be.

She fled from the cruel words, across the wide empty floor, not sure where she was going but hoping she was heading toward the ladies' room, where she could sniffle or even wail in private. Instead she found herself aimed in the direction of a middle-aged woman sitting at a table tucked away in the corner nearest the kitchen.

Shadows seemed to engulf that far side of the banquet hall where no chandeliers glittered, and no one had switched on the gold-painted wall sconces. Now, from that gloomy corner, the woman slowly raised her arm in the air and waved at Larrie to come over.

Curious, Larrie followed the beckoning arm into the darkness. When she got close, she spotted the 8½ x 11 sign, printed in reds and yellows, that was propped up on the woman's table:

THE SOUL'S JOURNEY
Madame Louisa
☯ Intuitive Interpreter of the Hands
☯ Tarot Card Reader
☯ Reiki Master

Larrie stopped abruptly. She did not need or want her fortune told. She started to turn away, not caring if she appeared rude.

"Wait!" Madame Louisa called out. "Don't go. I can help you."

Larrie turned anguished eyes toward the woman. "You can't help me," she whispered. "No one can."

"Oh, my dear, I see you've had a tragedy in your life. Sit down and let me talk with you, please." She stood and stepped around the table, revealing that her feet, much too tiny for her rotund body, were clad in white patent-leather Mary Janes.

How odd, Larrie thought, her eyes drawn to the shoes. She raised her head to look more closely at the palmist. The woman looked like an apple dumpling stuffed into a denim skirt and a bandana-print blouse. She had pink cheeks and round, dark eyes sparkling behind her spectacles. Her gray hair had been pulled into a long braid that snaked from her back over a rounded shoulder and was secured near its end with a red rubber band.

With a sweet smile, Madame Louisa urged Larrie, "Come, sit down. You're not afraid of what I might say, are you?"

Larrie's spine straightened. *Afraid?* she thought. *How can I be afraid of anything you might tell me when the worst thing that I could ever imagine has already happened?* Anger whooshed like a prairie fire through her veins. She strode to the chair across from Madame Louisa. Her chin jutted out in defiance. "I don't believe in fortune-telling."

Madame Louisa continued to wear the beatific grin of a Buddhist holy man. "Sit, sit. I don't tell fortunes. I interpret what fate has already written on your palm. I'm sure I can reveal something you need to know." She gestured for Larrie to sit down on the chair.

Although much later Larrie couldn't have explained why she did it, she obeyed and lowered herself into the seat.

Chapter 2

"What are you doing here?" Larrie challenged the woman with the first thought that entered her mind.

Madame Louisa moved her shoulders slightly. "The bride's mother hired me to amuse the guests. My husband, a magician, will be roaming between the tables during the luncheon doing card tricks."

While she talked, the palmist reached out to take Larrie's hands. The minute their fingers touched, she jerked back as if burned and cried out. Then she stared at Larrie, her black button eyes filled with awe. "You are—I never expected—"

"What? What am I? Am I ill?" Larrie felt alarmed, wondering what the fortune-teller meant.

But Madame Louisa shook her head and left the sentence unfinished. She cleared her throat. "I merely meant you have very high energy. It's leaping from you." She reached over and determinedly grasped Larrie's hands firmly in hers. She pulled them into the center of the table. She bent over and peered closely at Larrie's open right palm.

"Look at those lines. Extraordinary. Simply extraordinary. One in a million. You feel deeply. You feel everything. You feel all the time!" Her voice crescendoed, turning louder with excitement. "Look! See this! This line . . . how fascinating. What can it mean? It's telling me—" She looked up at Larrie, her eyes narrowing in suspicion. "This can be no coincidence. Somebody sent you. Who? I want to know who!"

Annoyance flashed into Larrie's face. "Nobody! Nobody sent me! I wandered over here by accident."

The palmist made a snorting sound. "There are no accidents. Who are you? Who are you really?"

"I'm nobody! Mackenzie's cousin, that's all. I don't like this. Maybe I should go." She tried to rise, but the woman gripped her hands hard, forcing her to stay.

Madame Louisa's voice brooked no disobedience. "No, you may not leave yet. You need to hear what I must tell you. You *were* sent to me whether you know it or not, so listen to your fate."

A shiver ran through Larrie. She didn't want to hear this.

The palmist's voice softened. "Don't be frightened, Ms. Nobody. You're going to live an impossibly long time. See here. This is your life line." She pointed to a skin crease that began at the edge of Larrie's palm between her thumb and index finger and swooped down toward her wrist but abruptly turned, crossing her palm and zigzagging before disappearing around the edge of her hand.

"Very unusual. And notice this." Her finger ticked Larrie's palm. "You have a line crossing your life line. That means danger. It's followed by a star. That means a crisis. Then comes a square, which indicates protection for you at a time when needed. All this happens at the beginning of the adult years, perhaps in your midtwenties." She looked sharply at Larrie, sizing her up. "Hmmm. You're at that age now. I'd say this will happen soon. Take it as a warning."

Larrie again tried to pull her hand away. Anxiety nibbled on her nerves. She felt as if she had to escape before ... before what? Something frightening, something she didn't want to know.

But Madame Louisa held her fast. "Don't be alarmed. You will survive. You must! Remember the line that shows you will have a very long life—but not the one you planned or ... hmmm, perhaps not even this one at all." She raised her eyes and locked them on Larrie's. "Does that have meaning for you? Do you understand?"

"I have no idea what it could mean." Larrie's eyes were wide and wild. This reading wasn't what she had expected. Absent were the tired platitudes favored by the Gypsy fortune-teller at the Luzerne County Fair each September when Larrie and her girlfriends slipped into her tent on the fairway. The olive-complexioned Romany with a scarf around her forehead always told Larrie the same thing: She had money coming, she'd find love, she'd have one, two, or perhaps three children, and travel lay in her future. No, that wasn't quite right. What the Gypsy always said to her was, "You shall take a long journey."

Madame Louisa said none of those things. Instead she momentarily released Larrie's hand and positioned her own hand, palm down, about three inches above Larrie's. "Feel anything?"

Surprisingly, Larrie did. Her eyebrows arched and her head tilted. *Oh, my*, she thought. To Madame Louisa, she said, "Yes. My palm's getting very hot."

The fortune-teller's trilling laugh became a merry brook running over small stones. "You're a healer! Why aren't you healing? You have a gift. You're not using your gift."

Larrie squirmed uncomfortably. "I've never healed anyone." *I can't even heal myself*, she thought.

"Well, you should. You must. When the earth's magnetic poles shift, it's going to be terrible. Destruction. Chaos. We need healers to train now."

Oh, my, Larrie thought again and frowned. *The*

woman is truly bonkers. She twisted uneasily in the chair.

Madame Louisa didn't notice. She had lifted Larrie's hand close to her face and was staring intently into the open palm. "Something I don't understand here." She traced a line going horizontally across Larrie's palm. "You need to be with people, a very strong need, but you have chosen to be solitary."

That was true. Larrie had shunned guests and well-wishers completely once Ryan's funeral was over, once everything was over and done. Now she felt unwilling to explain and stated flatly, "I see people all the time. When I want to. I buy and sell antiques—"

"*No!*" Madame Louisa screamed, her mouth becoming a round O, her eyes even rounder. "Antiques. No. No. All wrong! You shouldn't be around them. I had to pull a soul out of a mirror last week. You are too sensitive. You'll attract a—" She stopped abruptly, then continued. "I mean, you might attract something you can't handle. Wait a moment, please."

Madame Louisa dropped one of Larrie's hands and fumbled about in a large purse that sat by her feet. Finally she came up with a business card, which she pushed toward Larrie. "I hate to bring this out. I'm not here to drum up business, but here's my phone number. You're going to need to call me."

Larrie let the card lie untouched on the table. "Thank you for the offer, but really, I can't imagine that I'd be needing you. I've never found a soul or anything at all in the furniture I've had in my shop." She hesitated, honesty being bred into her bones. "That's not quite true. I did find a hundred-dollar bill once, taped on the underside of a dresser drawer."

At that point, Larrie successfully pulled away her hand, the one still remaining in Madame Louisa's, and got ready to stand. She had been foolish to sit down here. There was nothing important for her in the strange palmist's revelations after all—not that she really thought there would be.

Madame Louisa's eyebrows knit together and her mouth hardened into a disapproving look. "Young woman, you must listen to me. Watch out for those antiques. Now, I must finish the reading." She abruptly lurched over the table and grasped both of Larrie's hands, holding her fast. A tremor laced with foreboding raced up Larrie's arms the moment Madame Louisa touched her. Larrie's heart began to race. Now she felt very afraid.

"You will learn a lesson from the past," Madame Louisa began. Then she took one of her fingers and touched the watch on Larrie's right wrist. It was Ryan's watch, of course, and Larrie always wore it. It made her feel connected to him. "You don't understand time. It doesn't merely flow forward. It is not a river. It is not true that one cannot dip one's foot into the same water twice. You will learn that time is a great wheel, a circle, turning, turning. Do you understand?"

Larrie's chin sank toward her chest. Tears blurred her vision. She shook her head back and forth. She didn't understand at all. She had to accept the truth: The past was gone. She couldn't live in it. She couldn't get it back. She couldn't get Ryan back. Madame Louisa's calling attention to his watch had again churned up the deep well of grief inside her. The pain was unbearable. She wanted to go home, crawl into bed, and cry herself to sleep.

"Stop that!" Madame Louisa's voice broke through the fog of sadness gathering around Larrie. The palm reader gripped her hands so tightly it hurt. "Let go of your grief! You know nothing! The universe is huge, unfathomable. And love! Love is kind, love is everywhere, greater than the infinity of the cosmos, ever expanding. Listen to me, you *will* love again. And you have a gift!

You must use it. You have a fate. You must embrace it. See, it's right here." She poked her finger into the center of Larrie's hand. "You cannot escape it. It is something marvelous. Open your mind! Open your heart. It is written."

She abruptly dropped Larrie's hands. She folded her own in her lap, primly. She lifted her chin. "I have one more thing to tell you. I have a message for you. Ryan says his love will never die. But it is time for you to live."

Larrie gasped. "What did you say?"

"I said you must live."

"No! Not *you*. You said Ryan. I heard you. I did!"

Madame Louisa moved her shoulders in a dismissive way. "Did I? I don't remember saying that." She looked over toward the center of the room. "You should return to the others now. Take my card."

Preoccupied with her thoughts, hardly knowing that she did it, Larrie stood up and slid the white rectangle off the table. She put it into her pants pocket. Her heart pounded madly. Her mind raced. *The fortune-teller did say Ryan's name. I didn't imagine it. How could she know?*

In the very next moment, Larrie, terribly shaken, doubted herself and what her ears had heard. Perhaps the woman hadn't mentioned Ryan after all. Yet Larrie was so sure she had.

She scanned the room, trying to spot her mother. Feeling dazed and confused, she began to walk out of the shadowy area into the light. She had taken just a few steps when Madame Louisa called out to her.

"Remember! Beware! You must be careful around the antiques!"

Larrie didn't look back. She quickened her step, wanting to be away from the palmist and the unsettling things she had said.

Chapter 3

Larrie's mother, a not-quite-fifty, dark-haired woman named Anna Maria Smith, nodded her head as she listened to Mrs. Castellano, an elderly Italian lady, describe the details of her latest operation. To Larrie, now close enough to overhear the conversation, her mother seemed fascinated by every boring detail, and she probably was.

Larrie's mother was the kind of person who had long conversations with total strangers every time she went to Wal-Mart. She'd smile brightly at a fellow shopper pushing a nearby cart and comment on whatever jumped into her mind: "Is that thunder I can hear? Did you lose your electricity in the last storm?" "Are you thinking of buying that? I'm not meaning to butt in but the lids on those under-the-bed storage containers crack practically the first time you open them. I had to put mine back together with duct tape, you know." "Aren't these comforter and sheet sets a bargain! Even the king set is the same price!"

People answered as if they had known Larrie's mother for dogs' years. They not only answered, they told her their troubles and secrets right there in the aisle under the sign for the Smiley Face specials.

Instead of taking the risk she'd get roped into a blow-by-blow account of Mrs. Castellano's hernia repair, Larrie stopped before her mother noticed her approach. She took a deep breath. Okay, she had been a little spooked, and wasn't that just so silly? She stole a glance at the dark side of the room she had just left.

It was empty. The palmist was no longer there. But directly in Larrie's line of sight, not six feet away, Mackenzie Buffalino, the bride-to-be, stood looking back at her. Their eyes met with an empathy that nearly took Larrie's breath away. Mackenzie walked over and embraced her.

"Oh, Larrie. I'm so glad you came. I know—" She looked intently at Larrie, her dark brown eyes filling with tears, although not enough to spill over and make her mascara run. "I know it must have been hard for you to come. That you did means so much to me."

"Really?" Larrie was genuinely surprised. She and Mackenzie had never been close. In fact, she didn't think Mackenzie even liked her. Searching for a response, she seized upon a compliment. "You look very beautiful today. Really gorgeous."

Mackenzie's face turned radiant. Her eyes brightened. "It feels so good to hear you say that. I remember the time when my mother and I were visiting Aunt Anna Maria. She had broken her ankle, remember? You and I were in high school then, but of course you were always older—a senior, I think. I was looking through your mother's high school yearbook and found her picture. I said, 'Oh! I look just like your mother did!' And do you remember what you said?" Mackenzie paused dramatically.

Larrie had no memory whatsoever of the long-ago visit. That wasn't surprising. The entire Buffalino family seemed to be allergic to dogs, so Larrie usually fled with her pets when Mackenzie showed up with her mother. "I don't know. What did I say?"

"You said, 'No, you don't. My mother was much prettier!' I got so mad at you."

Larrie blinked. "Ahhh, geez. I don't remember. I'm sorry."

Mackenzie had stopped listening. She opened the little golden purse that hung on her tanned arm by a rhinestone strap. She pulled out a mirror and studied herself. She smiled at her own reflection. "That's okay. I can forgive you because even *you* can see I'm much prettier than your mother now!"

Before Larrie could answer—not that she had any idea what she could say that wouldn't be rude—Mackenzie had begun looking at something past Larrie's shoulder.

"It's about time! That stupid chocolate fountain has nearly ruined my shower. I think they're going to turn it on."

Larrie turned around and looked. One of the workmen flashed two thumbs-up, then dramatically hit a switch at the fountain's base. A humming began. The crystal fountain began a slow rotation. The gaggle of girls crowding around the table all clapped and yelled, "Woo-hoo!"

The young man's face got red. A goofy grin spread across it. He turned to another of the overall-clad workers and yelled, "Go on, Mike. Hose in the chocolate. It's all set."

A third repairman wore a puzzled expression on his face. He pulled at his ear. Larrie could almost hear him thinking before he said, "Hey, dude, I think, like, maybe, you know, dude, you're supposed to put the chocolate in *before* you—"

Just then the three-tiered fountain gurgled. A series of belchlike sounds followed. An ominous rumbling issued forth. A column of brown liquid started to fill the clear plastic tubing that ran up the center of the fountain. The melted chocolate hesitated and receded a few times before it surged upward at warp speed.

The ear-tugging worker's mouth dropped open. "Holy shit! She's gonna blow!" He dove for the floor, where he slid under a pink tablecloth. At the same moment the chocolate emerged from the top of the fountain and became Mount Vesuvius in full eruption.

Larrie gaped as molten chocolate launched from the top of the whirling fountain. The crowd of girls nearest the table became the first victims, sprayed with the brown liquid as effectively as if someone had fired at them with a garden hose. Their screams filled the room like an emergency siren wailing about a disaster.

Then, *bam*. A wad of chocolate landed in the middle of Larrie's chest, followed by a gob on the right shoulder and another slightly above her left knee. Each splat became a solid circle with artful rays arcing from it. *It's like paintball*, she thought with some detachment.

A screeched *"Oh, my God!"* from Mackenzie made Larrie whirl around. A generous sphere of chocolate had smacked the princess bride right in the forehead, slid down her face, and dripped with great accuracy onto the lovely tanned mounds of swelling breast that peeked above the neckline of the seafoam dress.

As Mackenzie attempted to wipe chocolate from her eyes, a second volley landed slightly higher than the first, hitting the updo hard enough to push it backward and drench it with goo. Mackenzie looked as if she had been tipped upside down and dipped into chocolate like one of the marshmallows on a long wooden skewer that had been destined for the dessert table.

Larrie froze in astonishment for a long moment. Then her mouth twitched and turned up into a grin. A bubble of laughter burst in her chest and peals of merriment issued from her lips. She laughed until her stomach ached, until her chest hurt, until she could barely breathe. She laughed until her knees got weak and she sat down on the floor. She laughed while the knot of pain inside her unraveled. She laughed while her imprisoned joy broke free and new hope was born.

Chapter 4

In high spirits, Larrie arrived back home. The afternoon sun lit the green lawn, made dappled shadows under the maple trees, and gilded the fading fuchsia blossoms on the rhododendrons in front of the white farmhouse with a rime of gold. The house itself sat contentedly along the old Tunkhannock highway, usually called the Old Highway—a forgotten road replaced decades ago by the interstate. Barn swallows swooped peacefully through the clear air. *Linaria vulgaris*, the variegated yellow wildflowers that her mother called Butter-and-Eggs, bobbed merrily in a light breeze. The flaw in this peaceful, nearly perfect landscape was the presence of a short, sturdy man.

Ticky Blackstone had an uncomplicated mind, a big heart, and terrible taste in women. Right now he stood in Larrie's driveway, a black do-rag tied around his head. Several sheets of new plywood lay across the wheelbarrow in front of him. A hammer and a box of nails sat atop the wood. He wore the same blue T-shirt that he had first begun sporting three days ago, after his latest romance hit the crapper. White letters across its back spelled out ASSHOLE TODAY, TOMORROW, AND FOREVER . . . JUST ASK *HER*.

Larrie's pickup truck pulled behind him. The ten-year-old red Ford had a dent in the rear fender, and rust was eating up the chrome bumpers. A splash of fresh mud nearly obscured SPARROW'S NEST ANTIQUES AND FABULOUS JUNQUE stenciled on the driver's door, which Larrie was opening. She climbed out, the bright sunlight making her squint.

"What're you doing here on your day off, Ticky?"

"Got a call from Ms. Lolly. She forgot to put the garage door up when she backed her car out, God love her. Don't worry—she ain't hurt none. But the wrecker from Wayne's took a good hour to pull the ass-end of her Honda free. Yer gonna need a new door, but this here plywood will make it secure long as it takes before you can get one."

"My homeowner policy should cover a new door, Ticky. I can get it done, don't worry."

But both of them knew there would be a hefty deductible, and that expense, along with the cost of the plywood, was going to cause Larrie some significant financial distress. For months now, money had been a constant worry. Part of the problem had been Larrie's mental state. Unable to get motivated and prone to moping around the house instead of doing all she could to make a living, Larrie had taken to following a carefully scripted budget and dipping into her meager savings.

But Larrie's depression-induced inertia hadn't been the biggest factor in her steadily falling income. With gas prices skyrocketing and the economy spiraling downward, the antiques business had gone into death throes across the country. Few people still went for weekend car rides and stopped at cluttered, dusty shops along the highway to browse for stuff they didn't really need.

Larrie wasn't completely broke, but she would have gone out of business like all the other antiques shops in the Back Mountain if she had to pay rent. She survived only because she owned the barn she had converted into a showroom. She owned her Civil War–era farmhouse on thirty acres as well, having bought the parcel and outbuildings with her own money when a booming economy and the popularity of the PBS television series *Antiques Roadshow* started a collecting craze across America.

These days Larrie was trying to ride out the downturn by hunting for bargains and buying damaged items she could repair herself. Mostly she sent the furniture and "smalls," what dealers called glassware, collectibles, and just about everything that wasn't furniture, to Traver's Auction Hall down in Dallas instead of selling it retail. By the time the auctioneer, Steve Traver, deducted his commission she didn't make much. Even so, she thought she could get by as long as she bought low and watched every penny she spent.

The fact that Aunt Lolly had had another accident was more worrisome than the cost of the garage door. It would set off a new round of "Isn't it time Lolly was put into a home" conversations among the relatives, with Larrie's own mother leading the discussion.

Larrie's face hardened at the thought. Storm clouds rolled across her brow. Aunt Lolly would be put into a home only over Larrie's dead body. The eighty-three-year-old wasn't senile. Her mind hadn't deteriorated a bit as the years passed. The problem with Leila "Lolly" Smith was that she often had her thoughts in the heavens someplace instead of here on earth with the rest of humanity.

Most folks had labeled Lolly eccentric even when she had been a young woman. A few called her crazy. Larrie knew Lolly marched to a different drummer. A retired Latin teacher, she was working on a new translation of Caesar's *Commentaries on the Gallic and Civil Wars*, part of her series called Ancient Rome for Modern Times. Far from being mentally defective, the woman had a brilliant mind; unfortunately it was housed in an increasingly fragile body.

"I was mulling over a particularly troublesome passage," Aunt Lolly explained sheepishly when Larrie located the tall, rail-thin woman in the apartment's galley-style kitchen. Lolly was dressed in a peasant skirt and embroidered blouse, recalling her political activism of the 1960s. Her faded red hair, once a glorious copper, still streamed down her back in waves. As she spoke, she was setting a pitcher of water and tea bags in the south-facing window to make a batch of sun tea. "I thought I hit the button of the garage door opener, but I was more focused on getting a new idea for wording the translation down on a notepad. Then I shifted into reverse and *jacta alea est,* the die was cast. I'm so sorry about the garage door."

"Don't worry about that. My concern was whether or not you got hurt."

"I'm fine. *Et tu,* Larrie? You look as if you fell into a mud puddle. How was the Buffalinos' bridal shower?"

A smile played around Larrie's lips. "As you often told me, Aunt Lolly, 'Man plans and the gods laugh.' "

A few minutes later, Larrie walked into her own kitchen. Sitting on the old country-store counter she used as a kitchen island, the answering machine had its MESSAGE WAITING light blinking frenetically. If the message had been left on her personal line, she would have picked it up without hesitation, as it probably would have been Melanie, wanting to know every detail of Mackenzie's bridal shower.

But the message was on the line for the Sparrow's Nest, and Larrie considered ignoring the insistent red flashing until Monday morning, or at least until tomorrow when she officially opened the shop for the day.

For the past year, that light had been blinking with

increasing frequency. At times she had to field several calls daily from people at different stages of desperation trying to sell their belongings and household goods. Most hoped to bring in enough cash to order heating oil or put gas in the car. Lately Larrie suspected some of them needed grocery money as well.

Larrie hated being the person who had to tell the callers that grandma's good dishes with the "twenty-four-carat gold" rims were probably worthless or that a yard sale was the only chance of bringing even ten cents on the dollar for the Franklin Mint collectible plates and Snowbabies. Larrie tried to sound encouraging when she turned down their offers of the dining room set or bedroom suite that had been in the family for decades, saying that although she just didn't have the space for it in her shop, some other antiques dealer might.

That wasn't completely untrue. Maybe the caller could find a buyer, but in most cases, it wouldn't happen. When it came to furniture, dining room and bedroom sets were the first to go. People decided they could live without their china closet, buffet, and table that seated six, or the furniture in the spare bedroom. But the market for those things was flooded, and customers were nonexistent.

Although Larrie had sympathy for the sellers, she couldn't afford to buy their white elephants out of charity. She perfected her ability to say no, having had to say it often. But every now and then a caller reported finding an oil painting in the attic or tin toys in a storage closet. Or the china cabinet in the Waterfall Depression dining room set that itself wasn't worth ten dollars held a stash of marvelous carnival glass. Or that "ugly" green umbrella stand that stood next to the front door for sixty years just might be made by Roseville and worth several hundred dollars.

The mere possibility that the caller had a treasure awakened in Larrie the same hopes held by the '49ers who had heard about gold being discovered at Sutter's Mill. It became a siren song she couldn't ignore. She dreamed she might hit the mother lode. She had to go and find out.

Today, seeing the blinking message light and aware that it was after business hours, as Saturday afternoon was fast sliding toward evening, she turned her back on the answering machine determined to march past it. But curiosity poked its bony finger in her ribs and she stopped. It poked her again. She turned around. She reached out her hand and hit the PLAY button.

A woman's voice, carrying a suggestion of a French accent and quavering with age, began to speak: "My name is Ms. Ydoboni, and I am calling from over in Centermoreland. My brother Josiah Ydoboni passed away and I'm in town to sell his estate. He traveled quite a bit and has some unusual things—"

Larrie rolled her eyes. "Unusual things" usually meant worthless tourist items such as painted wooden shoes from the Netherlands.

"—from India. On his most recent trip, he shipped back some pieces of furniture and decorative wares from the time of the British Raj. He also amassed a collection of native art and religious icons from the Punjab. Hmmm, and what else? I'm leaving something out. Oh, yes, the boxes. I have found some cartons filled with documents of that era. Would you call me back as soon as possible? I'm only going to be in town for a few days. My number is 696-5555."

Bright colors and exotic images exploded in Larrie's mind. *The British Raj! A nineteenth-century era of opulence and excess and wonderful things such as tea chests and tiger-teeth jewelry, rubies and ivory, carved hardwoods and golden statues of Hindu gods.* Larrie felt the heady rush of excitement and the crash of disappointment nearly simultaneously. She'd love to see what Ms.

Ydoboni had, but purchasing an entire estate of quality items would require funds far beyond her means.

She sighed heavily and picked up the telephone to return the call. All that Larrie could do for Ms. Ydoboni was recommend some dealers, like auctioneer Steve Traver, who had deeper pockets than she did.

As it turned out, Ms. Ydoboni wouldn't listen. "You are Larissa Smith, the one they call Larry, aren't you?"

"Yes, but I don't do much with higher-end antiques. You need someone from New York, maybe even from Sotheby's, if your brother's estate is as fine as you described."

"No, Ms. Smith, I want you. You come highly recommended. Too many dealers are ready to take advantage of an old lady like me. I have been informed that you are exactly the person I should deal with. I'm sure we can find terms that would be agreeable to both of us. Are you free this evening? The house has already been sold and I'm very anxious about getting it cleaned out quickly."

Larrie's heart sank. "I'm afraid I'd be wasting your time, Ms. Ydoboni."

"Let me be the judge of that, Ms. Smith. At least come over and go through my brother's things, then we can talk about your purchasing them."

It occurred to Larrie that maybe she could buy one or two nice pieces, although she was sure Ms. Ydoboni wouldn't let her "cherry-pick" the estate—that is, just buy the very best of the lot. She doubted she could afford to do that anyway, but still . . . This could be the opportunity of a lifetime. Her heart quickened. She simply had to go and look.

Besides her insatiable curiosity, she also had more energy tonight than she had since— She stopped the thought. A pang of sorrow twisted inside her, but the crushing grief that drained the life from her had gone.

She lifted her chin and faced the truth squarely. She had more energy this evening than she had at any time since the news came that Ryan had died.

And not surprisingly she had no other plans for her Saturday night. She might as well ride over to Centermoreland. There could be no harm in looking at Josiah Ydoboni's things. She felt light and weightless with the effervescence of anticipation. In fact, she was humming the "Toreador's Song" from the opera *Carmen* as she headed for her bedroom to change out of her chocolate-spattered clothes.

She pulled the palm reader's business card out of her pocket and tossed it on her dresser. She never gave a single thought to the palm reader's warning. But considering her choice of tunes, perhaps somewhere in her mind, her subconscious was trying to remind Larrie that in *Carmen*, a Gypsy tarot card reader had foretold the heroine's doom.

Chapter 5

The old lady said no.

Van Killborn felt the desperation of Aeneas as Troy was lost. He saw the walls breached and his hopes burnt down into ashes. He straightened the French cuffs of his white dress shirt and gathered his thoughts. The antique armoire he must obtain stood not more than ten feet away from where he sat on an uncomfortable green damask side chair.

He forced a smile in the direction of the wizened spinster in a black dress so old it had faded to rusty brown along the seams. She perched like a small bird on the Victorian sofa.

"But Ms. Ydoboni, I explained. The original *Lawrence* Killborn was my grandfather. Even though no Lawrence or 'Larry' is currently involved in running our fine art and antiquities showroom, our company *is* Lawrence Killborn and Sons. I should think that would suffice."

"Mr. Killborn, as *I* explained, my brother's will stipulates that his estate must be sold to an individual named 'Larry.' That person might have been your grandfather, since I found his card in my brother's safe deposit box, and thus called the number listed thereon. But when I learned that your grandfather had passed away and *your* name is Van, I told you not to come. You've undertaken a fool's errand. I cannot sell to you."

"But you do agree the price I offered you is fair? Not only fair, it is generous, is it not?"

From her perch on the sofa, the old lady chirped angrily, like a tiny wren defying the swooping attack of a hawk. "Yes, Mr. Killborn, it is an astonishing offer, and I have to wonder why. You are a businessman and I have never known a good one to be generous."

Van Killborn blinked his ice-blue eyes in surprise. A pink flush tinted his fair cheeks. He could barely control his annoyance at his own stupidity. He had offered this old woman double what anyone else would have, and it had proved to be a serious mistake. He had underestimated her. Now the hidden treasure that he, his father before him, and his grandfather before that had hunted since the 1950s might again slip away. He was so close. The prize was literally within his reach, hidden in a secret drawer of that armoire.

Van had to have it. His family's business, his future, and perhaps his life depended on it. But he had already made a serious tactical error and needed a convincing reason for having offered so much for Josiah Ydoboni's estate.

Van kept his handsome face from revealing his frustration. He showed his perfect white teeth in a smile. He decided to tell the elderly woman part of the truth. "I can afford to be generous, Ms. Ydoboni. I have a buyer, a collector of items from the Raj, whom I want to keep happy. Your brother's extraordinary possessions would please this important client of Lawrence Killborn and Sons. After all, a pleased customer will send referrals our way. But a *dis*pleased customer, as this one is bound to be if I return empty-handed and disappoint him, is bad business all around. You do understand my position now?"

"*Mais oui,* I understand your position more than you know," Ms. Ydoboni said primly, her mouth looking as if she were sucking on a lemon. "I cannot accommodate you, I'm afraid. And, as I have another appointment arriving any moment, I must ask you to leave."

My God, the old lady is throwing me out! Van paled, realizing how badly he had handled this. He stood, stiff with the rage he didn't dare to let show.

His grandfather had begun the treasure hunt more than fifty years earlier. Lawrence Killborn had linked Josiah Ydoboni to that armoire from the start. His grandfather never knew for sure where or when Josiah had obtained the massive old cupboard, but the biblical scholar had previously visited every home, warehouse, or furniture shop where the armoire had ever been. His grandfather had even talked with Josiah himself, not revealing his true interest but suggesting the scholar might act as the firm's agent on the subcontinent.

But something or someone had spooked the eccentric, bespectacled scholar and he broke off contact. Lawrence Killborn's spies had found him again, living near Lahore in the Punjab, but shortly afterward the man vanished, only to reappear in America, and then vanish again.

Van's father had continued the hunt without enthusiasm and only half believing the treasure really existed. But even as a child, Van had listened attentively to his grandfather's stories. He had never doubted the treasure was real. Over the past year, he had spent his own inheritance on the search, scouring two continents for Josiah Ydoboni without success.

Then the telephone call from Musette Ydoboni had come to the office, dropping like manna from heaven. It must have been fate. He himself had picked up the phone and spoken with her, his heart beating faster and faster as he realized the treasure he had searched for had literally found him. Now, here in this very room, where Van could see it and touch it, was the armoire that held the prize he sought.

Even with this setback, Van felt euphoric that he at last knew the exact location of the treasure. That put him just one small step from taking possession. Since the old woman wouldn't sell to him, he would simply find another way to obtain the estate. Realizing this, Van felt his natural good humor return; he was not a real villain, but simply a flawed, perhaps unethical, young man.

He gave the tiny crone a bow. "I'm sorry we couldn't do business, Ms. Ydoboni. Please do not hesitate to contact me if you change your mind."

The old lady hopped off the sofa, more birdlike than ever. "I don't mean to be ungrateful, Mr. Killborn. I realize you traveled a long way today to see me, but I'm sorry you felt you had to speak to me in person. I was very clear your firm's name alone wouldn't do."

"Being able to inspect Josiah Ydoboni's extraordinary collection for myself was worth the trip. When our firm lost contact with your brother all those years ago, my grandfather assumed he had returned to the subcontinent and been lost forever. I appreciate your willingness to let me inspect his magnificent things. It's been an honor. Are you absolutely positive I couldn't sweeten the offer enough to tempt you?"

The little woman shook her head. "Your offer isn't at issue, Mr. Killborn. It's simply not possible, according to the terms of the will, for me to sell to you. *Merci* and *au revoir*." She extended her hand to him.

Van took it. It reminded him of a claw, tiny bones covered by a thin layer of cool flesh. He could crush it with a strong grip, but of course he didn't. He was in perfect control. But inside him, where it didn't show, bitterness crawled up his throat like gall, like poison, like the dark thoughts he pushed away.

At least he was still able to push the dark thoughts

away and not act on them. Van always felt as if he had a good angel on one shoulder and a devil on the other. As his own desperation for money grew, he heard the devil's voice grow louder and he feared someday he'd listen. Then he would be lost to his dark side, and the devil would win.

Once Van had walked outside Josiah Ydoboni's stone house, a pitiful place barely bigger than a cottage, he watched a red pickup truck slow down and pull into the driveway behind his silver Mercedes. He waved and the truck stopped. The passenger side window lowered.

"Are you going out?" The voice he heard had round, sweet notes, like a flute's. It was a lovely voice, filled with music.

Van walked over and peered in the cab. An overly thin, very pretty woman sat inside. He felt something arresting about her eyes. They were ethereal, almost haunted, and a beautiful dove gray. She smiled but looked sad. Van thought her intriguing. "Yes. I'm about to leave," he replied, then realized this was Ms. Ydoboni's "other appointment." "Are you a dealer?" he asked.

"Yes. Are you?"

"I am. I'm from New York City."

"I guessed you came from out of town. I know everyone around here."

"I drove in this morning." Van couldn't take his eyes from hers. "You're here about the Ydoboni estate?"

The woman gave him another smile with shadows underneath it. "Well, I was. Am I too late? Did you just buy it?"

"No such luck. The old lady refused to sell it to me. And she won't sell to you either—unless your name happens to be Larry." He laughed.

The woman's amazing eyes became very wide. "But it is."

Chapter 6

Larrie took the expensively embossed business card the New York dealer handed through her truck window. She glanced at it and noted that his name was Van Killborn. He said he would be curious to know how she made out with Ms. Ydoboni. He had asked if he might phone her.

From the way he was looking at her, his eyes twinkling, Larrie thought for a moment that he was flirting with her, but that was ridiculous. What interest could she hold for him? He was extraordinarily good-looking and obviously wealthy. She was neither, although at one time, when she had fuller cheeks and no disquieting sadness in her appearance, she had been called "a wholesome girl."

He drove a Mercedes. She drove a beat-up Ford. He wore a tailor-made suit. She had on a Defenders of Wildlife T-shirt and a pair of Wal-Mart's Riders jeans. He dealt in fine art and antiquities. She dealt in junk. She called it "fabulous junque," but nothing in her entire shop was priced at more than three hundred dollars.

So when this attractive young man asked if he could phone her, Larrie laughed and said offhandedly, "Call if you want to. My shop's called the Sparrow's Nest. You can find the listing in the Yellow Pages."

Then she watched him walk away, noticing that he was

about six feet tall, broad-shouldered, and small-hipped. He climbed lithely into his expensive car, backed it out of the driveway, gave her a wave, and roared off down the road.

But by the time Larrie had pulled her truck into the spot he had vacated and parked, she had forgotten Van Killborn. She gazed with keen interest toward the cottage, its gray stone walls washed with a warm amber hue as the evening sun sank behind the green hills on the western horizon. The windows reflected the copper-colored light too, making the small house look magical. *A veritable fairy palace*, she thought.

Larrie's pulse began to pound. Her breath quickened. Something wonderful awaited her inside. She felt it. She knew it. She couldn't wait to see it.

"My brother was a biblical scholar," Ms. Ydoboni explained. "He spent most of his life in the Punjab, near Lahore in Pakistan, dangerous as it is there today. He was a driven man." She sighed. "Josiah was determined to prove that the Indian king Gondaphares mentioned in the apocryphal book Acts of St. Thomas really existed."

"And did he?" Larrie asked, immensely curious about both the brother and sister named Ydoboni. "Did he find any proof?"

Ms. Ydoboni sat herself down on the sofa again, her hands folded in her lap. She twisted a ruby ring on the middle finger of her right hand. "No. The last time we spoke he said he had found another piece of the puzzle, and it might be the key to unlocking the entire mystery. He had found someone in Baltistan—that's an isolated place deep in the Himalayas—who was a descendant of the king himself, or so he believed. My brother had booked his flight back to Lahore." A tear rolled silently down her cheek. "He had a heart attack on the way to the airport. He never made the plane."

"I'm terribly sorry," Larrie said. "But he must have had a fabulous life."

"Yes. I suppose there are worse ways to live than chasing a dream. But you have inspected his things. What do you think?"

"What do I think?" Larrie's eyes danced. "Oh, they are some of the most exquisite items I've ever seen! I can't even begin to tell you. That carved chess set with elephants instead of pawns, oh, it's so special. The magnificent inlaid tea caddy with the lapis lazuli pulls just took my breath away. Why, I couldn't even imagine something that extraordinary. And that majestic teak and mahogany armoire! It's fit for a maharajah."

"Well, yes, I believe it did belong to a rajah or at least a Prince Somebody. A bill of sale is still in the top drawer."

"It is? That adds to its worth, you know. It will provide a clear provenance, which is so important in showing an antique's authenticity. I don't think you should take less than two thousand dollars for it. I didn't get a chance to inspect all the boxes but they seemed filled with old books, figurines, and documents going back centuries, maybe even a millennium."

Larrie stopped talking abruptly. She shook her head and sighed. "Ms. Ydoboni, I must tell you, I simply don't have the funds to purchase your brother's things. I would love to, I really would, but I'm not the right person to handle antiquities. I studied them a bit when I was at Penn State, but I've always specialized in American antiques."

She paused and gave another little sigh. "I'm only a one-woman operation, and I only started my business a little over a year ago. I love what I do, but I don't have a huge bankroll to buy with." Her face brightened. "But I might be able to afford a few pieces of the furniture, if you'd be willing to separate them from the rest of the estate. I'm particularly taken with your brother's desk.

The whimsy in making its legs resemble a tiger's and the frieze of the tiger hunt carved around its skirt—I find it delightful. It's not as valuable as the rest of your brother's possessions, so maybe—"

"I know what my brother's things are worth, Ms. Smith," the elderly lady broke in sharply. "Making the most money on them is not the issue. If it were, I would have sold them to the young man who passed you in the front yard."

"That New York dealer? Why didn't you sell them to him if he made you a good offer?"

Ms. Ydoboni looked at Larrie with an expression that clearly said she thought Larrie was very young and naïve. "I didn't sell to Mr. Killborn because—" She hesitated and began again. "I didn't sell because that young man wasn't the right buyer for my brother's things. For one thing, he offered me far too much. I had to wonder why. That put me off." She shook her head and her gray curls bounced a little.

"Then there was a question of character. As charming as Mr. Killborn was, there was something about him—I don't know what." She shrugged her shoulders and turned her hands palms up in the French way. "I felt a *sang-froid,* an icy cold at the core of him. I can't be more precise than that. But it wouldn't have mattered if he were as saintly as the Dalai Lama. His name wasn't Larry. But I understand yours is."

"It says Larissa on my birth certificate, but yes, people call me Larrie. With an IE, not a Y, though."

"The spelling doesn't concern me, Ms. Smith. My brother's will specified that his estate must—I repeat, *must*—be sold to an antiques dealer named Larry. When I finally looked in the local phone book under Antiques, he had circled your ad in the Yellow Pages and drawn a large arrow in black marker pointing to your name. He had printed 'Larry' in the margin of the page. I have no doubt he meant me to call *you*. You and no other. If I had thought to look there originally, before I found the business card for Lawrence Killborn and Sons, I would never have called those New York people at all. I feel I made a dreadful mistake in doing that."

She focused her bright eyes intently on Larrie. "I am convinced you are the person who must buy my brother's estate. I have no doubts that he meant it for you, and for you alone."

"I don't understand your conviction at all, Ms. Ydoboni, but it doesn't matter if for some reason your brother wanted you to call me. I can't buy the estate. I wish I could, but I couldn't even get a bank loan for the amount it would cost." Larrie felt herself tumbling into a dark well of depression. With each new piece Ms. Ydoboni had shown her, she had become more and more euphoric. She wanted these wondrous things so badly. It had been a terrible tease to see them, to touch them, and to know she couldn't buy them.

"You don't even know my terms, Ms. Smith. Why don't you listen to them, and then tell me whether or not you can meet them?"

To Larrie's embarrassment, tears sprang into her eyes. "Because I know I can't," she practically wailed before gathering her emotions and reining them in.

"Will you at least listen to what I have to say?"

"Of course, but—"

"Silence, Ms. Smith. First of all, you may purchase the entire estate for the sum of one dollar."

"One dollar? No, I couldn't. I mean, why would you? It's not right. You're really giving it to me—"

"Silence, I said! I have not finished. You may purchase the estate for a single dollar but it comes with a stipulation. You may sell or send to auction any of the items in the estate except one. And that one you must keep for yourself—*forever*. You must keep it with you in your home, or if you should travel, you must take it with you. It is of critical importance that no one, I repeat, no one takes possession of it besides you. My brother was very clear on that. He even wrote me a note. He said—now, what exactly did he say?" The old woman's wrinkled brow furrowed more deeply. "Something cryptic about a circle?"

She looked blankly in Larrie's direction. "I can't remember the wording. It's part of the curse of getting old. But no matter. I'll read it to you. I have it right here." She fumbled in her pocket and pulled out a folded paper. She spread it flat and read:

> *Dear Sister,*
> *Remember, this one item must go along with all of my things to the person called Larry. But it cannot be sold. Larry must keep it. I made a promise to a fine old gentleman. It's all part of a plan. 'Betwixt and between a star skein of dreams, time's circle spins round. What goes up, comes down, till all is safe and sound, put in its rightful order. Couples join and villains perish—and the plan begun with this, is done.' Musette, I gave my word. Make sure it happens.*
> *Your loving brother,*
> *Josiah*

A tremulous sigh wracked Ms. Ydoboni's narrow chest as she folded the sheet and slipped it back into her pocket. "He had attached this to the item with a bit of sticky tape. It sounds just like him. He was a whimsical man, always talking in riddles." She raised glistening eyes to Larrie's. "Are you willing to do what he asked?"

Larrie's head was spinning. She couldn't get her thoughts wrapped around what was happening. Ms. Ydoboni was selling her all these things for the sum of one dollar. Just enough to make it a legal transaction. But why? It made no sense. She was a total stranger, not a rightful heir to the estate.

"Have you lost your voice, Ms. Smith? I made you an offer. Can you accept it under the terms I have put forth?"

"I—I don't want to seem rude, but I just don't understand. Why me? Why did this have to go to someone named Larry and how do you know I'm the right person?"

Ms. Ydoboni sighed deeply. "You are asking me questions I can't answer, my dear. I suppose there is a mystery behind my brother's insistence on the estate going to 'Larry.' You heard what I just read. He wrote that he promised an old man he would do this. Why? I don't know. But I do know you are the right person. I have a good feeling about you. Like my brother, you are someone who keeps a promise. I can see that in you. I see quite a bit, you know."

Larrie colored deeply at the woman's judgment of her character. "Do you mind if I ask what it is that your brother wants me to keep?"

"It will probably be easier to show it to you," the tiny woman said and slid off the sofa. She walked over to a small wooden coffer that sat next to the wall. A plain, unimpressive-looking box with a humped lid, it was constructed of a dull brown wood bound by leather straps. It wasn't very big, only two feet long by perhaps a foot deep and a foot high. And it couldn't have been very heavy, for as tiny as she was, Ms. Ydoboni intended to pick it up.

"Wait!" Larrie cried out, jumped up from her chair, and rushed over. "Let me carry that for you." She grasped the iron handles on either side of the box. They felt warm in her hands. In fact they seemed to get warmer as she held them.

"Where do you want this?" she asked.

"Just set it on the coffee table, *s'il vous plait*." Ms. Ydoboni pointed to the spot with her thin index finger.

Larrie set it down. She stroked her hand over the smooth rounded top of the coffer. The wood felt warm too. *How odd*, she thought.

Ms. Ydoboni pulled a brass key from a pocket in her black dress. She undid the lock, opened the front hasp, and lifted the lid. Blue velvet lined the inside of the box. Nestled in the soft fabric was an old, tarnished, rather battered Aladdin-style oil lamp. She lifted it and handed it to Larrie.

"Here it is."

Larrie took the lamp from Ms. Ydoboni. Whatever she had expected—and she had expected something extraordinary—this wasn't it. It felt warm to her touch, just as the box did. It had a handle on one end, a spout where the wick would go on the other, and a lid in the top where the oil would be poured in. She supposed the item was very old, but it wasn't at all pretty or valuable.

"Okay. It looks like an oil lamp."

"It is—an eighteenth-century one. Brass, I believe."

"That's it?"

"That's it. It was my brother's most cherished possession. Now, about my offer. Will you accept it?"

Larrie's thoughts were absolutely whirling. Blood throbbed in her temples. She couldn't believe the windfall that had landed right in her lap. Yet guilt tugged at her soul. "Are you sure about this?"

"You are Larry, are you not?"

"I am."

"Then this is what my brother wanted me to do. Please, Ms. Smith, give me your answer. Yes or no?"

Lights like darting fireflies danced in front of Larrie's eyes. "Yes," she said in a choked voice. Then she cleared her throat and snapped out loud and clear, "Yes!"

Chapter 7

Saturday night, in the darkest hours between midnight and dawn, Larrie dreamed the dream that had recurred almost every night since Ryan died. In it she floated high above the surface of the earth. Below her, she saw her farmhouse, a white T-shaped building with a gray shingle roof. Her barn cat, the yellow tabby that never got a name besides Kitty, strolled up the slate stone path toward the front door. A wide expanse of front lawn stretched to meet the road in a skirt of green. In the copse of woods behind the house, the leaves of the poplar trees danced in the wind.

Then Larrie moved away from the place she knew, gliding smoothly through the air along the Old Highway, following the gravel road as it dipped and turned, crossed a creek, passed black-and-white cows grazing in a hillside pasture, and curved east while it hugged the edge of an alfalfa field where Larrie's neighbor Cliffie Chapin drove his red Allis-Chalmers tractor up and down the rows.

Larrie flew farther, finding herself above rolling hills and the glistening ribbons of winding rivers, until she eventually crossed a wide sea with nothing below her but waves. Finally, in the distance, she'd see a city whose white spires and rounded turrets aimed up into the azure sky. She heard the sound of bells. She smelled a spice, although she didn't know which one. Once she thought she heard an elephant trumpeting.

But Larrie never reached the city. The dream would stop midaction as if a strip of celluloid film had been cut by a sharp utility knife. Larrie's eyes always flew open. She'd sit bolt upright in the bed. Darkness surrounded her, not the pellucid air of her dream. She was back in the blackness of her room, looking out at the night beyond the window, feeling both disoriented and disappointed.

She would rather be flying in the dream than back on earth. The experience seemed extraordinarily real, affecting all her senses sharp and true. She believed she had been carried by the currents of air high toward the heavens, able to witness but not feel the world turning below with all its sorrows. After having the same dream dozens of times, Larrie had become convinced that, although she never saw it, something had lifted her up into the sky. She wasn't flying under her own power, but she was carried along, while the wind moved softly past her ears, telling her a secret she could never distinctly hear—but sometimes she thought the wind was whispering *fly on fly on fly on*.

When Sunday morning finally dawned, Larrie awoke to find that the world outside had become a cathedral, its ceiling formed by a sky ablaze with fuchsia clouds outlined in silver. Larrie recited the rhyme her mother taught her: "Red sky in the morning, a sailor's warning. Red sky at night, a sailor's delight."

But if a storm was indeed coming on this clear, fresh morning, only the Technicolor sky foretold it. No breeze blew. No storm clouds gathered. Nothing threatening stirred.

A short while later Larrie stood in silent witness to

the glory before her, her coffee mug in hand, one of her dogs at her feet while the other two sniffed around the lawn, barking wildly and running in zigzags as they found the scent of a doe or a raccoon. Despite the dream or because of it, she had slept well, arising at first light to hitch up the cargo van to her truck. She had promised Ms. Ydoboni she'd arrive early this morning to pick up her brother's estate. Long before it was time to go, she was ready, her excitement growing at the prospect of possessing Josiah's magnificent, old, and marvelous things.

She flicked her eyes occasionally toward the winding road in front of the house. Ticky was due to arrive any minute. He was bringing Shem and Shaun, his "clod-hopping, shit-kicking country cousins"—his words—to provide the needed brawn. "All their brains is in their backs, Miss Larrie, but they sure do know how to work."

Just as Larrie finished her last swallow of coffee, Ticky's dusty Jeep rolled into view and rumbled into the yard. His cousins, twins in their early twenties, lumbered out of the rear of the open-sided vehicle. The young men were dressed in jeans with the knees torn out and T-shirts that might have once been brown but had faded to rust. Shem and Shaun were what folks in these hills called "towheads"—that is, they had hair as white blond as a dandelion puff, starkly contrasting with their deeply tanned faces. The knuckles of their hands were scarred and, more often than not, swollen.

Larrie had never heard either of them utter a complete sentence, and rumor had it they had landed in jail on many a Saturday night when their short tempers and quick fists started, or finished, a barroom brawl. But the boys were always well-behaved around Ticky, and the twins had helped Larrie before when she had been lucky enough to buy the entire contents of a house for a good price. They did work hard. Equally important, they worked cheap as long as Larrie provided bottles of Yuengling beer on ice for them along with their pay when they got done.

Larrie and her crew were in Centermoreland by nine, and the men expertly emptied the house without breaking a thing. Ms. Ydoboni watched, heaving a sigh every few breaths as her brother's possessions filled the cargo van. Larrie patted the tiny woman on the shoulder.

"Don't mind me." Ms. Ydoboni dabbed at her eyes with a tissue. "It's the end of an era, that's all. Did you put the lamp in a safe place?"

"It's on the seat of the truck. I promise to set it on my mantel just as soon as I get home."

The old woman turned red-rimmed, rheumy eyes toward Larrie. "You must keep it with you. If you go out, you should lock it up. If it were stolen, it would be . . . it would be a tragedy."

The likelihood of someone entering Larrie's house (since the door was usually unlocked, breaking in would not be necessary) to grab the shabby oil lamp was slim to none, but she answered Ms. Ydoboni in all sincerity. "Because the lamp was your brother's and because it will always remind me of your kindness, I will cherish it. I promise to keep it safe." She paused. "I wonder, do you know its history or how your brother happened to have it?"

The elderly lady shook her head. "He never talked about it. He showed the lamp to me just once after he brought it home from India. He told me it could bring either sorrow or joy, like love. He had fun with me by speaking in riddles, as I told you before." Her eyes got a faraway look. "He had an unhappy experience with love himself, and that is why he remained a bachelor. It happened long ago, in his youth, when he was a student. He met the woman in England, and they wanted to marry, but she was a Sikh from the Punjab, you see."

Larrie didn't see, but she didn't know very much about the religions of India. "What happened?"

Ms. Ydoboni didn't answer right away, but turned her gaze toward an open window where the earlier sunlight had vanished and been replaced by a filtered grayish light. "In the end, the young woman chose the match her parents arranged. But my brother said he wished her every happiness, and he was very sure she found it. He never said anything else about her."

Larrie felt there was much more to the story, but it was a tale that would never be told. "I bet the lamp was a token of their love, that's why he never wanted it sold."

Ms. Ydoboni glanced up at Larrie, her expression unreadable. "If you wish to believe that, by all means do. But I suspect the lamp was something else entirely."

"Like what?"

Ms. Ydoboni moved her bony shoulders under the black dress. "I wouldn't even pretend I know the answer." Her voice became so soft that Larrie could barely hear it. "All I do know is that my brother felt strongly it must be given to 'Larry.' To you."

Larrie said her good-byes, gave her thanks to Ms. Ydoboni once again, and drove off with Josiah's things. Within a half hour, she had positioned the cargo van in front of the big nineteenth-century barn that housed the Sparrow's Nest, her antiques store. Shem and Shaun hopped out of the crew cab and pushed open the double doors to reveal the empty area waiting to be filled by the Ydoboni estate.

The skies had darkened to the color of lead as the lowering clouds squeezed the light out of the day. The sailor's warning had been accurate after all. A cool breeze raised goose bumps on Larrie's arms. The threat of a storm worried her. She turned to Ticky. "We'd better hurry. If you feel even one drop, don't take anything else from the van. I won't risk any of these things getting wet."

"You're the boss, Miss Larrie."

After the men had worked for a while, Larrie directing where each piece should be placed, she looked over her shoulder and noticed a black box truck approaching on the Old Highway. It slowed and stopped in front of the Sparrow's Nest. Ornate gold lettering on its side spelled out:

LAWRENCE KILLBORN & SONS

Dealers in Fine Arts and Antiquities

5075 Madison Avenue

New York, New York

Van Killborn emerged from the passenger side of the cab. A wide grin lit up his face. He strode toward Larrie and called out, "You did it! You got the estate. I suspected you might. I took the chance of just dropping by."

Puzzled, Larrie stared at him. "But why? You said you might call."

The breeze ruffled Van's sandy-colored hair, tousling it across his forehead in a charming way. He spoke quickly and loudly as New Yorkers do, a hurry in his voice. "It was just as easy to drop in as to phone you. I wanted to make you an offer. No, don't look that way. I don't want everything you bought. I know you'd never sell it all so soon—I certainly wouldn't. I just want four pieces of furniture. Wait! Don't shake your head. Let me tell you which ones. The tea caddy with the lapis lazuli pulls, the ebony chest inlaid with ivory, that marvelous tiger-paw desk, and the huge teak and mahogany armoire. I can see by your face you don't want to sell. Don't refuse me yet. I will probably offer you more than you paid for the entire estate."

"It's not that—" Larrie finally got a chance to say.

"Would fifteen thousand dollars make you say yes?"

Larrie's expression registered her shock. "Fifteen thousand?"

"I have a buyer. Even if I don't make a dime on the transaction, it's worth it to me to keep him happy. What do you say, Ms. Smith? It is Ms. Smith, isn't it? That's what your ad in the Yellow Pages said, 'Larissa Smith, owner.' I'm Van Killborn, by the way. I should have introduced myself when we first met. I apologize."

Van spoke so quickly that Larrie could barely follow him. She took his extended hand. It was firm and cool. They shook, and he held on for a moment longer than necessary.

"Nice to meet you, Van. Yes, I'm Larissa Smith. About your offer—"

"Twenty thousand. Say yes."

Larrie shook her head. "It's not the money. And I'm not saying no. What I need to say is 'not right now.' I have a policy—I learned the hard way, you see—that I never sell an item I've purchased until I've had a chance to inspect it thoroughly. I'm not saying there's hidden treasure in any of that furniture, but I need time to evaluate what I actually have. You can understand that, can't you?"

For the briefest of seconds, faster than the wink of an eye, anger flashed across Van's face, so quickly Larrie didn't consciously know she had seen it—but she immediately felt uneasy. Glancing away from him, she saw two large men climb out of the Killborn truck. Both wore cheap jean jackets and had suspicious bulges under their left arms. They lounged against the hood of the big truck and watched Shem and Shaun finishing the emptying of the cargo van.

Van's charming smile had returned. "I understand your position. I'm disappointed, of course. I had brought moving men and the van with me from New York, believing that Ms. Ydoboni would sell to me. When she wouldn't, it was worth waiting to speak with you. And you did say you weren't saying no, right?"

"I'm not saying yes either. You do understand that? And I won't have an answer for a while, a week at least." She hesitated then. She was tempted. Fifteen or maybe even twenty thousand dollars would ease her financial crunch. She doubted she could sell the four items at retail for half that sum, and she couldn't predict when or if she would find a buyer in this tight economic climate. She'd be a fool not to take Van's offer. She looked at the dealer. He seemed terribly disappointed.

"Oh, buck up, I'm a softie." She smiled. "You know what? Give me two days to inspect the furniture and maybe do some research on it, and I promise I'll have an answer for you."

Van beamed, incandescent with delight. "It's a deal. It's worth waiting around for that, and it'll be even more worthwhile if you'll go out to dinner with me tonight."

The color fled from Larrie's face. Thoughts collided in her brain. *I'm not ready. I should go. I can't do this. Yes, I can. No, I'll be betraying Ryan's memory.* "I don't think it's a good—"

"I know you don't know me. But we're both dealers. We'll talk shop. I want to hear your opinion on the market. I want to hear what you like to buy. Say yes, Larrie. Dinner will be all business, I promise." He held up his hand. "Scout's honor."

Larrie looked at him closely. Danger lay in misjudging others, she knew. This man, definitely of the Greek god type, appeared to be without guile, open and hopeful, well-educated and friendly. He was no one to fear, and he was a stranger in town. She should accept to be courteous, and the dinner would be between two colleagues discussing their profession. It wouldn't be a date date. "Okay, I guess. I mean, sure."

"Great. I'll come by at seven. Is that too early?"

Larrie couldn't suppress a smile. "Around here, folks think anything after the Early Bird Special is late. Seven's fine."

Meanwhile, behind Van, his two workers were now laughing and nodding in the direction of the barn. "Get a load of those rednecks. Wonder if they're as dumb as they look." One of the New Yorkers spoke loud enough so everyone could hear him.

Larrie froze, sensing trouble, then swiveled her head to see Shem and Shaun standing like young bulls about to paw the ground, two country boys with dour faces, short fuses, and knives in their boots. Ticky, his gestures frantic, was urging his young cousins to go into the barn. They had gone deaf to his words, their attention riveted on the New Yorkers.

"I see me some dumb-ass Eye-talians," Shaun said through gritted teeth.

Shem leaned over and picked up a crowbar that was lying next to the barn door. "Yeah, me too," he said.

Oh, crap, Larrie thought. Her eyes had grown large and anxious. She implored Van, "I think you'd better—"

Van spun toward his truck, his voice a bellow. "Hey! Hey! You two! Get in the damned truck."

One of his men opened the truck door. Van glanced briefly back at Larrie and started to say, "It's okay—" But he stopped short when instead of getting in the cab, the worker reached behind the seat and came out with a baseball bat. "Hey!" Van yelled, as fear spread across his face. He took a step toward the truck, but clearly the men weren't paying any attention to him as they charged toward Shem and Shaun.

Suddenly Larrie's hair was standing on end. A strange tingling danced across her skin. The world exploded with the brightest flash she had ever seen. It was followed by a boom so loud it was as if a cannon went off next to her ear. In the next second, the heavens opened up and hail the size of marbles came down. Larrie felt as if she were being pelted with rocks. She ran for the barn. Van and his men sprinted for their truck. The hail changed to rain that fell as wide, blowing curtains of water pouring from the gray clouds.

Larrie, rivulets of rain running down her face, her clothes drenched, reached the sheltering barn. Ticky, Shem, and Shaun were already inside. They slammed the double doors shut behind her.

Just then the lights in the barn went *click click*, went out, came on, went out and stayed dark.

"Lost the 'lectric again," Ticky said as they stood there in a murky gloom, rain drumming angrily on the roof, the items from the Ydoboni estate turning into looming shadows around them. "You know, Miss Larrie, we came near to a real bad sit'ation out there."

"Yes, I know."

"Those knuckleheads had guns."

"I thought they might."

"Don't look like movers to me."

"Not to me either."

"Don't look like the type of workers who'd be with a rich dealer like that. So who do you think they are?"

Larrie was wondering the same thing. The two men hadn't listened to Van or acted as if they were working for him. He was afraid of them too. She looked at Ticky. "I don't know who they are. That's something I'd like to find out."

A few minutes later, Larrie, her emotions churning and her foot tapping impatiently inside the darkened barn, heard the Killborn & Sons' truck start up and drive away into the violent storm.

Chapter 8

The power stayed out even after Ticky and his cousins
finished moving furniture, got paid, had a beer, and drove
off. Larrie carried out the remaining tasks of sweeping
and dusting, then left the barn and drove her pickup a
few hundred feet to park in the driveway. She grabbed
the coffer containing the lamp off the passenger seat,
and toted it in the house.

The storm had ended long ago. The sun had returned,
making shadows on the lawn and slanting through the
window blinds, providing light enough for her to see.
She set the wooden box down on the floor in the living
room, opened it, and took out the lamp. She held it up.

Centuries of smoke and gunk had made the brass
nearly black. The rounded sides had dents and dings.
The spout had been bent at an angle. Larrie talked out
loud to herself, a habit she had acquired while spending
so much time as a solitary creature. "It's not going to
add anything to my decor like this, but maybe if I get the
grime off it, it will look a lot better."

Larrie put the lamp down on a richly grained slab of
burled wood set on a tree stump that she used as a table
next to the sofa. She went into the kitchen and rummaged around under the sink until she found the metal
polish and some soft cotton rags. All three of her dogs

followed her back into the living room, dancing around and barking at nothing, or at least nothing Larrie could discern. Then they plopped down on the rug while Larrie started to rub the lamp. "There's some writing on this thing." She directed her remark to Taco the Chihuahua, who was absorbed in licking his private parts and ignored her. Sadie, the Heinz 57 Varieties mutt, rolled over on her back and looked at Larrie upside down, her pink tongue lolling out of her mouth. Only Teddy the loyal Chow watched intently.

"Thank you, Teddy, for caring," Larrie said. She polished the brass vigorously. Writing appeared, encircling the top of the lamp around the lid, although the language was foreign, Urdu maybe, and the words remained unreadable. *How fascinating, and quite pretty*, she thought, observing her handiwork.

But it had taken an enormous effort to clean that small patch of the brass. Fatigue suddenly overtook Larrie. The events of the day had drained her more than she had realized. She put down the polishing cloth. *I'll finish this up tomorrow*, she promised herself. *I need a short nap before tonight. Before my "date,"* she thought, and a wriggle of anxiety moved inside her.

She wondered if she had made a mistake by agreeing to dinner with Van Killborn. She didn't feel any chemistry with him, and that was a relief, really. She was making too much of what would probably be just a few hours talking about antiques with a man who was her own age, and good-looking, and who seemed to like her. She had the impression he did like her, and that started the worm of anxiety moving again.

She sank onto the couch, stretched her legs out along the soft cushions, and felt her eyes sliding shut. She was drifting off, tumbling down into oblivion, when the barking dogs made her eyelids flutter open. *Damn those dogs*, she complained to herself. *What now?*

She didn't rise but turned her head in the direction of the noise and immediately felt confused. She couldn't believe what she was seeing. Standing next to the sofa table was a man who simply could not be real.

Oh, I'm just dreaming, Larrie decided as she beheld him. He was Caucasian, but deeply tanned and dressed like an Indian native of the last century. Bells encircled both ankles. His tight white *churidar* trousers rode low on his hips. His bare stomach sported a full set of six-pack abs.

Wow! What a sexy hunk, Larrie thought and smiled. This was definitely a dream and one of her better ones. The man's unruly hair was long, thick, and dark. His eyes shone like obsidian. He had a deep cleft like a devil's thumbprint in his chin. He winked at her. He was every inch a rogue.

"Who are you?" Larrie muttered, her eyes becoming heavy again. She felt utterly relaxed. She would have purred had she been a cat.

A rich deep baritone replied, "The genie of the lamp."

Sleep was fast carrying Larrie off. "Hmmmm," she murmured. She stretched her graceful white arms above her head. "Aladdin's lamp. Of course it must have a genie. Hello, genie."

"My given name is John Trelawny, but call me Jo."

A poem by Robert Burns popped into Larrie's head. It was one of Aunt Lolly's favorites. Larrie had heard it hundreds of times. With her eyes closed, she recited, "'John Anderson, my Jo, John/When we were first acquent/Your locks were like the raven/Your bonnie brow was brent . . .' " Her voice trailed off on the last line.

She was nearly fast asleep when she felt lips softly cover hers. The genie of the lamp was kissing her, she thought. He was a very good kisser. She brought her arms forward, encircled his neck, and kissed him back.

His mouth tasted clean, male, and a little like cinnamon and cloves.

What a lovely dream, she thought in the middle of the kiss as the genie's tongue parted her lips and slipped inside her mouth. She sighed and kissed him harder while he explored and tickled, sucked and nipped. He kissed her harder too, bruising her mouth ever so slightly, not enough to hurt, but only to excite her.

Larrie began to tingle in places she hadn't tingled in a very long time.

Oh, this is so very nice, she thought, and to her great surprise a moan escaped from deep inside her.

The genie's hand slowly lifted her shirt and since Larrie didn't wear a bra, easily found her small firm breast. Larrie kept her eyes closed tight. She was asleep, she assured herself as she wondered how far the genie would go with this. *Is this a woman's wet dream? Can we have them?* She smiled and reveled in the sensation of the genie's fingers stroking her expertly, feeling her questions were now moot as she was clearly aroused.

Then the dogs started barking again. The hand stopped. The lips vanished from hers. Her arms were suddenly empty. She opened her eyes. The power had come back on, and the room was brightly illuminated from the overhead fixture. Naturally, there was no genie kissing her. No one was there at all. Larrie felt a stab of irrational disappointment. *It's too bad you can't request your dreams*, Larrie thought. She'd like to have this one again.

With the clock ticking toward the hour when Van was due to arrive, Larrie stared at herself in the mirror, feeling slightly depressed. Like Aunt Lolly, she had fair skin with a tendency to freckle and "Red Irish" hair, even though her Smith ancestors were Highland Scots, a brave and belligerent race.

And, as observed at the bridal shower, Larrie *had* cut her own hair, making it very short on the sides, long on top, and uneven everywhere. She'd done the amateur shearing around three a.m. one night, in a fit of grief, and even if she had known how to cut hair, her eyes had been so blinded by tears she couldn't see what she was doing anyway.

As unlikely as it sounded, cutting off her long hair had made her feel better. As she stood in the bathroom barefooted, piles of her red hair on the cool white tiles, she viscerally comprehended the Jewish mourning custom of "rending of garments." The cutting was a way to make the internal grief visible on the outside, and once outside, it began to lose its power to keep tearing a soul apart.

But looking at her own reflection right now, Larrie despaired about what to do with her raggedly shorn, ginger-colored hair so it would look good enough for a dinner with a sophisticated New York dealer. At first she'd thought she'd mousse or hairspray the heck out of it and go punk or spiked or whatever it was the young and pierced were doing this year. She had also seen that some girls frosted their locks with bright blues, yellows, and purples, but she drew the line at experimenting with the turquoise fabric dye that had been sitting in the laundry room for years. However, she admitted it had crossed her mind.

She ended up slicking the short hair back on the sides. The bangs that she had forgotten to trim recently were full and nearly in her eyes. The accidental hair style and her waif-thin body made her look gamine in an Audrey Hepburn way. Dressed simply in skinny black cropped pants and a white sleeveless blouse, Larrie could have starred in *Breakfast at Tiffany's.*

But to her own eyes, she was a disappointment, a shadow of her former hardy self. In her misperception,

Larrie was no different than most people. She didn't see herself as others did, but through a glass, darkly.

She put on some wide sterling cuffs for jewelry, slipped silver hoops in her ears, and loaded her fingers with estate jewelry that wasn't very valuable, but that she happened to like. She dabbed on a little mascara and some lip gloss. That was it. She was as ready as she'd ever be.

She strolled down to the kitchen to putter around while she waited for Van. She went to pass by the brass lamp which she had set on the mantel. She stopped in her tracks and looked at it before she reached out absentmindedly and gave it a little stroke. It felt unusually warm, warmer than the summer night air. She peered at it curiously. Where she had polished it, it seemed to glow unusually bright.

She smiled, and per her habit of having a conversation with inanimate objects, she cocked her head and began her monologue: "Hey, genie of the lamp! Are you in there? I just wanted to say you're a great kisser—and kissing a dream man is the only intimacy I am ready for. I am going on a date. But to tell the truth, I'm not looking forward to this 'date' at all. It's a test, you see? If I can get through a simple business dinner without a total meltdown, I think that's a good thing. Don't you?

"Cat got your tongue? What did you say your name was? John, but you're called Jo. You know, Jo, I never had anybody in a dream tell me their name before. You're the first. It was a real humdinger of a dream, that's for sure! I would love for you to come see me again. In fact, I insist on it. So come on, now, out of there!" Then she laughed, reached out, gave the lamp another little rub, and then went on past into the kitchen.

She picked up the phone and called Melanie. She had to tell somebody she was going out for dinner with a guy she had just met, and that's what best friends were for.

Larrie started off by giving Melanie a short version of buying the Ydoboni estate, because books rather than antiques were more Melanie's thing. Then she launched into the big news—she had said yes to having dinner with another antiques dealer who wanted to talk shop.

Larrie, who couldn't see wasting time while she talked, held the receiver between her shoulder and her ear so she had her hands free. She opened the pantry and started purging foods beyond their expiration date and rearranging the canned goods while she told Melanie that she honestly believed that talking about antiques tonight was Van Killborn's motive. She rattled on, barely pausing for breath, telling Melanie for the hundredth time that she wasn't ready to date, and this wasn't really a date because there was no earthly reason this guy would have any interest in *her*, in a man-woman way. They didn't travel in the same circles; they lived in different worlds. She was surprised he asked her in the first place and she figured that he was just buttering her up so she'd sell him the furniture he wanted.

Finally Melanie sighed loudly and followed the sigh with a snort of disgust. "Larrie, you're so dense. Oh, sure, he's 'buttering you up.' Why? So you'll sell him the furniture at a primo price, far beyond what you can hope to get by selling it out of the shop? Get real! Did you consider that maybe he wants to see the gorgeous redhead he stumbled on in the middle of Podunk Nowhere? Meeting you was as if he found a diamond in a box lot of costume jewelry, to put what I'm saying in terms you might understand."

"Melanie, no way. I'm sorry, but you've got it wrong. I'm only gorgeous to you and my parents."

Another huge sigh, a brief silence, then Melanie began to chuckle. "Well, hey, Larrie, it's a lot better than being pursued by Norb Tichmarsh." The balding, wimpy high school attendance officer had called Larrie for weeks, trying to get her to go out with him. Melanie's laugh, a beautiful silver bell ringing, came over the line.

Larrie started to laugh too. "You got that right!" she hooted.

Finally Melanie said, "Look, Lar, just have a good time and stop analyzing, okay? Whatever it is, it is."

At that point, a movement in the doorway to the living room caught Larrie's attention. She looked over—and screamed. As big as life, the genie of her dreams leaned insolently against the doorjamb. A lopsided grin showed very white teeth in his tanned face. His arms were folded across his bare chest, which was as magnificently muscular as Larrie remembered. He winked at her.

Larrie blinked. The doorway was empty. The man had vanished.

"Larrie! What happened? Are you okay?" Melanie's voice sounded frantic.

Larrie's fingers clenched the phone receiver. *Oh, shit. I must be hallucinating. I've gone totally bonkers.* Her breath got short. Her chest got tight. She squeaked out the words. "I—I—dropped a can of creamed corn on my foot, that's all. I'd better go. Van will be here any minute."

She wasn't paying attention to Melanie anymore. She felt that she had to get off the phone and check out the living room—on the unlikely chance somebody really was in there.

"Call me tomorrow. I need to hear everything," Melanie demanded.

"Right. Sure. Will do. I gotta go, Mel." Larrie's heart was pounding. She hung up and rushed into the other room.

The genie lounged casually with his back against the mantel. "What took you so long, luv? You asked me to come round and see you." His British accent announced him to be aristocratic, arrogant, and impossibly sexy.

Dizziness overtook Larrie and the room started to spin. She grabbed the back of a chair to steady herself. She stared. What appeared to be a solid flesh and blood gorgeous guy really was standing half naked in her living room.

Nothing made sense. The dogs, who barked viciously at a passing butterfly, were not making a sound. Sadie snoozed in an armchair. Teddy was drooling and gnawing on a rawhide chew as he lay on the hearth not far from the man's bare feet. And Taco was jumping up on the man's shin, demanding attention.

The man picked the little dog up. Taco licked his face. The man stroked the little dog's forehead and then gently put the Chihuahua back down.

Larrie stared dumbfounded. "I must be dreaming," she finally said aloud.

Jo, the genie, turned brown eyes with impossibly long lashes in her direction. "You look awake to me. Do you think you're asleep?"

"I am not asleep! Don't be ridiculous."

"You suggested that. I didn't."

"I'm trying to come up with some rational explanation for you."

"You think my being the genie in Aladdin's lamp isn't rational?" He grinned his engaging grin again, showing deep dimples in his lean face.

"Of course it's not! It's crazy. The story of Aladdin is a fairy tale. Oh, God, I've had a breakdown. That must be it." At that point, Larrie's legs gave way and she sat down on the floor with a thud. She fought the panic rising inside her. "Oh, damn. Oh, crap. Oh, shit," she said to no one in particular.

Suddenly she heard a merry jingling. She saw bare feet on the floor next to her. The noise came from the bells encircling one tanned male ankle. At the sight of the smooth brown skin, Larrie's stomach gave a little flip. She couldn't be near this figment of her imagination without instantly getting turned on. She must be mad. She jerked her head up to see the genie looking down at her.

He wore a mocking smile. *What's the joke?* Larrie thought. He didn't seem the least concerned that Larrie was edging closer and closer toward hysteria.

"You don't swear particularly well. You have no imagination. I can teach you some authentic limey oaths. You'll be swearing like a sailor in no time, luv." His British accent made everything sound delicious.

"What? No! And stop calling me 'love.'"

"Right-o, luv. Let me help you get up."

Suddenly he was standing behind her. He put his strong hands on her sides. His touch was warm, firm, and definitely real. It made Larrie's heart flutter. He lifted her easily to a standing position and released his grip, but he stayed standing just inches away. Larrie could feel the heat from his body.

He spoke again. "You're as scrawny as a chicken."

Larrie whirled around. The man was very close. "Why must you insult me? It's bad enough I'm hallucinating." Then her face threatened to crumble. She squeezed her eyes shut. She opened them. The man was still there, still smiling, still cocky. "This is crazy. I'm crazy. I have to be."

The man gave her a pitying look. "You're not crazy. At least, you're not crazy because you see me. I'm a one hundred percent genuine genie. I can't vouch for your mental state in other respects since we just met. But you didn't strike me as unbalanced—at least you kiss like a perfectly ordinary woman."

Larrie's eyes widened. "What! That really happened? You kissed me and—and—you—you—put your hand—" She backed away, outrage obliterating all other emotions. "You have some nerve. Where do you get off coming in here and kissing me while I was asleep? You! You! Whoever you are!"

"I'm Jo Trelawny. You remembered it just a few minutes ago when you stopped, gave the lamp a rub, and requested my return. Naturally I obeyed. It's what I do."

"What *are* you talking about?" Larrie tried to make sense of the man's words, but they were utterly fantastical.

"I am the genie in the lamp—not by choice, you understand. But there you have it. I mean literally. You have *it*. The lamp. Therefore you have me."

"I still don't understand." Confusion was making Larrie's thoughts addled when she heard a car crunching up the gravel in the driveway. It had to be Van's Mercedes. The dogs, barking frantically, all raced to the front door. She glanced at them for a brief moment. When she looked back toward the genie, nobody was there. The lamp sat on the mantel just as it had before she called Melanie.

Jo Trelawny, the genie, was gone.

Chapter 9

Van's heart thumped loudly in his chest when the woman called Larrie flung open her front door. She was far too thin for his taste and anxiety pinched her lovely face, but she was a knockout. Van had an eye for potential. He could spot the masterpiece hidden beneath a deceptive surface, and he had seen from the first that this particular woman could break hearts. He hoped she would not break his.

He noted that she looked amazing tonight, 1950s retro and charming, but he found it hard to concentrate on her beauty when he was in danger of being ravaged by three vicious dogs.

"Teddy, down! Back! Sadie, no. No!" Larrie grabbed the two big dogs by their collars. "I'll lock them in the kitchen," she called out as she dragged them away. That left a singularly ferocious Chihuahua to dive at Van's ankles. By the time Larrie returned, Taco had Van's pant leg in his teeth and was shaking it with deadly intent.

"*Taco!* What has gotten into you? I'm so sorry. He never does this. Did he bite you? No? Thank goodness for that. Your pants don't look ripped, just a bit damp." She snatched the little dog into her arms.

"You don't need a bodyguard with that kind of protection," Van said, brushing off his slacks. He was relieved to see they weren't torn. "It's probably wise, a woman living way out in the country all alone."

"I'm not"—she hesitated and glanced over her shoulder toward the fireplace mantel—"really alone." Then she turned her lovely face toward Van. "What I mean is my great-aunt lives on the property. But never mind that. I'll put Taco with the others, grab my handbag, and we can go."

Van's silver Mercedes sat sleekly in the driveway. He gallantly opened the door for Larrie, then moved around to the driver's side, hoping he wouldn't step in anything. He suspected he needed to take note where he walked, but he couldn't see very well.

Although some illumination came from the glowing windows inside the house, the dusty country road lacked streetlights. Looming shapes and gloomy shadows, all nebulous and indistinct, filled the rural, alien landscape. Van, who lived in a city where the lights never went out, inwardly cringed. Eyes seemed to be watching him. There had to be wild things in the dark.

He was just reaching for the door handle when somebody planted a hand between his shoulder blades and shoved hard. He pitched forward and thudded into the side of the car, barely managing to grab the door handle and stop his fall.

He whipped his head around. He could see nothing. "Who did that!" he yelled angrily. He heard nothing in reply but the distant barking of a dog.

It sure felt as if somebody pushed me, he thought. He stood still another moment. Nothing living moved. He slid into the car.

"Are you all right?" Larrie asked. "It looked as if you slipped or something."

"I'm fine. But I could swear somebody pushed me." He laughed nervously. "Must have been my imagination. You don't have any ghosts out here, do you?" He smiled in her direction.

A little frown appeared between Larrie's eyebrows. "Ghosts? My goodness, no. We're up on a mountain, though. It might have been a gust of wind."

"The wind? Must have been." Van turned the key in the ignition. The starter clicked, but the lights didn't go on, the engine didn't turn over. He tried again. The expensive car sat like a worthless hunk of silver metal, inert and silent.

Van glanced over at Larrie. "That's odd. It ran fine on the drive up here."

He turned the key on and off a few more times, then shook his head. "I have less than ten thousand miles on the car. It's nearly new. I don't understand why it's not starting."

"Do you need gas?" Larrie asked, her voice encouraging. "I keep a five-gallon can in the storage shed."

Van stared at the unlit, useless dials of the dashboard. "No, I filled up this morning." He turned to Larrie. "It won't do any good for me to look under the hood. I'm not a car guy. I guess the problem must be electrical. There are no lights at all. I better call the roadside emergency number. Mercedes will send someone out." He exhaled heavily. "I'm really sorry. It doesn't look likely that we'll get any dinner."

Van felt miserable and increasingly anxious. He needed to talk Larrie into selling him the Ydoboni items—that was part of why he asked her out. Big money was riding on his getting what was in that armoire. And the client—Van didn't even like to say his name but it started with a G and ended with a vowel—nobody crossed him, and nobody disappointed him. It wouldn't do to return to New York empty-handed, not if Van valued his kneecaps, or even his life.

Van wished the business of the furniture didn't exist

as an issue between him and Larrie. He genuinely liked this slender, ethereal-looking woman and coveted her in the way he did any rare and beautiful thing. He wanted to spend time with her. Now he felt cheated and let down.

Unexpectedly, Larrie reached out and gave his shoulder a little pat. "I can see how disappointed you are. Buck up, Van. You go on and call road service. The night's not over yet." Her voice alone lifted his sagging spirits. She was a great girl.

Using the car's Tele Aid, he made the call, hoping someone could get out here quickly enough to save the evening.

The operator's reassuring voice over the speaker-phone promised that help would be dispatched. A long pause was followed by the revelation that help would take some time considering the vehicle's remote location. The service would find an authorized provider and get back to Van. Then he and Larrie sat in an awkward silence waiting for the return call. It came after a short interval, the operator informing Van that the tow truck would arrive in about an hour.

"An hour! Can you believe that? I could have gotten Wayne here in fifteen minutes," Larrie said. She noticed Van's questioning face. "Wayne Smith owns a towing rig in Tunkhannock. He's a relative. But then who isn't around here!" She laughed. "My family settled this area before the Civil War. Everybody's my cousin, I think!"

Van wasn't really listening. Disappointment put a ragged edge on his voice. "There goes our dinner. My plans for the evening are ruined."

"They're just changed, not ruined. Now that's not so bad. We can use my truck to run down to the Ranch Wagon and back in thirty minutes. We'll grab some foot-longs and fries. It's such a beautiful night, we'll have a picnic right here in the yard while we wait for the service truck." Larrie's voice sounded high and bright, and to Van, even a bit relieved.

He shrugged his shoulders under his lightweight sports jacket. "Sounds like a plan. But I wanted to treat you to a good dinner, with wine and soft music. A beautiful woman like you deserves more than hot dogs."

"I'll take a rain check. Come on, there's no use crying over spilled milk, as my Aunt Lolly always says." She opened the door and got out. Van slipped the ignition keys into his jacket pocket and followed Larrie to her truck. The grass, already wet with dew, quickly soaked through his good Italian leather loafers.

The driver's door squeaked loudly on its hinges when Larrie got in. Van hauled himself into the passenger side. A clipboard sat on the console along with a pile of badly folded maps. The cab smelled of dog. He didn't want to think about the probability of dog hair on the seat.

The engine roared when she started it and ran with a rough, thumping sound. "It's a diesel," Larrie yelled to Van over the noise.

"Right."

He made an effort to talk over the din as Larrie drove expertly down the dark roads toward Dallas—not Dallas, Texas, but a small town about five miles from her farm. After Larrie replied with, "What? Huh? Can you talk louder?" a few times, Van settled for watching her. He tried not to stare, but sent as many glances as he could her way. She had a naturalness missing in the women he dated in New York City, yet her defined cheekbones and long neck gave her an innate elegance. With her angularity and bone structure, he could see her dressed in something couture. He'd like to show her off.

She was naïve though, he felt sure of that. He knew he was a good manipulator. He always did well with sales. She wouldn't suspect anything, and he should be able to convince her to part with the items he wanted.

He rationalized that desperate times called for desperate measures. Besides, he was paying her extremely well, and therefore not really cheating her.

Or rather, he wouldn't be cheating this sweet woman if he didn't know what was in the armoire. He pushed his guilt away. He had to do this. When he found the treasure officially—and he would be terribly "surprised"—he could even pay her a "finder's fee" out of the goodness of his heart. After all, this kind of thing happened all the time in the antiques business.

He recalled one of the most famous incidents. In the late 1980s, a fellow bought an old painting for four bucks at the Adamstown, Pennsylvania, flea market. When the frame fell apart in his hands, one of the official copies from the first printing of the Declaration of Independence fell out from behind the picture. Sotheby's authenticated it, then sold it for $2.42 million. What did the flea market seller get? Nothing except a bad case of heartburn. That was part of the game called dealing in antiques.

Remembering that, Van felt better, smiled to himself, and settled back in the seat as the noisy red truck rattled through the night.

When Larrie and Van finally got back from the Ranch Wagon, Van carefully carried a greasy paper bag that purportedly contained their "dinner"—two foot-longs with chili and the works, plus two orders of fries. Another bag, not greasy, held the Mike's Hard Lemonade they grabbed at a supermarket. It was the only alcoholic beverage available besides a few popular brands of beer. Van had made a face at the purchase. He never drank this kind of thing, but there wasn't a wine store open in the entire state of Pennsylvania on a Sunday night.

The Mercedes sat exactly as they had left it. The road service truck still hadn't arrived.

Larrie pulled her big red Ford onto the lawn and turned off the engine. "It's a beautiful night to stay out here, but we can carry the food inside to eat if you'd prefer a real table and chairs."

Van remembered the dogs. He imagined they'd bark the entire time he was in the house. "Outside is perfect."

"Come on then, we'll have a tailgate party. I used to do it all the time before the Penn State games."

"I'm not much of a football fan," Van said.

Larrie looked at him as if he had landed on earth from another planet. "Penn State is one of the Big Ten schools. You've heard of Joe Pa, Coach Joe Paterno, haven't you?"

He looked at her blankly. "I went to Bard College as an undergraduate. It stresses the arts."

A flash of something, pity perhaps, crossed Larrie's face before she composed her features into neutrality. "You probably had lots of other ways to have a good time besides freezing your butt watching a college game. Out here in the sticks, there's not much else to do. But come on, this will be fun. I promise you."

With that, Larrie climbed out of the cab and met Van behind the truck. She had a small emergency light on her key chain and handed it to Van to hold while she expertly lowered the tailgate.

"Aim the light over here," she told him and leaned inside. She pulled out two high folding chairs. She leaned them against the truck. Then she flipped up a cooler top and pulled out paper plates, napkins, and some plastic cups for the Mike's Hard Lemonade. He noticed her hands seemed to shake a little. He was surprised that she was nervous and wondered why.

Finally she took out a Coleman lantern and set it up. She turned toward Van and with a great flourish lit the wick. "As God said on the first day, 'Let there be light!' Whoa, that's way too bright." The white glare lit up their faces in a garish way and clearly revealed their surroundings, which proved to be just a couple of bushes and an old tractor tire on its side that was being used as a planter of sorts.

Larrie quickly extinguished the lantern, and except for the narrow beam from the key chain light, blackness returned with a vengeance. Van shivered uneasily. She asked him to aim the light back into the truck bed and then rummaged around in another box. She pulled out two votive candles. "This will be better. Enough light to eat by, but not enough to destroy the beauty of the night."

"If you think inky blackness is beautiful."

"What? Oh, you haven't looked up. Look up, Van. It's a gorgeous night."

It was. The sky held innumerable tiny diamonds displayed against black velvet. Van tipped his head back and gaped. The only celestial objects visible from the bottom of Manhattan's canyons were the moon and one or two of the very brightest stars. He remembered something like this from Boy Scout camp ages ago. A plane's lights winked red and green amid the glory. "I see the Milky Way and the Big Dipper. Definitely better than the planetarium at the Natural History Museum."

Larrie snorted in an unladylike manner. "Planetarium! You're a city boy, Van. This is the real thing. The moon will be up later. It dims out some of the stars, so enjoy the show while you can."

Van began thinking that being alone in the dark with the beautiful Larrie had its advantages over a crowded restaurant. He wondered how she'd feel if he made a move. He would try something, he decided. He just had to wait for an opening. Nothing radical, of course. He didn't think she'd sleep with him, not tonight anyway, but all the women he knew were pretty easy and found their way into his bed after the second or third date. He figured he'd see how she responded to a kiss and take it from there.

Another thought occurred to him. Since he wouldn't have a vehicle, it might seem appropriate for her to ask him to sleep over. He could score. He had to play this exactly right.

To start the process, he reached for a French fry just as she did, making sure their hands touched. She jerked away as if he had scalded her. He kept his face from showing anything, but he was taken aback. She made that biblical reference a few minutes earlier. Maybe she was religious—maybe a Bible thumper in some evangelical sect. He better take it very slowly with her and not screw up the business he needed to conduct by scaring her off.

He figured he better get her talking about herself. She'd probably say right away if she were a Jehovah's Witness or something. He needed some insight into what he was dealing with. "So, what should I know about you?"

A number of emotions—sadness, worry, confusion—chased across Larrie's face. Then she turned her silver eyes toward Van. "You should probably know this is the first time I've gone out with any man—for any reason—in a very long time. You see—" She took a deep breath. "My fiancé, Ryan—he died. He was—" Another heavy breath. She coughed. "—in the Mideast. In the war." She turned her head away.

"I'm sorry to hear that." Van thought it explained a lot. She was grieving, a little scared, lonely, and very vulnerable. He was sure she could be seduced if he was smart about it. This was better than he had hoped. He pictured her slender body naked in his arms. "But that explains the watch."

Larrie looked down at her right wrist. "Yes, it's his. I guess it looks odd to be wearing two wristwatches, but his doesn't run. I keep it set to the day and time—the last time I saw him."

"It's not so odd. I've seen it before."

"You have? I thought I was the only person who ever did such a thing."

Van very quickly reached out and gave her hand a squeeze. "Not at all. I've seen it a few times. Watches are loaded with symbolism, you know. There's even a trendy watch that's called 'Memento mori.' In Latin that means 'Remember you will die.' In other words, savor every moment of life because all things end."

A sigh escaped from Larrie's lips, but she forced some brightness into her face, her eyes catching the candlelight and twinkling with unshed tears. She sipped the hard lemonade and changed the subject. "You said you wanted to talk antiques."

"Absolutely. You just made a major score with the Ydoboni estate. You beat out a top New York dealer, you know. How did you get started in the business?"

Larrie lit up as if someone had turned on a light switch inside her soul. "You don't really want to know!"

"I do. Tell me, please." Van liked watching her with her face animated and devoid of sadness. He was happy to just listen.

Larrie took another gulp of her lemonade and began. "Okay, you asked for it. I slipped into antiques through the back door, you might say. Unintentionally. I never planned on this career. I was going to be a great artist. A painter. I loved the work of Mary Cassatt when I was still in college. There are some wonderful examples of her work in Philadelphia. Oh, I know, I can see it in your face. I seem to never get out of the state of Pennsylvania. I dream about it sometimes, but I seem to be stuck here.

"Later, after—" She stopped and took a deep breath, then went on. "After Ryan's death, I found myself drawn to Frida Kahlo. She put her internal self on the canvas, you see. Anyway, to get back to my career choice. I always loved going to yard sales. While I was growing up, my mom and I used to do that every Saturday morning. It was our special thing. We'd get up before dawn and take Dad's pickup. It was treasure hunting. You can understand the thrill of that, can't you?"

A frisson of something like guilt passed over Van. He nodded. "I can."

"I began to collect cookie jars when I was twelve. That's a crazy thing to do since they take up so much room, but I just love them, the animals mostly. I also started noticing that every second or third yard sale had a head vase for sale. You're making a face. I know they were mass produced and mostly from Japan. Sort of kitsch, right? But the faces, the colors, those hats!" She laughed when he looked disapproving, then wrinkled her nose at him, as if she thought *he* was a snob not to appreciate the tackiness of the glued-on earrings and false eyelashes.

Then she went on. "As I was saying, for no good reason except that they tickled my fancy, I'd buy every head vase I found that was perfect. I didn't bother with anything that was chipped or cracked. By the time I finished high school, I had over two hundred vases. In late summer, when I was ready to start classes at Penn State, I sent my entire collection to Traver's Auction to sell in hopes that I'd get enough money for my textbooks."

She clapped her hands suddenly, startling Van a little. "Would you believe it? I got a check for almost seven thousand dollars! I kid you not. Some of the vases I had picked up for fifty cents. I had a few Relpo vases in that lot that brought more than three hundred fifty dollars each. The Jackie Kennedy by Inarco really floored me. I got seven hundred dollars for her. I was hooked for life."

Van thought Larrie was cute to get so excited by a

fifty-cent head vase. A fragment of an Etruscan statue would bring ten times her seven thousand dollars, and Van had sold one for exactly that, seventy thousand dollars, when he was sixteen. But he didn't tell Larrie that. "That's terrific," he said, trying not to sound patronizing, "but you finished college, didn't you?"

"Oh, sure, I did. With honors too. At first I thought I wanted to go work for one of the big auction houses in New York, Sotheby's or Christie's, you know. Or maybe get a job in a Soho gallery. But by then Ryan and I had set a wedding date, and we didn't want to raise our kids in the city. So I got the bright idea to open an antiques store. Ryan helped me set it up before he left . . ." Her voice trailed away like a fading puff of smoke.

She didn't look at Van anymore. She turned her eyes toward the darkness of the night outside the candlelight. Her voice had become flat and emotionless when she started speaking again. "After Ryan died, I threw myself into getting my business started. I went to the Missouri Auction School and got my appraiser's certification so I could do that too. I researched every item I bought and built up a good reference library.

"I realized I wasn't grieving or dwelling on myself when I traveled around looking at other people's things or got caught up in bidding at an auction. But the biggest thing that's happened to me after—after Ryan— I've discovered I prefer the past over the present. I came to love what's gone: a time when people took pride in their work and cared deeply about the things they made. I came to understand people's lives from the contents of old houses—the canning jars, the crocheted and tatted table linens, the game tables, the good dishes and luncheon sets, the massive dining room suites, the ticket stubs, the fountain glasses.

"Those kinds of things told me that in the past people had friends over for lunch, they got together to play pinochle or bridge or canasta, women met to paint china or make quilts, and men and women of all ages went to the local movie theater that was on every Main Street in every little town, then stopped at a soda shop afterward.

"I liked what I saw. I liked that people rode trains and trolley cars. I liked the bikes, scooters, red wagons, and skates that showed me a past when kids went out to play without supervision and without fear. I read the post-marked letters and postcards from the decades when the postman brought mail twice a day. And I saw a time when newspapers, dozens of them, had a morning and evening edition ... When families ate meals together and everybody got together for Sunday dinner ... When you knew your neighbor ..." She sighed and stopped for a moment. "That was a better, sweeter life."

She turned back to Van then, focusing her shining sil-ver eyes on his. "I have decided I don't like this century or the world we've created in it. I don't really want to be in it, I guess, so I deal in antiques."

She talked on for a while after that, but the spark was gone. Finally, she gave up talking about herself entirely and asked Van, "What about you? No wedding ring. You're such a handsome guy, you must have your pick of women. Are you divorced? A confirmed bachelor?"

Van laughed. "I'm happily single, at least for now. I haven't had a serious relationship in a while. I started working longer and longer hours and traveling a great deal. That lifestyle doesn't make for lasting relation-ships. You see, I've been trying to keep the antiques business going. It's been in our family for three genera-tions. Right now we're dependent on a few big clients. This economy has made us very vulnerable. That's why I hoped— Hey! What's that?"

"What?" Larrie's voice was alarmed.

"The curtain in your house just moved. I swear I saw somebody inside. Didn't you say you lived alone?"

"Maybe it was one of the dogs. They jump up and look out."

"You shut them in the kitchen, remember. I saw somebody in *that* window. The one right in the front of the house." He pointed.

Larrie looked very worried. "Are you sure?"

Just then the front door began to open.

Chapter 10

Larrie was as jumpy as a cat in a roomful of rocking chairs. Her earlier hallucination, or whatever it was, of the genie in her living room had shaken her as violently as a terrier shakes a rat in its jaws. She couldn't understand what was happening to her. Despite appearing to function normally, she must have somehow lost her grip on reality.

She wondered if agreeing to go out with Van had precipitated a mental crisis. What else could have caused her unstable state of mind? Yet she could scarcely credit that a dinner with another antiques dealer could have flipped her over the edge.

And the "date" itself had been anticlimactic. Van had proved to be easy company and a thoroughly nice guy, only definitely not her type. She had enjoyed the evening, even though she had to keep telling herself it was unfair to compare Van with the boys she had grown up with, and especially with Ryan.

But she just couldn't help it. Van was different from any of them, city-bred and out of his element, like a stranger in a strange land even though he was only 130 miles due west from Manhattan. Clearly he wasn't comfortable around dogs. He certainly got spooked when he nearly took a tumble getting into his car. Imagine, thinking someone had pushed him. And he had jumped every time an owl hooted or some small, harmless creature rustled in the grass.

Larrie didn't think less of him because of that. She'd be just as uneasy in the middle of Manhattan, thinking a mugger was going to attack her any second.

But when his car wouldn't start, she had been surprised that he had no idea what to do. Ryan would have jumped out and had the hood up on the recalcitrant Mercedes in seconds. He would have said derogatory things about "furrin" cars and complained about the new cars' internal computers that kept men from fixing their own vehicles; meanwhile he would have been grinning and enjoying the challenge of something mechanical that refused to work.

As it turned out, the problems with the Mercedes had been a welcome distraction from the "date" she had dreaded. She had felt relieved that she didn't end up at some fancy restaurant. All things considered, she congratulated herself on emotionally doing better than she expected. She hadn't had any panic attacks, strange visions, or weird hallucinations. Except for one teary moment, she hadn't slipped into a sad place.

In the end, she sat happily on the folding chair next to the tailgate they were using as a picnic table. She ate hot dogs and fries. She enjoyed Van's gentle, undemanding presence. She began to talk a lot. Mike's Hard Lemonade had no doubt provided the necessary social lubricant.

The clarity of the sky and its shining carpet of stars added to her giddiness. She became light-headed, almost tipsy, when she pointed out to him several constellations besides the obvious Big Dipper with the North Star twinkling brightly beyond the "pointer stars" at the tip of the handle.

Larrie's favorite constellation was Cassiopeia, whose biggest stars formed the letter W. It was always easy to find. She sometimes wondered why it appealed to her so much, since the story behind it was such a terrible one. Queen Cassiopeia, the wife of Cepheus and the mother of Andromeda, was chained to this star throne in the heavens for eternity as punishment for boasting that she was more beautiful than all the Nereids. When the earth rotated and the stars seemed to move, the poor vain queen hung suffering upside down. Larrie thought the image was wonderfully macabre and yet poetic too.

And after she told Van how she had gotten started in the business, she had also chatted about her passion for sturdy American pottery and the carnival glass of the 1920s and 1930s. She told him she relished finding inexpensive, everyday things from the American past best of all. She didn't care a whit if she ever came across popular antiques, like Stickley Mission furniture, that, despite the economy, commanded high prices. She prized the quirky and unique as long as it was authentically old and well-made.

Larrie let herself relax. In the back of her mind, she knew the roadside service truck would arrive any minute and the night would be over. She didn't have to worry where this conversation or the evening was leading.

She was well aware that most women would have trouble keeping their emotions in check around Van Killborn. He was, by any standard, a stunning-looking man, nearly a Nordic god with his ample height and broad shoulders, sandy blond hair and square jaw. Yet as attractive as he was, he ignited no spark in Larrie. She laughed to herself. The only sexual desire she had felt in over a year had been with a genie in a dream!

She waxed introspective when she thought about that. She had to stop beating herself up for her grief. She had to give herself time. In fact, the alcohol had started to create a warm glow inside and Van was looking better to her—if still no more sexually desirable—as the minutes ticked by.

Then he had seen the figure at the window and asked her why someone was in the house if she lived alone.

With her heart beating wildly, Larrie too saw the curtains being moved and a person briefly appear. Larrie's thoughts careened like a pinball back and forth. For one insane moment she thought, *It's the genie!* Was that possible? It certainly looked like a man. A second later, the figure was gone.

Larrie jumped to her feet. To do what? She didn't know. "Maybe it's the dogs," she suggested, knowing it wasn't. She heard a noise from the house. Her breath caught in her throat. The front door swung slowly open. A tall figure appeared, a dark silhouette against the light inside.

"Yoohoo! Larrie? Is that you out there?"

"Yes, Aunt Lolly. It's me." Larrie went weak with relief.

"I heard voices. The dogs were barking," she called out.

"I'm out here with a friend, Aunt Lolly," Larrie answered.

"I won't bother you then. Good night, dear." The door shut.

"It was my aunt," Larrie stated the obvious to Van.

Van looked decidedly puzzled. "I could have sworn I saw a man behind the window curtain."

"Aunt Lolly's quite tall."

Van frowned. "I must have been mistaken. But I was certain— Hey, there's the service truck. At last."

A towing rig rumbled up the driveway and parked behind the Mercedes. The driver climbed quickly out of the cab. He was wearing a T-shirt and jeans accessorized with a utility belt.

"Hey, Wayne," Larrie greeted him. "Guess you got the service call after all."

"What you doing with a Mercedes, Larrie? You buy one for Lolly to replace the Honda she crashed through the garage door? Hahaha."

"You're a comedian, Wayne. The Mercedes belongs to one of my colleagues. Wayne Smith, meet Van Killborn. He's an antiques dealer from New York City."

Wayne extended his big paw and shook Van's hand. He gave Larrie a sly glance. "You selling antiques at night now, Larrie?"

Oh, great, the whole town is going to know by tomorrow that I was out with some fancy New Yorker, Larrie thought. She put her hands on her hips and snapped, "Mind your own business, Wayne, and do what you're getting paid for. Look at the car. Engine wouldn't turn over. No lights. Dead as a doornail. You'll probably have to tow it to the dealer in Scranton."

"Ay-up. You think a vehicle that cost as much as a damned house should start, now don't you." He walked over and put the hood up. He pulled a flashlight from the utility belt and peered in. "Hmmmm," he said. "Hmmmm. Well, don't that beat all. Hmmmm."

"What are you 'Hmmmm Hmmmm-ing' about, Wayne?" Impatience colored her voice.

"Nothing wrong with the car. Somebody disconnected the battery. Cable's off."

Larrie turned to Van, a question on her face.

"Don't look at me!" Van protested. "I don't know a thing about it. I'm from New York City. I didn't even own a car until this year."

It wasn't that Larrie didn't believe him. He had no reason for sabotaging their date—in fact, just the opposite was true. He wanted to go out to dinner with her. But if he didn't do it, and Larrie knew she didn't do it, she couldn't imagine how anyone else could have either.

"Maybe it fell off?" Van asked.

Wayne gave Van a look that plainly said *this guy is*

obviously a total idiot, but then Wayne's face slowly changed. He seemed to be giving serious consideration to what Van asked. "Well now, you might have something there. It might have fallen off, *if* somebody had jerry-rigged it to do that before you drove out here, so that at some point the cable separated from the negative terminal and broke the circuit."

From the lack of comprehension on Van's face, Larrie realized Wayne could have been speaking Greek. She jumped in to interpret Wayne-speak. "You mean somebody deliberately tampered with the car so Van would get stranded, not necessarily here. Maybe on a dark road somewhere."

"Anything's possible. But I don't see no tape or nothing. 'Course it's pretty hard to inspect the battery in the dark. It's a lot more likely somebody popped the hood right here and pulled it off. Only take a couple of seconds. Think Aunt Lolly did it? She's a little, you know—"

"Wayne Smith! Aunt Lolly is *not* 'a little, you know.' She's as sane as I am."

Wayne raised an eyebrow.

"Unless you want that flashlight stuck someplace the sun doesn't shine, you better knock it off, Wayne." Larrie was more touchy about her own mental health than she had been a few hours earlier.

Wayne put his hands up in mock surrender. "I was teasing! Shoot, Larrie, I don't know how this happened, but it weren't nothing serious. Somebody playing a joke, I guess. If you opened the hood, you could have fixed this yourself."

"I never even considered it, for heaven's sake. Just put the damned thing back on, please." She looked over at Van. It was hard to tell what he was thinking.

"I suppose I better get going once it's fixed," he said at last.

"It is getting late."

"You did say you'd give me a rain check." His face looked a little brighter.

"Sure, Van, if you're still around. Maybe later in the week. We'll see."

The light in his face faded. "Right." He paused a minute. "Do you have time to give me another look at the Ydoboni estate?"

"You mean you want to make sure I didn't scratch or break the things you offered to buy when we moved them?"

Van stammered, "Well, uh—"

"Don't apologize. If I offered all that money to buy something, I'd certainly want to make sure it was still okay. Wayne, we're going to head to the barn. You need Van up here for anything?"

Wayne was closing the Mercedes' hood. "He needs to sign a paper so I can get paid. And hang on just a minute. I'll make sure the car starts. Who's got the keys?"

Despite his city ways, Van was a good athlete, especially skilled at racquetball and tennis. He pulled the car keys out of his jacket pocket and tossed them in a graceful arc to Wayne's open hands.

A small folded piece of paper came out unnoticed with the keys and fell softly to the grass.

Chapter 11

Van looked appreciatively around the huge space inside the old barn that Larrie used as a showroom for the Sparrow's Nest. "When was this built? Look at these mortise and tenon joints and the wooden pegs. It's magnificent."

Larrie was busy creating a path through the piles of furniture. "In 1864. Man by the name of Charles Herdman. He came home from the Civil War and built it. My house too."

"How did you find that out?" Van stared in awe at a huge beam, more than a yard wide, that anchored the building down the center. "They don't have lumber like that anymore, that's for sure."

Larrie pushed her ginger-colored bangs back off her forehead with her hand. The night air was cool, but the day's heat had been trapped inside the old structure. "It was a funny thing how I found out. I mean, I knew the Herdmans lived in the house for generations. Lulu May Herdman married a Patton, and she lives right down the road. She told me she learned to roller-skate in my upstairs hallway."

As she talked, Larrie cleared a walkway and led Van over to the area where Ticky and his cousins had put the Ydoboni furniture and dozens of smalls. "I was poking around in the attic one day, not long after I moved in, and I found an official-looking paper between the joists up there. It was military, I could see that right away, but I figured it was from World War II, because it wasn't faded or brittle. When I got it into the light I saw that Charles Herdman of the Wisconsin Thrifty Volunteers was 'hereby promoted to lieutenant' in 1863. Hey, Van, help me move these boxes. They're blocking where we need to go. Put them over by that bookcase. We can get a better view of the armoire.

"Back to my story, that's how I knew his name was Charles Herdman and he fought in the Civil War. Try not to take a deep breath while you're holding that box. It's dusty.

"Then a couple of months later, I was replacing the front door to my house—it was split and warped and I just couldn't save it. Wouldn't you know, a brand-new penny tumbled out from the lintel above it and rolled across the floor. Well, the coin looked brand-new, but it was from 1864. They did that back then—put a new penny in the plaster over the front door for luck.

"That's how I knew about the history of the place. Deductive reasoning and blind luck. There we go, that's the last of the boxes. Just stack it with the others. While you're over in that section, take a look at that post." She pointed to a thick, rough-hewn support beam next to the boxes from the British Raj. The words *C. Herdman, 1864* had been carved into it.

Van traced his finger over the words. "I'm impressed. I really am. This is wonderful."

Then Larrie laughed. "You asked me about ghosts. I forgot about something. One night I was working late down here, in the tack room, which is over there in the back of the building. It was after midnight, and all of a sudden I heard what I thought were heavy footsteps. They went real slow: *Thump. Thump. Thump*. Then they stopped. A moment later I heard it again: *Thump*.

Thump. Thump. It sounded like someone walking in heavy work boots."

Van's face went very pale. He looked around at the shadowy corners and up at the gloom that obscured the ceiling thirty feet above them. "You mean this place really is haunted?"

Larrie laughed again. "Heck, no! I poked my head out of the tack room. I didn't see anything at first. Then I heard the sound again: *Thump. Thump. Thump.* Turns out my little dog Taco had jumped onto a Lincoln rocker. The thumping was the rocker moving back and forth on the wooden floor. I don't believe in the supernatural—" She stopped abruptly. She didn't believe in ghosts. She never had thought twice about the paranormal. But either that genie up in the house was real, or she was losing her mind.

Grim lines appeared around Van's mouth. His eyes became worried. "You might not believe in ghosts or angels or demons, but I don't mind saying that I do. Like I said, my family has been in this business for over fifty years, and we've come across—across—*things*, mostly jewelry or pieces of furniture, that aren't quite right. My grandfather said they had a curse on them. I think they had absorbed negative energy. I don't know. It just wasn't good to be around them very long. Remember what Shakespeare wrote in *Hamlet*: 'There are more things in heaven and earth, Horatio, than are dreamt of in your philosophy.' "

Larrie stared hard at Van. He was beginning to sound like that fortune-teller at Mackenzie's shower. "What about things like—like spells, or witches, or—or genies? You think they could actually exist?"

Van raised and lowered his wide shoulders in a casual way. "I really don't know. But I do believe that folklore and myths represent the truth as our ancestors understood it. I'd say it's very likely witches exist. So something like a genie? I'd keep an open mind."

A visible shudder passed through Larrie.

"You okay?" Van asked.

"I had the oddest sensation. As my Aunt Lolly would say, I think somebody has just walked over my grave."

Larrie stood back as Van carefully inspected the four items from the Ydoboni estate he had offered to buy. As Larrie watched him, she thought how she especially liked the tea caddy and would have loved to keep the tiger-paw desk, but she had learned long ago not to get attached to the purchases she made for the Sparrow's Nest. She wasn't collecting furniture for herself; she was in the business of buying and selling. Usually she softened the pain of parting with something that she badly wanted to keep by telling herself that someday she'd find another just like it. *They didn't make just one*, she'd tell herself.

She suspected that was true of the tea caddy with those blue teardrop pulls of lapis that called to her soul. Other very similar tea caddies probably existed. The massive teak and mahogany armoire, so heavy that it took Ticky and both cousins lifting together to move it, most likely had duplicates or close copies out there too, maybe, if they survived. But in the case of many of these marvelous things from the British Raj, however, they probably did make only one.

Especially the tiger desk! That was a work of art and surely unique. She didn't want to give it up. Yet she would sell it, sell them all unless something radically changed in the next few days, after she had a chance to go over these things at her leisure. She couldn't afford to turn down the money Van had generously offered. She sighed heavily.

Van must have heard her. He looked up. "I know it will be hard to part with your treasures. Honest, I do. If you sell them to me, I'm going to feel the same way when I have to turn them over to my client." He ran his fingers over the tiger's snarling face on the skirt of the desk. "What hands carved this? Who was the genius able to put the essence of the cat into the wood itself? I can't help but wonder."

Larrie squatted down next to Van and admired the vibrant beast that looked nearly alive on the wood. "I love that piece especially. I feel absolutely drawn to it. The other things are pretty too, but not like this."

Something changed in Van's face. "I do want them all, but I'm willing to negotiate. I mean if you only want to sell me—at least some of them—we can talk about it. The huge armoire especially might be hard for you to get rid òf at a decent price. It's not a good fit for modern rooms, you know."

Larrie smiled and stood up again. "I'll keep that in mind. Are you satisfied we didn't damage anything? No scratches?"

Van stood up too and brushed dust off the sleeves of his sports jacket. "They're still perfect. Your helpers are more adept at furniture moving than they appear."

Larrie's temper flashed. "You mean they look like rednecks who've been inbred for generations? Your movers look like mob enforcers."

"Whoa! I meant no offense. I just meant—"

"Look, Van, it was pretty clear what you meant. And now that *you've* brought it up, I *think* your 'movers' were armed. I *know* that they were muscle-bound goons who nearly provoked a serious fight this afternoon. So who are those guys and why are they with you?"

Van didn't answer right away. Larrie considered that he was either thinking up a lie or mulling over whether or not he should tell her the truth. What he finally said was, "You're observant, Larrie. I don't think these guys have ever moved furniture. They're not my usual helpers. The client sent these two guys to our showroom with the demand that they go with me."

Larrie's eyes widened.

"Yes, that's right, he 'demanded' I use them. As I explained, our business has become dependent on just a few major buyers. If we lose this client, we could lose our company. That's how important he is to us.

"I didn't like bringing them. I didn't have a choice. Not really. And I'm not sure what the client told them, but they watch my every move. So you can see the pressure I'm under—"

Uneasiness wrapped around Larrie like a shroud. She wondered if she was being manipulated. Van was making sure she knew that if she refused to sell to him, he'd be in financial trouble. Or even in physical danger. Something about this situation, about Van, bothered her, but she wasn't sure what it was. She hadn't seen the "cold at the core" in Van that Ms. Ydoboni mentioned. Yet she didn't completely believe everything he said either.

The earlier warmth she had felt toward the handsome dealer cooled. "I'm sorry you're in such a fix, Van. I told you I needed a couple of days to make up my mind about the sale—"

"Larrie! Don't misunderstand me. I'm pressured, but I don't want to pressure you. You do what you have to do. Believe me, I'm sorry if you got the wrong idea. Don't be mad. I can see it in your face. You've been terrific about this. Please, Larrie, don't hold it against me. It was great being with you tonight."

His voice sounded completely sincere. His contrition seemed genuine. His apology was convincing. Larrie felt her irritation ebbing away. What was she being so prickly about? He had offered her a king's ransom for things she intended to sell anyway. Her manner softened.

"I had a good time too. I'm not mad. I just have the stereotypical redhead's temper. But I don't want any misunderstanding between us—or any more trouble between those men and Shem and Shaun. Somebody could get badly hurt. I mean that."

Van walked close to Larrie, close enough to look into her eyes. He spoke in a tone as sincere as a stockbroker promising an investment will definitely make money. "Don't worry. I'll handle those goons. They're my problem, not yours."

Larrie searched his handsome face with her eyes. She wanted to believe him, she really did. But deep inside her, like a worm in an apple, a wriggling doubt twisted around. Those men could become her problem too. She just didn't know how.

Chapter 12

The note from Aunt Lolly lay on the kitchen counter next to the phone.

> *Larrie, dear,*
> *You have found yourself such a nice young man.*
> *A bit counterculture perhaps, but knowledgeable about Latin. A true gentleman. So rare these days. I promised to bake him an apple snitz pie.*
> *Love you*
> *L. S.*

Larrie couldn't imagine what in the world Aunt Lolly meant in the note. She hadn't even met Van, so how would she know he knew Latin? Even if Aunt Lolly overheard their conversation, Larrie was almost positive he didn't mention anything like that. Of course, since his business was antiquities, Aunt Lolly might have assumed he knew the classics, and no doubt correctly.

But the rest of the note was baffling. Van as counterculture? He was wearing a linen sports jacket and Italian loafers. He was the very epitome of mainstream American.

And why on earth would she be baking him a snitz pie? Larrie felt sure Van's food preferences ran to

gourmet cooking, fine wines, and properly aged bou-
tique cheeses, not a Pennsylvania Dutch dried apple
pie. He never touched his hot dog, she remembered. He
definitely wasn't a home-baked goods kind of guy. She
couldn't imagine *his* mother up to her elbows in flour
turning out pastries.

In fact, Larrie had gotten the impression that his family was very male-oriented. He talked of his grandfather
and his father. He had such pride in "Lawrence Killborn
& *Sons*." Van never said a word about any siblings or
his mother. If a man was close to his mother, he usually
talked about her right away.

Larrie suddenly realized she was thinking about
Van Killborn a lot. She also decided that not all those
thoughts were positive, even though Aunt Lolly evidently approved of him—although on what basis Larrie
couldn't begin to imagine.

But she was too tired to figure it out tonight. Lolly
usually made perfectly good sense once she explained
her thinking. Larrie would ask her about it in the
morning.

A pesky beam of sunlight made the world entirely
too bright to sleep. Larrie was about to put her pillow
over her face, when an awareness slowly roused her.
Sunlight? What time is it anyway?

She rolled over and directed her half-opened, bleary
eyes at the bedside clock. *That can't be right.* She looked
twice. *Nine o'clock?* It was hours past when the dogs had
to be let out.

Larrie scrambled out of bed, disoriented, her brain
still foggy. Why didn't the dogs wake her? They always
started barking at first light. She never had to set her
alarm. Where were they?

She hastily dressed in a pair of jeans, pulled on a T-
shirt, slipped her feet into a pair of flip-flops, and rushed

downstairs. "Sadie! Teddy! Taco! Where are you! Sadie!" Her voice had a frantic, hysterical tinge. Then she heard their answering barks, faint and distant, from outside on the lawn.

Who let them out? she wondered, then answered her own question. *Aunt Lolly must have come down. But she never stops by early enough to let them out, never.*

Larrie flung open the front door. The day looked fresh-washed; the air felt clean, the green grass had a startling intensity. She whistled. The dogs came running, their ears bouncing, their tails wagging. They bounded right past her and headed straight for the kitchen.

Good morning to you too, she thought. "Canine ingrates," she groused, and followed them, thinking how much she needed her morning coffee. She'd feel so much better once she had it.

But the minute she stepped into the kitchen, three things clamored for her attention all at once: One, a snitz pie sat on the counter; two, nearly a quarter of it was missing; and three, especially three, a man sat there, a plate in front of him holding a large piece of pie. He had begun to lift a forkful to his mouth.

"You!" she cried out. "What are *you* doing here?"

Jo Trelawny, genie extraordinaire, looked up. He appeared to be quite surprised that she was yelling at him. Then he turned his attention to Taco, the Chihuahua, who was standing on his hind legs next to the chair. Jo scooped the dog up onto his lap and gave the little pup a piece of piecrust.

Then languidly, almost insolently, he got around to answering. "As I explained last evening, before your beau interrupted us and you completely ignored me, you rubbed the lamp and told me to come back. I must obey you. I therefore returned. You rushed out of the house without a word to me. You never sent me away, so I'm still here."

"What in the world are you talking about!"

Jo tilted his head, apparently puzzled. "You struck me, when we first met, as being of normal intelligence." He shoved a few forkfuls of pie into his mouth, put the dog back down on the floor, then wiped the crumbs off his lips with a section of paper towel. "Bloody good pie! Your aunt is a fine baker. She's old, but she's sharp as a razor's edge. You, conversely, seem to have no memory whatsoever."

"Memory! We're not talking memory here. We're talking wackadoodle dandy! You're not real. Ohhhhhh. I don't know why I'm hallucinating!" Larrie had turned white as a sheet. She put her hands on her temples and held her head. She thought maybe she should scream and opened her mouth—

Suddenly the genie was standing directly in front of her, his hands covering hers and gently holding her head still. "Shhhh. Don't. Don't scream. Breathe. Calm, now. You'll be okay. Your reaction isn't all that unusual." He peeled her hands away from her head and held them in his. "Listen, please. You can feel my hands, right?"

He was staring at her intently. Larrie looked into his deep brown eyes. His hands were strong. She detected some calluses. She could tell he worked with these hands. She rather liked being held by them. In fact, his touch was igniting a flame inside her, but she didn't want to admit it. She nodded at him.

"Good. And you can smell me, right? What do I smell like, if I may ask?"

Larrie wrinkled her nose. "Your breath smells of apples. Your skin smells spicy, like patchouli or cloves. And you smell—" Larrie leaned forward just slightly and put her nose close to his bare chest. "Male." That salty, earthy smell made her stomach do something very odd, like a little flip.

"You see!" Jo Trelawny smiled widely with his generous mouth. "I'm real."

"I don't believe that, but if you are, you're trespassing." Larrie pulled her hands free, deciding that her reaction to Jo was dangerous, unsettling, extraordinary. She intended to stop these crazy feelings before they went any further.

Jo's long dark hair tumbled across his forehead. His chestnut eyes twinkled. He was still grinning at her. He didn't seem to be taking anything she said seriously. "Surely I am not trespassing. You invited me here."

"I did not."

"You rubbed the lamp. Don't deny it."

"Of course I rubbed the lamp! I was trying to clean it!" She glared at him. This man, this whatever-he-was, had the ability to infuriate her. He was obviously the type who had to be right. She could tell immediately he would argue until he proved his point, and he would never hesitate to say "I told you so." Why did she dream up a man like *this*? Ryan had always agreed with her, or if he didn't, he patronized her and let her have her way.

Her imaginary genie—since he couldn't possibly be real—was saying something and interrupting her train of thought. *How rude of my hallucination to butt in constantly*, she thought.

"You see! You admit you rubbed it. And what happens when you rub Aladdin's lamp? Every schoolchild knows. The genie appears and grants you three wishes."

"I have *Aladdin's* lamp?" Larrie's skepticism was palpable.

"No, of course not. Not the same one. Aladdin's lamp, that was just a story in *The Book of One Thousand and One Nights*. But it's the same thing."

"You see! You admit Aladdin's lamp was a story."

"You are absolutely impossible, woman." He finally

gave her a mildly annoyed look which soon melted back into a charming grin.

"No, *you're* impossible. You can't exist. And neither can your three wishes."

"I do, and they do. I assure you. And the wishes are yours, not mine."

Larrie stood there getting lost in looking at him again. Why should she find his smile so attractive? She shook her head to clear it. "Wishes? What good are wishes to me? What would I wish for anyway?" She turned her head and looked away, pangs of sorrow hitting inside her like raindrops.

The genie took her gently by the shoulders and turned her back toward him. He took his finger and softly wiped a stray tear from her cheek. "Let me tell you about wishes," he said in a kind voice. "Wishes, real wishes, aren't when you say, 'I wish I had a piece of pie.' That's not a wish, that's a want. I can grant you a hundred pieces of pie and a thousand wants. I can clean your house. I can feed your dogs. But wishes, the best wishes, are the hopes you nurture in your very soul. They are secret dreams that blossom into the most perfect rose of desire. Wishes that come true can transform the wisher. Wishes can change everything. And I get to grant you not one incredible, life-altering wish, but three."

"Like what?" Larrie's eyes were shiny as new silver coins, the tip of her nose had turned the pale pink of a rosebud, her lips looked as sweet as a perfect peach.

"You are quite adorable, you know that." Without warning, Jo lowered his head and kissed her.

For the briefest moment, Larrie didn't move. A bolt of lightning ripped through her. She gasped and pulled back in shock. "What! What do you think you're doing!"

"I remembered kissing you yesterday. I admit I liked it. It's been a while since I've kissed a white woman.

And you know, I don't think I ever kissed an American before."

Larrie gaped at him. She was speechless. She not only dreamed up an arrogant know-it-all of a man, her imagination had created a Don Juan. It was inexplicable. "Maybe I should go see a doctor," she muttered to herself.

"Are you feeling ill?"

Exasperation overtook her. "I am not ill! I am going crazy!" Larrie sank down on one of the chairs at the old store counter that had become her kitchen island. A cup of hot, black coffee suddenly appeared in front of her.

The genie was now sitting across from her on the other side of the counter. "Would you like a piece of your aunt's pie? You might feel better with some food in your stomach. You're too thin. Maybe you're consumptive."

"Consumptive? What century are you from?"

"A much better one, if you want to know the truth. I was born in 1880. In London. I'm British."

"I couldn't exactly miss that accent," Larrie murmured. She looked up at the clock ticking away on the far wall. It was about ten past nine. She spoke aloud to no one in particular, and certainly not to Jo Trelawny. "Why the hell did I dream up an Englishman. I must be soooo crazy."

She shook her head, smelled the aroma of fresh-brewed coffee, and decided she might feel better if she drank some. She didn't even try to figure out how it got in front of her. If she could dream up a genie, she could dream up coffee.

To her shock, the coffee burned her mouth. "Oh!" she cried out. "It's hot!"

"It's steaming. I fail to understand why you don't accept the proof of your own eyes. And mouth." Jo Trelawny crossed his arms with their well-developed biceps across his muscular chest and began to pout. "And you need to believe I'm real."

Larrie narrowed her gray eyes. "Why? What's it to you? I'm the one with the mental problem."

"I have my reasons," Jo responded. "It's very important. Your aunt had no second thoughts, by the way. She asked me some insightful questions about London and the late Queen Victoria. I answered them. She had an odd fascination, for a female, with steam engines. We talked about London Bridge station. She's been there, you know. We talked about my schooling. She was quite satisfied I am who I say I am."

"You probably made it all up. Aunt Lolly doesn't have a suspicious mind."

"I resent your questioning my integrity."

"Excuse me? From what I've read, genies have earned an unsavory reputation. You are not truthful, ethical, or trustworthy. You deliberately lead people astray."

"That's a Muslim *djinn* that you are referring to. An evil spirit. I am a genie of the lamp. It's quite different. And I will have you know that prior to my years as an explorer on the subcontinent where I had the misfortune to become enchanted, I was both an officer—in the Bengal Lancers—and a gentleman." He sat up very straight and looked down his rather long nose at Larrie. "My father was a duke."

Larrie put the cup down, feeling more and more like Alice at the table with the Mad Hatter. Come to think of it, didn't Alice eat a hallucinogenic mushroom? While confusion buffeted her about, her gaze landed on the pie. She did feel sort of hungry. Maybe she had low blood sugar, and snitz pie was her favorite. She loved the rich apple and cinnamon flavors and the sweetness that was cut with a hint of lemon. She picked up her fork and cut into the flaky crust. As she ate, she decided if she pretended the genie didn't exist, maybe he wouldn't.

After popping a few forks filled with pie into her mouth, she peered up from under her lashes.

The genie was still there. His skin was darkly tanned. His chest was bare. She remembered he wasn't wearing shoes and had bells around his ankles. His manner was slightly crude, his hands were rough, his clothes belonged to a peasant, and except for his toney accent—which any good actor could learn—he didn't appear as if he had an ounce of blue blood. She muttered, "If your father was a duke, I'm the Duchess of York. So call me Fergie."

The genie reacted as if struck with a blade, a wounded creature unfairly pierced. "I *am* the youngest son of a duke. And of course you are not the Duchess of York. I happen to know her. We're related through her grandmother, the Countess Claudine Rhédey von Kis-Rhéde. The Duchess of York is Mary of Teck, but she's called May. Why, we've waltzed together in Madras. She's the Empress of India, or rather she was, when I was there. I don't know why you want me to call you Fergie. Is it a nickname?"

Larrie gazed at the genie sitting across the counter from her. "Forget it. I was making a joke. It doesn't matter who your father was or who you say you are. I don't believe in you—I don't believe in your very existence. I think I've had a nervous breakdown. And I really don't know what to do about it. I don't seem to be having any other symptoms except seeing you."

"Exactly! Your mental faculties are not impaired. I need to prove to you that I'm real. Why don't you deliberately wish for something? Make one of those big wishes I spoke about. I'll grant your wish and then you'll be convinced."

Larrie's mouth suddenly became dry as sand. The pie stuck in her throat. She choked it down. Despite what she had said earlier, she had a secret wish. She wished for a miracle. She had wished the clock could be turned back. She had tried to bargain with God. She had wailed and sobbed as she had wished with all her heart and soul to erase the past year entirely. If only she could see Ryan again, to hold him, to have him back. Her eyes filled with tears. She dropped her fork and it clattered to the counter. Without thinking through what she was saying, she barely whispered the words, "All right. I wish to go back in time."

Chapter 13

Melanie O'Casey had begun to think that her best friend had vanished into thin air. She was worried enough that she took a personal day and didn't go in to her job as head librarian—as the *only* librarian—at the Bowman's Creek Library, where she was also the only paid employee.

Melanie rarely took a day off for any reason. Her absence left the operation of the library entirely in the hands of volunteers—not that the elderly ladies who helped weren't competent. But the library had become Melanie's entire world. She oversaw the daily lending operations, the bookmobile, the Reading Is Fun children's program, the computer literacy program, the book drive and annual auction, and the ceaseless fund-raising.

The BCL devoured her time and made her feel useful. Yet her busy hours did not fend off loneliness or stop the ache that throbbed in her chest when she read to the children at story hour. She wanted a family of her own. She wanted a relationship with not just a man, but with a wonderful man who shared her interests and appreciated her talents. She wanted an engagement ring, a bridal shower, a white wedding, and a honeymoon. She wanted a house with a fenced yard where her children could play. She wanted the whole enchilada.

Fat chance, she thought, her choice of words deliberate. Melanie O'Casey hadn't even been on a date since— A sigh escaped from her lips. Since Lyle Siglin took her to the Halloween party in Ms. Ralston's class. In junior high. Before her hormones kicked in and she put on all the weight.

Melanie, a sturdy, substantial woman, stood five feet ten inches tall and carried a hundred pounds beyond what the height/weight charts indicated as "normal." She thought of herself as Rubenesque. Everybody said she had "such a pretty face" because from the neck up, Melanie was a knockout. She had long, straight black hair, eyes such a deep blue they were almost violet, and eyelashes so thick and lush she didn't need mascara. Her complexion was classic peaches and cream. Her lips were a perfect Cupid's bow.

From the neck down, she despaired. If only she had been born in a different century, instead of an era where all the role models were anorexic. She had read somewhere that Queen Victoria had a fifty-two-inch waist, and nobody dared to call *her* fat.

She often thought it was unfortunate that the phrase *pleasingly plump* had disappeared from the English language. That description fit Melanie perfectly. She was gently rounded and soft where a woman should be soft. That meant that her shape, devoid of hard edges and muscle definition, wasn't desirable, especially to "wonderful" young men.

Recently Melanie had been contemplating one of those stomach stapling or gastric bypass operations. She mentioned it to Larrie, who reacted with horror.

"You're *beautiful*, Melanie! You're completely healthy. You can't risk your life by doing something that radical, simply to change your appearance. Not every man wants a woman to look like a Barbie doll."

"Get real, Larrie. Guys want tits on a stick. I've got big bosoms on a balloon."

But this Tuesday morning, as she squeezed herself behind the wheel of her PT Cruiser, she wasn't thinking about her own life, she was thinking about Larrie's. The last time she had spoken to her best friend was on Sunday night, before she went out to dinner with that New York guy.

Melanie had been surprised when Larrie didn't contact her first thing on Monday morning. When she didn't get a call by noon, she started phoning Larrie. She only reached Larrie's machine. She left several messages. She never got a return call. Finally, late in the afternoon, she called Larrie's Aunt Lolly, which was a hit-or-miss strategy, depending on what planet—Earth or La La Land—Lolly was on that day. The conversation went something like this:

"Melanie O'Casey? Of course I know who you are. I was right there when Wayne Smith threw that rock and knocked your front tooth out. You were in first grade. I can hardly tell you have a crown, dear. It looks very natural."

Melanie put her hand to her mouth, suddenly self-conscious. Damn Lolly for bringing that up. "I was wondering, do you know where Larrie is?"

"Not exactly."

"I've been trying to reach her all day. She's not answering her phone."

"She can't answer it. She's not home."

Melanie took a deep breath and worked on keeping the impatience out of her voice. "I figured out that she wasn't home. Where is she? Do you know?"

"I told you, dear, I don't know exactly."

"Can you tell me what you do know, even not exactly, Ms. Smith? I'd really like to get hold of Larrie."

"I don't think you're going to be able to do that. She left early this morning with her young man."

"She did?" Astonishment sideswiped Melanie. The date must have gone a lot better than Larrie anticipated if she had gone out with that New York dealer again so soon. "They left together? Really?"

"Yes. She flew out of the window with him. I think it was around nine thirty."

Oh, Lordy, it must be one of Aunt Lolly's bad days, Melanie thought. "Let me get this straight, Ms. Smith. She *flew—out the window*?"

"Yes, dear, that's right. With her new boyfriend. They were on some kind of rug, I believe, but I only caught a glimpse of them. They were moving quickly. He's very impressive. Quite a Renaissance man. I suppose he engineered it. If they're not back by dinner, I'll ask Ticky to take care of the dogs. He's here fixing the garage door. I need to go now, Melanie. I wouldn't worry about Larrie. He's a nice young man."

"Wait! Wait!" But it was too late. Aunt Lolly had broken the connection.

The conversation had disturbed Melanie. When there was no word from Larrie by Tuesday morning, Melanie took her personal day. She knew something had to be dreadfully wrong.

Now, approaching Larrie's house in her PT Cruiser, Melanie spotted the old red Ford truck in the driveway. Clearly Larrie hadn't taken it anywhere. Her handyman, the strange banty rooster of a man called Ticky Blackstone, his face long and solemn, stood behind the truck peering forlornly up and down the Old Highway. With nearly identical expressions, three dogs sat at his feet, looking up and down the highway too.

Melanie pulled over and climbed out of her car. "She's not here, is she?"

"No, Ms. O'Casey. She didn't come home last night. Didn't call me or nothing. So I stuck around after I fed the dogs. Figured I'd better not leave the place unguarded. I had my .38 in my vehicle. I took it out, loaded it, and sat down in the shop, waiting."

The color drained from Melanie's face. "Why did you think you'd need to guard the place? With a gun?" Her voice squeaked, her throat having gotten tight with fear.

"You know how it is. I wasn't taking no chances. Those New York knuckleheads that was out here on Sunday? I don't trust them. They're nothing but thugs. And she's out with their boss? Didn't come home? Something's got to be wrong. I think you ought to call the police. That's what I think."

Melanie nodded her head in agreement. "It's not like Larrie to stay out and not tell anyone. On the other hand, she left of her own free will as far as I can tell. I'm going to try to call this guy. I'm sure I can get a phone number from information. She said his name is Van Killborn. If he doesn't have any good answers, then I'll go to the cops."

Ticky snorted. "Yeah, well, it's *not* like Miss Larrie, no way. You know how it is. She wouldn't worry Lolly like that, not that Lolly's worried, 'cause she don't seem to be. Look at it logically. Miss Larrie would have called me. I don't know if she wanted me to open up the shop today. I don't know nothing. It's not like her. And what do you make of this?"

Ticky fished around in his breast pocket with his thumb and forefinger. He pulled out a folded piece of paper from behind his pack of Camels. "I found it on the lawn next to the driveway yesterday morning, soon as I got here. I was waiting to give it to Miss Larrie. Think it means anything?"

Melanie took the paper from Ticky and carefully opened it. It was frayed along the creases as if it had been folded and unfolded a thousand times. She read:

Small places in big things
You have to look for wings
Near a rose in the middle
Use the key to fiddle
And the treasure you look for
will spring

Melanie thought for a minute. "It's a riddle. I don't know what it means. Maybe Larrie dropped it. Maybe she found it tucked into a drawer of some old furniture. She never mentioned it to me, so I don't know."

She shook her head, dismissing Ticky's discovery as completely unimportant. "I don't think it has anything to do with her not coming home. But I'll hold on to it until I see her." She put the paper in a pocket of her plus-size jeans. "I think that New York dealer has everything to do with her being gone though. He's taken advantage of her. She's vulnerable. Look what she's been through."

Ticky nodded, his face solemn.

Thinking about the fragility of her friend's emotions, Melanie realized that her own anger, which rarely emerged, had ignited and started to burn brightly in her chest. She glared at Ticky. "Just wait until I give that guy a piece of my mind."

"You're not going to have to wait long."

"What are you talking about?"

Ticky put his hand up to shade his eyes. "See that silver Mercedes coming down the Old Highway?"

Silver Mercedes? Melanie turned and could barely see a car approaching amid the cloud of dust being kicked up on the dirt road. "I see a car coming this way . . ."

"I bet it's that Killborn guy. Wayne, you know him, got called out here Sunday night when a silver Mercedes wouldn't start. Said Larrie and this here city dealer were real chummy. Funny thing, nothing was wrong with the car 'cept the battery had been disconnected. Wayne thought it was real odd and all."

Sounds like this Van Killborn was up to something. And now Larrie's in trouble. Melanie blamed herself. She should have gotten on the computer and checked this guy out before Larrie spent time alone with him. Maybe this guy was a serial killer. Maybe the Killborns were connected to the mob or something. They were from New York and everything. Her temper began to flare like a rocket on takeoff at Cape Kennedy.

The minute the car pulled into the driveway, the dogs became a Greek chorus in full voice, and Melanie was on the move. She bore down on the Mercedes like a battleship going full speed ahead—if in fact a battleship had size 44 D breasts bouncing like melons as she ran. As the man inside opened the car door and stepped out, she screamed, *"What have you done with Larrie!"*

Surprise and incomprehension and perhaps something like awe spread across Van Killborn's face. "What? What are you talking about?"

"Don't lie to me, you—you—" At that point, Melanie noticed, really noticed Van Killborn. He stood up tall. His blond hair shone in the sun like a young Apollo's.

"You—" was all she could say.

"Who are you?" Van asked. He regarded her quizzically as if he recognized her but couldn't quite place where he had seen her before.

Melanie stopped short. Her body jiggled. She tried to restore her dignity. "I'm Larrie's best friend, Melanie O'Casey. I demand to know where she is."

"I'd like to know the same thing. She hasn't returned my calls. I have got to talk to her. It's urgent."

"Why are you lying to me! Larrie is with you!" Hysteria gripped Melanie by the throat. She suddenly felt overwrought. Tears filled her eyes and spilled over to run down her cheeks.

"What? *No.* Larrie's not with me. I haven't seen her since Sunday. Hey, what are you crying about? What's going on?"

At this point Ticky stepped forward. He had a gun in his hand. "You better start talking, mister. We need some answers, now."

Van threw his hands up in the air over his head. *"Don't shoot!"* he yelled.

Melanie, wiping her tears away with her fingers, turned to Ticky. "Put that thing away, Ticky. Somebody could get hurt."

"Somebody could already be hurt," Ticky muttered and tucked the weapon into the waistband at the back of his pants. He stuck his face belligerently toward Van. "There are two things I hate in the world, humid weather and liars. Guess which one you are. Where is she, you murderer?"

Van lowered his hands, but his face had turned deathly pale. "I told you. I don't know!" He looked at Melanie. "What's going on here?"

"Nobody's seen or heard from Larrie since yesterday morning. Since she left with *you.*"

"With *me?* Not me! I was talking all yesterday morning with New York. I stayed in my hotel room. I never left the place until late afternoon. I had room service bring my lunch. I can prove I never came here. Who said I did?"

A blush crept into Melanie's face. As if she had been painted by Renoir, her cheeks took on a subtle wash of the most delightful rosy hue. Van was staring at her, which made her even more uncomfortable. "Larrie's great-aunt said you and Larrie left together." Then she stared at her feet and in a nearly inaudible voice she murmured, "Through the window. On a flying carpet."

"What? Is the woman out of her mind?"

Melanie dared to peek at Van from under her coal-black lashes. "Uhhhh. Probably."

"I need to talk with her. I need to clear this up right away."

Ticky was heard then, his voice a growl. "You're going to get your chance. Here comes Lolly now."

Like a willow in the wind, Leila "Lolly" Smith approached, her tall, thin figure swaying, her hand holding an unusually large straw hat on her head. Her once red hair, now streaked with gray, streamed down her back, some of its tendrils tossed about in the breeze. She had found a floor-length lilac gown to wear, all tulle and satin, but quite wrinkled. She looked extraordinary.

Van stared. "It's Ms. Haversham." His voice was incredulous.

"You read Dickens." Melanie regarded Van with interest, her heart beginning to pound crazily in her chest.

"It ain't no Ms. Haver-whatever. That's Lolly," Ticky said, removing the pack of Camels from his shirt pocket. "She likes to bum my cigarettes," he added.

"I heard voices, and the dogs barking," Aunt Lolly announced as she reached the group. Bright spots of rouge stood out garishly on her powdered cheeks. "I thought Larrie had returned." She stopped and took a Camel from Ticky's offered pack. "Thank you for the ciggie. I do so want a good smoke."

Ticky lit it for her, taking care not to ignite her hat.

She puffed and exhaled. "Hello, Melanie. Is this your boyfriend? I thought I saw his car here the other night."

"My—? No! This is *Larrie's* boyfriend."

"I'm not Larrie's boyfriend. I'm a colleague," Van corrected. "But I did invite her to dinner on Sunday." He gallantly extended his hand. "I'm Van Killborn."

Lolly shook his hand warily. "You're too good-looking. I imagine you've gotten away with much more than you should have." She turned to Melanie. "Don't judge a book by its cover. If you're going to marry him, you have a great deal of work to do first. He's got a rottenness at the core."

Damn Lolly! Melanie thought, feeling terribly embarrassed. "I met Mr. Killborn a few minutes ago. I'm not marrying him. I don't even know him."

Lolly puffed away and regarded the top of a nearby pine tree. "Really? The way he was ogling you, and the way you were stealing glances at him, well, anyone with half a brain could see you two have something going on." She gave Melanie a piercing look. "If you haven't had sex with him yet, you will. Don't let it go to your head. A handsome man paying attention to you. Remember what I told you."

"*Ms. Smith!* He's not someone I would ever—I never—I would never—"

"Wait a minute! I don't even know you people and you're judging me!" Van sounded indignant. "*She* says I'm rotten at the core. This guy points a gun at me and calls me a murderer." He was only a few inches taller than Melanie. He looked straight into her face. "And you find me repulsive."

Melanie didn't move. She couldn't move. She was turned to stone by his startling blue eyes. She had never seen eyes so beautiful. "I—I *don't* find you repulsive. You're very attractive. But you'd never, I mean, look at me. I'm so—"

"Incredible," Van breathed. He looked her up and down, staring openly. "I see it now. You're the spitting image of my mother. I mean when she was young. I've seen pictures. She was killed along with my brother in a boating accident in Corfu. I was only seven. I wasn't there. Do you bake?"

Their faces were only inches apart. "As a matter of fact, I do. I create specialty breads. The store-bought stuff is dreadful, don't you think?"

A beatific expression lit Van's face. He couldn't seem to tear his eyes from Melanie. "Do you cook too?"

Melanie nodded. "I had a job in a four-star French restaurant during college. I worked my way up to sous-chef. I'm quite good."

"Really?" Van was smiling. He couldn't seem to stop smiling. "You know, I thought you were a Valkyrie when I saw you running toward me like that. You should have been carrying a spear. My mother was Scandinavian. Not blond like me. That's from my father's side. She had long black hair, like you."

"Hey!" Ticky interrupted. "What about Larrie? What did you do with Larrie?"

Van wrenched his attention from Melanie. "I told you, I haven't seen Larrie since Sunday night." He turned to Aunt Lolly. "They tell me *you* said I went out with Larrie yesterday morning."

Aunt Lolly's eyebrows rose. "I said no such thing. Why would I?"

Melanie cut in. "That's *exactly* what you told me when I phoned and asked where Larrie was."

Aunt Lolly took a final drag on her cigarette. She threw it down and tromped on it angrily with the 1960s white go-go boots she was wearing. Her manner showed she was decidedly annoyed. "People never really listen. I said she left with her young man." She pointed a bony finger at Van. "He is *not* Larrie's young man."

Chapter 14

The too hastily uttered "I wish to go back in time" had no sooner left Larrie's mouth than the room exploded in a bright light. Suddenly she was sitting on a Persian carpet—four feet off the floor. Jo was kneeling behind her, his muscular thighs acting as her backrest. Her blood rushed through her temples. Below her the dogs were barking wildly. *Is this a vision or a dream?* she wondered.

The carpet started to glide forward and left the house through the open kitchen window, which was indeed a very large opening but normally contained a screen. They passed right through it like magic. Larrie gasped. Then the carpet angled upward.

"Hang on for the ride!" Jo called out gaily, and Larrie gripped the edge of the carpet for dear life. She glimpsed Aunt Lolly watching from a window in her apartment over the garage. Afraid to release her hold on the rug and wave, Larrie gallantly smiled instead, but out of the corner of her eye she saw that Jo was blowing Aunt Lolly a kiss.

Up and up they flew into the morning sky until the farmhouse with its gray shingled roof seemed very small below them on the green patch of lawn. Gripped with a sense of *déjà vu,* Larrie instantly knew she had seen this before. *My dream! This is my dream!*

Only it wasn't her dream, even if she was, in fact, dreaming. This experience was different. For one thing, a young, handsome man was positioned behind her, his hands now resting on her shoulders. In her dream she had always been alone, disconnected from the world and trying to leave her pain behind. Here, rising higher and higher and flying faster and faster, she was acutely aware that the unusual man named John, called Jo, and professing to be a genie, was behind her, keeping her steady, keeping her safe.

Rushing through the sky, she felt exhilarated and alive. The wind whipped through her hair. Her every sensation was heightened. She believed the intensity of her feelings had to do with Jo, though she wasn't sure why.

The carpet itself, her personal aircraft for this strange, wondrous ride, felt solid beneath her. Its deep pile, woven in wool of reds and blues on a cream background, created a vivid and pleasing conveyance. Nothing about this experience was insubstantial or dreamlike; everything had shape and form. And above her the sun beamed down with a radiance that nearly blinded her.

Larrie was positive she wasn't asleep. But could this actually be happening? Real people didn't fly on magic carpets. That only took place in novels and fairy tales. So how could she explain what was happening to her?

She couldn't explain it. She probably couldn't stop it. She decided she might as well enjoy it, because what was occurring to her was astonishing: She was flying on a magic carpet with a genie at her back.

As in the dream that repeated night after night, Larrie found herself flying along low rolling mountains. She crossed the winding silver ribbons of the Susquehanna and the Delaware. She traveled very far until she rode through pellucid air above an endless, rolling, eerily dark sea.

"Where are we going?" she dared to ask Jo at one point.

"As you wished, into the past, long ago and far away." His fingers tightened on her shoulders.

Long ago and far away? "But I didn't mean—" she began to say. "I meant—" The words stuck in her throat as the pie had done. She had wanted to turn back the clock to last year, before Ryan's death. Evidently she had botched the wish, badly. She hadn't wanted to go back decades or centuries. She swallowed the words she couldn't say and blinked away the tears. It had been a vain wish after all.

She bowed her head and sighed. Disappointment weighed heavily upon her. Despite her best efforts not to cry, a few crystal tears slipped down her cheeks and landed on the deep pile of the flying carpet. Then a kind hand pushed strands of hair from her wet cheeks.

Jo's low voice sounded very close to her ear. "Don't despair, dear Larrie. Your fate is just as it should be, as is mine. Life had given us vinegar on a sponge when we needed to quench our thirst. We have tasted the bitter gall. But when the sweetness comes again, we will prize it all the more because we know its absence." His lips briefly brushed her cheek like the brushing of a petal and left a tingling where they touched.

"I believe I'm getting a sunburn," she said at last after flying above the wine-dark sea and beneath the blistering sun for a very long while. She thought it decidedly odd she could get a sunburn in a dream, but the skin on her face had begun to feel tight and uncomfortable.

"My apologies." Jo's voice came from behind her. She heard bells, and believed they were the ones encircling Jo's ankles. A hat with a wide brim and ribbons that tied under Larrie's chin appeared on her head.

"Are you thirsty?" he asked.

Larrie nodded. "I could use a drink." A bottle of spring water appeared in her hand. She noted that it was a thick glass bottle, however, not a plastic one. The water inside was cold and tasted fresh on her parched tongue.

"Look ahead of us." Jo leaned down and put his cheek close to hers. He hugged her shoulders with one arm and pointed with his outstretched hand to a coastline with jagged mountains beyond it.

The carpet suddenly seemed to quiver in the air. In the twinkling of an eye they had left the sea behind and were above land. The wind smelled of spices. Palm trees waved below on a broad flat plain. Oxen pulled plows through light green fields, turning up a deep brown soil. Temples with white minarets glistened against the blue sky.

"Where are we?" Larrie asked, struck with wonder.

"India. The Land of Five Rivers—the Punjab. I'm taking you back to my home."

Inside the one-story building with a wide covered veranda surrounding it, the air was cool. The flying carpet had become just another rug on the highly polished floor. To Larrie, the room where she now stood looked more British than Indian.

Elegant hardwood panels covered the walls. On one of them hung a large portrait of a older man in a military uniform with a great number of medals on his chest. Next to him was a truly huge portrait of a woman dressed formally in white standing by a chair. A small dog, similar to Larrie's Chihuahua Taco, lay at her feet. The paintings had been arranged amid a number of stuffed tigers' heads, whose enraged snarling mouths and glass eyes seemed to blame Larrie for their demise.

A turbaned servant scurried in. "Sahib Trelawny! So good you have returned. You have been absent many days."

Larrie whirled around to find Jo Trelawny behind her.

Amazement poured through her like water. He was no longer half naked with bells around his ankles, his manner and dress rough and crude like a peasant's. Instead he wore a finely made khaki shirt and British walking shorts. High sturdy boots shod his feet. A white silk cravat peeked jauntily from his neckline. At that very moment, he was removing a white pith helmet from his head and tucking it under his arm. He pulled off a pair of thin leather gloves. He had a pistol in a holster at his waist.

Aside from some dust on his boots, his attire was immaculate. He stood impressively tall, his presence commanding the room. His voice held authority when he spoke. "It's good to be back, Tara Singh. Would you have someone bring us tea? We've had a long journey. Since Lady Larissa will be my guest, please have a room readied for her."

The servant, a middle-aged Sikh sporting a full black beard, nodded. "A separate room, sahib?"

"A separate room."

The Sikh called Tara stared at Larrie. She was wearing a pair of jeans, an old blue T-shirt that had the Penn State Nittany Lion roaring across her chest, and flip-flops on her feet. Jo Trelawny looked at her too. "Lady Larissa's luggage was lost in transit from America and she has only her outfit for, uh, for deck sports. Can you find something appropriate for her to wear here?"

The Sikh bowed his head. "Yes, sahib." He bowed toward Larrie. "Memsahib." He left the room on silent feet.

Once they were alone, Larrie, feeling confused and for some reason put out, said, "I thought you were a genie. I thought you had to obey me. You seem to be in charge here."

Jo's smile showed his white teeth in his tanned face. "I am the master in this house. And I thank you for allowing me to return to it. But I am your genie. You may do with me whatever you please. Your wish is my command." He leered at her. "I can cancel my order for the separate bedroom—you don't even have to wish it. Just say the word."

Larrie stiffened. "You are out of line, Mr. Trelawny."

"I beg your pardon, Ms. Smith." But he kept grinning.

Then he strode to a long table against the wall and picked up a decanter. "Would you like a brandy? We have tea coming, but I feel the need for something stronger." He poured amber liquid into a glass.

"A drink at this hour? It is barely past breakfast. Or it was when we left my kitchen." She glanced at her own wristwatch. "My watch has stopped."

"I don't carry a timepiece," Jo remarked and glanced toward a tall window, his face unreadable as he sipped at his drink. "It appears to be nearly teatime here." Then he turned and studied Larrie from sultry eyes under those incredible lashes.

Larrie felt her cheeks get hot. *It must be the sunburn*, she thought. She said, "What year is this?"

"It is the end of April, 1906."

"It's 1906? That's more than a century ago. Or so you say. I suppose you can prove it."

"Proof?" Jo was silent a moment, and he seemed to be studying her. "You have a healthy skepticism. Not a woman to be fooled easily."

Larrie nodded. "I have learned the hard way to be cautious. In the antiques business, the gullible and naïve end up with damaged goods, reproductions, and fakes. So yes, Mr. Trelawny, prove I am where you say I am and the year is what you say it is."

"You can ask Tara, or—let me see. There is usually a copy of the *Times of India* about." He looked on the table where the decanter and glasses sat. "Ah, here we are." He picked a newspaper, studied it for a moment, then fell silent. He lifted his eyes to Larrie's, his face serious. "It's dated a week ago. I'd better warn you. The headline is quite disturbing. It's a terrible thing to have happened."

He walked back across the room and handled the *Times* to Larrie.

She looked at it and felt a shock. The banner headline screamed EARTHQUAKE HITS SAN FRANCISCO. Below it she read the subtitle: "Early morning quake levels city April 18. Thousands believed dead."

She felt faint. Her stomach churned. "I—I can't be dreaming this. I mean I knew San Francisco had an earthquake at the beginning of the last century. But I didn't know the date. How could I make this up in my mind? Can it be true that you have taken me back in time?"

Jo nodded. "It's true. You have your proof. Do you believe yet?"

Larrie didn't know. She honestly couldn't say whether the strange things that had occurred in the past few days were real, or whether she had shut herself up entirely in the recesses of her own mind and had become trapped there.

She looked around her. The room looked quite grand although not at all exotic. Outside the long windows she could see tall palms, their fronds waving gently, and bright sunlight. "How long will we be here?"

Jo's face revealed nothing of his feelings. "That's entirely up to you. It has been a very long journey. I hope you won't be in a rush to leave. To be frank, I would like to take care of some important matters as long as we're here. Matters of a highly personal nature." He sighed. "But when you're ready to go back to your quaint farm in America, you simply have to make the wish to return."

Larrie stared at him hard. This John "Jo" Trelawny was shrewd, she thought. He was up to something. But what? "Let me get this straight. I have three wishes. You mentioned that."

"Absolutely. Three wishes are standard."

"I have already used up one to get here. To get back home, I have to use up another. Correct?"

"Yes. Your going back will require a second wish."

"That leaves just one." She regarded him intently. "What's going on, Jo?"

"I don't know what you mean. You knew you were wishing. You intentionally decided to make a wish. I granted your wish."

Larrie shook her head. "No, I don't think so. I think you manipulated my wish to fulfill one of your own. You wanted to come back *here* at this time, on this date. I think the question I need answered is why."

Tea arrived on a cart pushed by a young woman in a brightly colored shirt with tight trousers beneath it. A scarf covered her dark hair. The cart held a china teapot, which Larrie recognized as one made by the English company James Sadler & Sons; a silver creamer and sugar bowl, probably plate but possibly sterling; a stack of pretty china cups and saucers; and a rose-painted plate piled with small cakes. On a bottom shelf was a package wrapped in brown paper and tied with string.

The young woman kept her head bowed shyly. She picked up the parcel and handed it to Jo. "For the mem-sahib," she said in a voice like a flute.

"Thank you, Amita. You can go now."

She gave Larrie a curious look, then scurried from the room.

Jo opened the paper. "It's your clothes." He passed them on to Larrie. "Punjabi women wear what Amita had on. The shirt and pants are called a *salwar kameez*. The scarf is a *dupatta*."

Larrie examined the clothes. The shirt, beautifully

embroidered with silver and blue thread and made from a fine yellow cloth, would reach to her knees. The pants were blue. The scarf, shot through with silver threads, was also blue. Nestled beneath the clothes she found a delightful pair of silver slippers with needle-nose pointed toes that turned up like the prow of a gondola.

"They're beautiful," she murmured. "I'll have to find my room and change."

"No need." Jo clapped his hands. The air moved slightly and took on a glow. Larrie looked down at herself. Her jeans and T-shirt had vanished. She was clad in her new garments.

Jo stared at her then. His eyes brightened. "Astonishing."

"Yes, my goodness, it is astonishing. You must have used magic, but I could have just changed in a normal way."

"No." Jo strode over and stood in front of her. "*You* are astonishing. Even with those freckles across your nose, you look beautiful. You quite take my breath away." His arms went around Larrie. His lips lowered toward hers.

She shoved him hard with both hands, pushing him back. "What do you think you are doing!"

"I was about to kiss you."

"Well, you can't! You can't go around kissing me whenever you feel like it. I'm not—I'm not like the women you obviously are used to kissing."

"Your words are a knife that cuts into my soul." His face looked very hurt.

"You're lucky I don't have a real knife, Mr. Trelawny. I might cut you somewhere else."

His eyebrows shot up. "I was too forward. I apologize." He looked contrite for a moment. Then he stared at her again. "It's just that you are so kissable. I can't resist. But I'll wait. Soon you'll come to me, begging to be kissed."

"When hell freezes over, I will. You are very full of yourself, Mr. Genie."

Jo laughed. "I am. That I am. It has gotten me into some jams." The joy suddenly went out of his face. "It got me into that lamp, you know."

"No, I didn't know. How did you get in there?"

"Come. Sit down on the divan. I'll pour the tea and tell you the story."

Larrie walked over to the sofa and sat. "I know you're going to tell me a story. But will it be true?"

Jo waved her hand dismissively. "I have no reason to lie to you."

I'm not sure I believe that, Larrie thought. *You might have a very good reason to lie to me. Maybe you need my other wishes too.*

"One lump or two?" he asked, holding the delicate porcelain cup decorated with rosebuds in his large, callused hand.

"Two."

"I might have guessed you'd like it sweet." He winked at her. "Milk or lemon?"

"Milk."

He handed her the cup which Larrie, out of habit, lifted up high enough to check the maker's mark. As she suspected she would, she found the crossed swords of Meissen, Europe's first porcelain manufacturer.

Then Jo picked up his own. He drank his tea black. He took a swallow, made a displeased face, and set the cup back on the tea cart. He returned to sipping his brandy.

"Where should I begin?"

"Tell me why you're in India. Start there," Larrie suggested.

"That's easy. I came with the army. I was an officer with the Forty-first Bengal Lancers. I thought it quite a lark. After all, I was young then and liked to fight. Tara, whom you just saw here, served too. The Sikhs are fierce warriors. Good men to have on your side."

Larrie sipped her tea. It tasted very sweet and satisfying. The journey must have been longer than she believed it was. She felt hungry and reached for a cake on the tea cart. She bit into it, savoring flavors of oranges and cardamom. She glanced at Jo. "You are still young."

Sadness drew down over his dark eyes "I look the same age as when I was enchanted, but I've lived more than a hundred years inside that lamp. I have served many masters. I am ancient and quite weary."

Larrie's quick empathy felt the pain which his cocky manner had previously hidden. "Oh," she said softly. "I'm sorry."

Jo sighed deeply. "As am I." He roused himself and gave her a small smile. "To return to my story. After a few years in India, I 'went native,' as they say. I became enamored with the country. I enjoyed the women, who knew so many tricks of lovemaking. I resigned my commission. I offered Tara a position, officially as a valet but more like my secretary and general factotum. He joined me when I became an explorer and an adventurer.

"After many excursions through the jungles of the south, I had gotten a wild desire to climb the mountains to the north of here, the highest in the world. We went off into a region called Baltistan, the land some call Little Tibet."

His voice grew soft. His eyes got a faraway look. "Strange things happen there. The air is thin. The narrow mountain passes take one above the clouds. The snow is white, the bare rocks are dull brown or black. The only color is the jade green of the glacier-fed rivers. The jagged peaks and terrible crevasses create a severe and beautiful landscape. I tracked ibex and snow leopards. I witnessed strange and wondrous visions. And—" His voice choked a little. "I met a woman. Her name was Rani. She was very young and very beautiful. I—never mind. Suffice it to say, she loved me. I stayed with her for an entire winter, but when spring came to her village, I left."

Larrie felt her heart give a hard thump. "Did you love her?"

Jo shrugged. "I liked her a great deal. I cared for her. But love?" He looked at Larrie. "I have never fallen in love, not as the poets describe it or as it appears in romantic novels. I suppose it exists, but I don't know what it feels like. I don't know if I am capable of experiencing it. I suppose I'm not."

"That's terrible."

Jo shrugged again. "Not to me. One doesn't miss what one has never had. But that lack in me has had its consequences."

"What do you mean?"

Jo looked at her. "I'll get to that in a moment. It turned out that the Baltistani woman who loved me had an uncle, a guru named Harkrishnan ji, who possessed extraordinary powers. I was not aware of that when I left the mountain village and returned here, to the Punjab. I began a business of sorts, bringing in British goods and exporting local wares. I wanted to go adventuring again, and I needed to raise some cash."

"You said your father was a duke. Aren't you rich?"

"Ha! I'm the youngest son of a duke. I haven't a farthing from my family."

"Are those your parents in the portraits on the wall?'

Jo turned his head toward the paintings. "No. The man is my grandfather, Edward John Trelawny. The woman is my grandmother, Marguerite, the Countess of Blessingham. I was very fond of them. My father wasn't as sentimental. After my grandparents both died and he came into the estate, he gave their portraits to the servants. I bought the paintings back from a maid for a few pounds."

"And your parents? Where are they?"

Jo's face got stiff. "My father is in London, I suppose. My mother . . ." His voice became hard. "My fair lady mother lives with her lover, in Glasgow, I think. I don't speak with either of them. And they want nothing to do with me."

"That's terrible! Can I ask you why?"

"You can ask. It's an ugly tale. Do you really want to hear it?"

"Yes, if you are willing to tell me."

"I don't mind. It's the truth, after all. Plainly put, my mother didn't want me, I'm sure of that. The servants told me she threw herself down a flight of stairs when she was carrying me in her womb in hopes of aborting me. I never remember her giving me one hug, one kiss. When I was around her, she either looked at me as if she hated me, or ignored me as if I weren't there. I was sent off to boarding school when I was six.

"When I was very small, I thought I must have done something very wrong to make my mother hate me so. Later, I heard bits and pieces of the things that happened before I was born. Mrs. Jenkins, the housekeeper who was always good to me, finally told me the whole tale. My father's first wife had died from a fever. He had been left with two young sons and a debt-ridden estate. He wanted a rich wife.

"He courted my mother, but she rejected him. In fact, her maid had told Mrs. Jenkins that she laughed at him when he asked for her hand. She had been quite cruel and called him old, bald, and fat. However, she didn't have a choice. Her parents forced her into the marriage. His parents, my grandparents, weren't keen on the match. My mother's family was in trade and were not nobility. And my mother, although very pretty and well-mannered, was still very young.

"My father insisted on the marriage. My mother's family had a lucrative shipping business, and he was assured a partnership. He had the title her family wanted. Her family had the money he needed. And so they were wed.

"The maids heard my mother begging my father not to touch her on their wedding night. They heard her screaming too. They heard her screaming every night until she became pregnant with me. Once she was with child, she moved into her own suite and had a lock put on her door."

Jo got up abruptly and went to the side table. He filled a tall glass with brandy. He looked at his grandfather's portrait while he talked. "Before I went into the army, my father invited me to come for a visit. I thought he wanted to wish me well, congratulate me on my commission. Instead, he had a plan that I would marry a girl, the daughter of one of his friends. She was not even sixteen. The marriage would be a profitable business alliance for him, and he said it would be financially lucrative for me as well." Jo took a long drink of the amber fluid. "I asked him if he also wanted me to rape the girl on my wedding night as he had my mother. He ordered me to leave his house. We have never spoken since."

"I don't know what to say."

"Why should you say anything?" He brought the glass of brandy back to the chaise, sat down, and leaned back on the cushions. He remained silent while he warmed the brandy glass in his hands, then finished it off with a long swallow. When the glass was empty he said, "This is turning into a long tale. Let me finish.

"Harkrishnan ji, the young woman's uncle, found me. It took him a long time to do so. He showed up

on my doorstep, here in the Punjab. He told me that
his niece, who had loved me, had died—bearing my
son. 'She didn't lose her life because you left,' he said.
'Her living or dying was not in your control. Yet she
had lost her joy. There the blame is yours, for you were
the source of her happiness. A joyless life was crueler
than death.'

"I was appalled, of course. I never would have walked
away without providing for her if I had known she was
carrying my child. I am not a complete cad." He saw
Larrie's questioning look. "No, I wouldn't have married
her. I was not of her world, nor she of mine. But I asked
her uncle if he wanted money to care for the boy. He became very angry. He said no, he had come to teach me a
lesson. Then he said he was going to turn me into a genie
and imprison me in a lamp.

"Fool that I was, I laughed at him. I told him I didn't
believe in his magic." Jo turned haunted eyes to Larrie.
"As you don't believe in magic, or me."

A chill ran through Larrie's blood. She felt disturbed
and uneasy.

"As you have witnessed, I was wrong to have doubted
him. I was enchanted that night, a week or so ago from
this day at the end of April, 1906. I have been a genie
ever since."

"I'm sorry," Larrie said yet again.

"Don't be. In my case, accountability is absolutely
necessary, but absolution is not required." He sprang
up from the divan. "That's my story. Now, to matters at
hand. You asked me to prove that you are where I say
you are. Come, let me show you the village. You must
see the Punjab."

Larrie rose slowly from her seat. Her face revealed a
growing anxiety. "I know you wish to stay here a while,
but my family is going to be frantic. To them I have simply disappeared."

"Not a thing to worry about!" Jo stretched out his hand to her. "We can tarry in the past as long as we want. When we go back to your present, I'll return us on the same day we left. No one will even know you've gone."

Chapter 15

Once he was back in his own home, brandy warming his insides, Jo Trelawny had become like a man who, having reached a high mountain summit, stood on a precipice. He felt exhilarated, yet fully aware of the gravity of his position. He had accomplished his first goal, to return to the past, to his life as he had left it. He had landed a few days beyond where he had aimed to appear, but it was close enough. Little had changed in the slow-moving Punjab while he had been absent.

Unwittingly, the newest owner of the lamp had given him a chance to escape from his soul-wrenching enchantment. It had been a stroke of fortune to end up in the possession of this American girl. Since Jo was neither an evil person nor a man without conscience, he felt a twinge of guilt at manipulating her, but he believed he had no choice.

None of his other masters over the decades had provided an opportunity like this one. The scholarly old man, Josiah Ydoboni, had stored the oil lamp in a locked cabinet. Unlike all the others who had owned the lamp, Ydoboni never even made a single wish. The endless confinement had nearly driven Jo into madness. He watched the years roll by as his life stayed in limbo—a limbo that consisted of the tiny dimensions of that horrible lamp. No cruel god could have dreamed up a worse punishment.

Now, all had changed. A warm wind enveloped him. A familiar path lay beneath his feet. He was home. Jo took a deep breath of air, of freedom.

He stole a glance at the woman whose hand he was holding. Now he was leading her from the confines of the house into the vibrant, color-drenched world of India. Shot through with happiness, he squeezed the woman's fingers. He owed her a deep debt which he had no idea how he'd ever repay.

She had the most unexpected effect on him too. She had felt so good against him when he had held her in his arms. She lacked a classic beauty of creamy skin and graceful manner, but to him she was exceptionally lovely with her blazing red hair and strange silver eyes. He had the irrational desire to try to kiss her again, but it wasn't the right time or place. He resisted his impulse.

Larrie looked questioningly at him. "What is it?"

He swept his unoccupied hand toward a water buffalo pulling a plow in a field near the road, a group of small children hiding shyly behind the nearby bushes, the Kusum tree with its early red leaves beginning to go green, the delicate lavender of Himalayan columbine, the crimson and yellow flowers growing in profusion everywhere, the palms swaying gently above them. And as the *pièce de résistance*, he silently pointed out a herd of elephants in the distance, sheltered by some trees.

In a soft, low voice, he said with his lips very close to Larrie's ear, "What do you think? Is it real enough for you?"

The woman didn't answer right away. She stopped on the path and dropped his hand. She looked around. "I can only say that if I am dreaming, it's like no other dream I've ever had. And if I've gone mad, then madness is close to the divine."

"Well said!" Surprised at her insights, Jo realized that this plucky woman, whom he had thought as simple and shallow as most pretty young girls, was deeper than he had judged her to be. She also had a devil of a temper. He laughed to himself. She had threatened to cut off his manhood a few minutes earlier.

Jo reached out his hand, and she willingly placed hers back in it. He was finding the company of Larissa Smith delightful, and he had not expected that either. If only he were not a genie, he would usher her about, take her dancing, pull her laughing into his bed. Of course, as a genie, he could still bed her, but it was different than being an ordinary man. As a genie, he wasn't his own master but hers. That might spoil the lovemaking somehow, he thought.

Lovemaking. Love. The images brought his thoughts back to the story he had told her. It was all true. What he hadn't said, what was worse than his enslaved enchantment as a genie, was the knowledge that the dark spell could be lifted, but not knowing how to do it. He knew this because, in the seconds before he had been struck by a bolt of energy so powerful it had rendered him senseless, the guru named Harkrishnan ji had told Jo to always remember that he had it within his own power to break the enchantment.

When Jo came back into consciousness, he had found himself less than three inches tall and lying on the guru's open palm. Panic overwhelmed him. He jumped to his feet. He pleaded with the wizened mountain elder to tell him what he had to do.

"How can I undo this? How can I break the spell you have struck me with?" Desperate and afraid, he would have done anything if only his captor would just return him to his life.

For a moment the holy man studied him without compassion. Then he said, "This enchantment is your schooling, teaching you what must be learned. You have been careless and selfish. You must be transformed before you can return to your place in the world of men. So hear me, you pathetic helpless creature I could crush like a bug." The holy man began to tighten his fingers, perhaps to instill fear in his prisoner. "Two things must happen for the spell to be lifted."

"*I'll do them!*" Jo yelled as loud as he could, for his voice was barely a squeak issuing from his place on the man's hand.

"You cannot *do* them. I told you to listen carefully to what I say. First, since you would not believe, you must make another believe in what you did not."

"You mean believe in magic? In genies?" Jo thought that sounded possible. He felt heartened. "What else? What else?" he cried out.

"You must—"

A clap of thunder boomed so loudly the world itself reverberated with the sound and suddenly all was dark. The words, those crucial words that could free Jo, went unheard. Jo found himself locked in the chamber of the brass lamp, with no light, no human kindness, no joys. His release came only when the lamp was rubbed and he emerged to become a *jinn* and a slave to whoever possessed the lamp.

Tormented in this way, Jo had passed over a hundred years. The tedious incarceration in that lamp had cost him his future and hopes. It had cost him nearly everything except his wit. He had plenty of time to think about what might break the enchantment. And yet, as intelligent as he was, he could not figure out what words would have followed "You must—"

He had concluded that his only hope for release was to find the old guru and make him repeat what he had said. Jo had thought of little else for a century. Now, if he could convince this woman to stay in the past long enough, he would track the fellow down. The guru, old and on foot, could not have traveled very far in less than a week. Jo swore he would get the answer he sought—and then his freedom.

"Where are we going?" Larrie's voice broke into Jo's thoughts.

"Just walking about. And if you agree, I should like to check on my business. I have a warehouse for my export trade in the village." That's what Jo said. What he kept to himself was that he needed to make inquiries to find the guru. He'd have to find something to keep Larrie occupied while he did.

An idea began to form in his wily mind. All women liked children, didn't they? He thought the ones he saw hiding outside the house might be just what he needed. Without Larrie noticing what he did, he beckoned with his free hand for the children to follow.

Chapter 16

Larrie Smith realized she wasn't in Beaumont, Pennsylvania, (pop. 600) anymore. Whether she had really ended up in the Punjab in 1906, she didn't know. Yet she was beginning to believe she had.

With her feet stirring up dust from an unpaved road no wider than an oxcart, she walked hand in hand with Jo Trelawny, the warm pressure of his fingers feeling comforting and pleasant. She could let go of him—perhaps she *should* let go—but she liked the feel of him. A sharp pang of grief shot through her even as she enjoyed Jo's company. It had been a long time since a young man had held her hand.

She and this handsome Englishman—it was hard for her to think of him as a genie when he dressed in Western clothes—moved along at a brisk pace toward a cluster of buildings in the distance. Larrie assumed that was the location of Jo's warehouse and their destination, but now, distracted by astonishing sights such as two chattering monkeys in the top of a tree, Larrie went along silently and didn't ask.

She soon became aware of the sounds of giggling. Larrie glanced behind her. The children whom Jo had pointed out hiding shyly behind some bushes had begun to follow them. She gave them a little wave.

The group of no more than a dozen boys and girls ranging in age from six or seven years old to no more than ten or eleven ran up closer, and finally, timidly, a little girl slipped a small hand into hers. "Hello," Larrie said.

The child didn't answer but looked up at Larrie with huge, dark eyes. The girl's hair was dark too, but with a reddish cast. Her arms and legs were stick thin, but under the tattered shirt or chemise she wore, her belly seemed large.

This child is ill, Larrie thought. She glanced back at the other children and saw they too had rusty-colored hair and a malnourished look. Having been raised on a farm and around animals all her life, Larrie knew about vitamin and mineral deficiencies. She had a rescued squirrel die from lack of sunshine's vitamin D, mother sheep that had gotten milk fever from calcium loss, and she and her father had battled kwashiorkor, a disease caused by a protein deficiency, in weaned calves. *Kwashiorkor*, she thought, *that's exactly the problem.*

"Jo." Larrie turned toward the man walking at her side. "What do these children eat?"

He gave her a quizzical look. "I don't know. Why do you ask?"

"They're not well."

Jo shook his head. "It's a poor land and a poor village. This is India, you know."

"No, I don't know." Her eyes flashed with annoyance. "I just arrived. And it's supposedly a hundred plus years behind the world I came from." Suddenly irritated with him, she dropped his hand. She thought he was an impossible person, whether he was a genie or a man.

Deliberately ignoring Jo, she turned her attention to the little girl whose bare brown feet were dirty with the road's dust. To Larrie, she appeared to be an exceptionally beautiful child. Larrie bent down and looked directly into the child's face. She pointed to herself and said, "My name is Larrie. Lar-ee. Can you say Larrie?"

"Lar-ee," the child repeated.

"What is your name?" Larrie put her index finger gently on the child's shoulder.

"Mayree," the child answered.

"Mayree! How pretty." Then she noticed that the other children had moved closer. She stood up. Holding Mayree with one hand, she stretched out the other. A tall, very skinny boy ran up and grabbed it. He grinned at her.

His face is so thin, she thought and her heart squeezed in her chest.

Larrie again began walking behind Jo. With the rest of the children trailing behind her, she felt like the Pied Piper. She wished she had candy in her pockets to give them, but she had nothing. So she just held the two small hands and decided to sing. She thought "Somewhere Over the Rainbow" was appropriate, so she launched into it with her clear soprano that had been well-trained by the choirmaster in the Lutheran church she used to attend.

The children seemed to love it. When Larrie finished the song, the little girl holding her right hand squeezed it and said, "You sing more, memsahib?"

"You speak English?" Larrie asked, delighted.

The girl nodded. "A little bit, memsahib. Sing now?"

Thus encouraged but limited by songs whose lyrics she knew, Larrie chose "Blue Skies," and pretended she was Barbra Streisand as she belted out the melody. The children behind her all clapped.

Larrie forgot momentarily about Jo until he cleared his throat loudly and interrupted her impromptu performance. Larrie stopped singing about bluebirds. It was her third time through the chorus but the children still giggled and seemed to enjoy it. She glanced at Jo and realized they had entered the village. They all now stood in front of a ramshackle building of old stone and boarded-up windows.

"This is my place. I need to talk to Ghurki, a fellow who works for me. Will you stay outside with the children?" Jo paused and gave her a meaningful look. "Your, ah, singing is attracting attention."

Larrie noticed that men and women had emerged from the small buildings lining the street and were staring at her from the doorways. Larrie lifted her chin. She certainly would not be quiet because she was embarrassing the big Sahib Trelawny. "I think I shall sing 'Getting to Know You' next," she announced.

Jo looked at Larrie's squared shoulders and determined face. "You'll give the villagers something to talk about, anyway," he muttered and hurried away into the building.

Larrie sang her song; then she asked Mayree, "Did you learn English in school, Mayree?"

"No, memsahib. In an English house. No school."

"You mean you don't go to school?"

"No school."

"You mean there is no school?"

The little girl nodded, her eyes grave.

Larrie looked around and saw a shady spot under a tree that had large leaves and crimson blossoms. She clapped her hands and motioned for the children to follow her. They did. Once under the tree, Larrie thought she could give an impromptu lesson in addition. She figured mathematics was a universal language and knowing it was always useful.

She started with $1 + 1$ which she figured all the children knew. She held up fingers. Then she progressed to $2 + 2$ and went as far as $5 + 5$, when she ran out of fingers. They caught on and soon joined in the game, for Larrie made the lesson fun, laughing when they held up the right numbers, walking around and hugging them all, and generally having a fine time. She decided she needed sticks or pebbles. She had some vague memories of observing a Montessori class and remembered they did something with sandpaper numbers and different-sized dowels. She could make flash cards, and if she could find the materials, she could create a simple abacus for next time.

Next time. With a start, Larrie realized she was already envisioning teaching the children again, but perhaps she wouldn't be able to. She doubted that she would be here, in this place, in this century.

In any event, she would speak to Tara Singh about the children's diet. She had some ideas about improving that too. Getting some iron skillets to their mothers immediately occurred to her. Eating food prepared in cast-iron cookware was an easy way to ingest supplemental iron and she suspected the children, with meat obviously lacking in their diet, were probably anemic.

Moving on to subtraction with her attentive "class," Larrie had no idea how much time had passed before she heard Jo calling to her.

"Ms. Smith! Ms. Smith, we need to go now." He stood in the road outside the shade of the tree. He was frowning and didn't look pleased.

"Oh," she said aloud. "Just a moment." She turned to Mayree, who Larrie now knew was the only child who understood any English at all. "I must go. But can you tell me where you live, sweetheart? I'd like to talk to your mother."

The child stared at her with solemn eyes and didn't answer.

Larrie tried again. "Your mommy? Your mama?"

"No ammee."

"You don't have a mother? Where is your father?" Larrie searched her memory for a different word for *father*. "Your papa? Baba? Abba?"

"No abu," Mayree said sadly.

"And your home? Where you sleep?"

Mayree now stared at the ground and shook her head.

By this time Jo, evidently agitated and wanting to go, walked over to Larrie and the children. "I really need to be going." His voice was impatient.

Larrie didn't budge. "Mayree says she has no mother or father, and nowhere to sleep."

Jo glanced at the group of raggedy children sitting cross-legged in the dirt. "These are all orphans. Sometimes a local family takes them in or lets them sleep with their animals. Other times they live on the streets or in the fields."

"That's terrible! No wonder they are malnourished. This situation is unacceptable!"

"No, Larrie. This is India. There are thousands of children like these. It's how it is here. Come on." He turned to go.

Larrie grabbed his arm. He halted and turned to find her eyes ablaze and boring into his. "Saying 'This is India' is no excuse. These children are in this village. They are your responsibility."

Jo's mouth gaped, and he stared at her. "My responsibility? They are not my children."

Larrie's emotions felt explosive, like drops of water popping in a hot pan. "You are educated. You are well fed. You wear fine clothes. Although you say you have no money, you live in a grand house with servants. Call it noblesse oblige. Call it compassion. I don't care. But *yes*, Jo Trelawny, these children—" She stopped mid-sentence and looked at the group of boys and girls who was watching the sahib and memsahib with great interest. She mentally counted them and looked back at Jo. "These ten orphans, ten helpless hungry souls, are *your* responsibility." She folded her arms across her chest and glared at him. "And I am not going anywhere without them."

As he marched into his house, Jo's face was a thundercloud. He called out for Tara Singh. When the servant appeared and asked, "Yes, sahib?" Jo barked out, "Lady Larissa wants you to feed these children." He gestured behind him to Larrie and the orphans approaching up the front walk toward the open door.

The turbaned Sikh kept his face impassive, but there was a twinkle in his dark eyes. "Where to feed them, sahib?"

"Not in the main house! On the back veranda. Feed them there."

"They need good food, milk, and eggs, Tara," Larrie said as she slipped in the door behind Jo, herding the children in around her. "And, Tara, if you have a moment, I wish to talk with you about these boys and girls." She lifted her chin in the way she had and glared at Jo. "With *your* permission, Sahib Trelawny, of course," she added with sarcasm, since he knew, and she knew, she was his master after all.

"Of course," he echoed. "Please do whatever the Lady Larissa wishes, Tara," he added and headed for the brandy decanter. Larrie and her charges followed the bearded Sikh out of the cool dark interior of the house and around to the covered veranda at the rear.

Larrie talked to the Sikh as they went. "What food can you prepare for these children? Have you milk?"

"No, memsahib, but we have yogurt. It is for the servants. Sahib Trelawny doesn't eat it as a rule."

"Yogurt is excellent. Fruits? Nuts?"

"Yes. We have mangoes and some almonds."

"Good, good. That will do for now. In the morning they must have eggs. Omelets, I think. With toast and jam. If we have no milk, perhaps some juice."

"In the morning? The children are staying here?"

"Yes, they most certainly are. And they all need baths. Does Sahib Trelawny have a tub?"

"The master's tub? Are you sure?"

"I am very sure. Baths for every one of them. In the tub. But after they have eaten. These children are hungry."

The group had reached the screened-in veranda. Tara told the children in their own language that they should sit down on the wooden floor. Then he disappeared into the house. A short time later Amita appeared with a large platter of fruit. Tara followed her with ten bowls of yogurt on a huge tray.

Larrie worried about the children's dirty hands, but she hadn't asked for water and cloths to wash them, and she couldn't bear to make them wait any longer to eat.

"Did you bring spoons?" she asked Tara.

"Yes, memsahib."

"Then please tell the children to use them for the yogurt. I suppose they must eat the fruit and nuts with their fingers."

"Yes, memsahib." Tara put a bowl of yogurt along with a large spoon into each child's eager hands. He didn't seem to disapprove of what Larrie was doing, and she wondered if the Sikh resented Jo's having so much when the people around him had so little.

"What do the people in this village eat?" Larrie asked the Sikh as she watched the children devouring the food.

"Millet mostly. Vegetables if the crop is good. We have many fruits almost always. Mangoes, like these. Grapes, dates, and nuts too."

"What about meat? I suppose you cannot eat beef. Or pork."

"No beef. No pork. A chicken sometimes or lamb at a feast for the Muslims. But the Hindu eat no meat. As for the Sikhs"—Tara raised his palms upward—"some eat meats, some do not."

Larrie thought about this. She didn't know what religion the children were, but meat was a luxury in any event. A vegetarian diet would be more practical, as long as it included milk and eggs.

Larrie didn't have all the answers, but she had some ideas buzzing through her brain. "Chickens!" she said without preamble and startled Tara. Mostly she was thinking out loud. "We need a flock of hens, with a rooster or two, of course, so we will have chicks. Meanwhile the hens will lay eggs, plenty of eggs."

She fell silent and gazed upward while her mind raced. "Hmmm, not cows." Then she turned her silver eyes toward Tara and began speaking again. "We must get some goats. Goats are perfect. Goat milk can be drunk fresh and made into cheese. We can also make goat milk yogurt."

She couldn't read the expression on the Sikh's face. She wasn't sure he agreed with her goat suggestion, so she spoke more quickly. "Now I realize that billy goats smell dreadful and they get into mischief. We had ours eat the bedsheets off the clothesline once. But that is exactly the point. Goats can eat just about anything, and are happy eating what cows would never touch. Yes, we must have goats."

She stood quietly for a moment, her forefinger tapping her upper lip. She was still thinking. At last, she spoke. "I am sure more will occur to me later, but I will tell Sahib Trelawny to order large sacks of lentils. The children must not eat only millet. They must combine them with lentils. They need a complete protein."

"Complete protein? I do not understand this," Tara said. "An American custom?"

"No. It just means that millet alone is not enough. Millet and lentils make children well and strong. And I need you to obtain some iron pots to cook them in."

"Iron pots?"

"Yes, Tara. They will help prevent anemia. Iron-poor blood."

Tara shook his head at the lady's odd notions. "I will find some blankets for the children to lie on."

"Thank you, Tara. That's very thoughtful."

Jo Trelawny came to the rear of the house in time to see Amita and Larrie scrubbing three squealing, splashing children in his copper bathtub. He frowned again and laced his fingers behind his back. He did not come to the veranda, but stood some ways off and watched for a long while before he called out, "Ms. Smith, if you would be so kind, I need to talk with you."

Chapter 17

Larrie felt happy when she heard Jo's voice, and her heart made an unexpected leap. She straightened and wiped her soapy hands on a dry cloth. She left the children's baths for Amita to finish and walked over to Jo.

"You wanted to say something to me?" Despite her initial joy at Jo's appearance, Larrie remembered her disappointment and dissatisfaction with this British nobleman who needed a lesson in social responsibility and compassion. Her disapproval showed on her face.

"Yes." Jo nodded.

Larrie stood there unsmiling. Her voice and manner were cool. "Well, go on and talk."

"I need to talk with you alone." He took her arm and marched her around to the front of the house and into the main parlor, lit now by oil lamps and filled with shadows. To Larrie's surprise, as soon as they were inside, Jo told her he needed to leave in the morning.

Her face hardened. "You're leaving without me?"

"I'm traveling on horseback into the mountains. It's dangerous country. It's no place for a woman. I will likely be gone a few days. I'm going with Singh. You need to stay here."

Had Jo known Larrie better he would have seen the signs of her temper rising, but he missed the slight flaring of her nostrils, the widening of her eyes, the color beginning to stain her cheeks. He did notice her eyebrows shooting upward, but he never had a chance to step back before the force of her anger hit him.

"I don't think so!" Larrie's quick feelings had skyrocketed and her words came out like bullets. "Let's get something straight. You are not going *anywhere* without me. You are the only way I can ever get back home. I have no intention of being stranded in the wrong century in a strange country. So you can either forget about going, *genie*, or I am going with you."

By this time, Jo had blinked and stepped back. "I, uh, I thought, uh—"

"And tell me, *genie*, why can't you just fly wherever you're going anyway? Or transport yourself by magic? What's this business about horseback?"

At this point, Jo, who was a man as well as a genie after all, was getting an attitude himself. He reacted to Larrie's tone of voice even though she was the master of the lamp, and therefore master of him. He veritably growled in response. "If you'd think about it, *mistress*, you'd see that the answer is obvious. I can fly when *you* want to fly. I can't fly anytime *I* want to fly any more than I can let myself out of that lamp or turn myself back into a man. A magic carpet ride is *magic*. I can perform magic *for your sake* or at *your* bidding, not my own."

"Oh, really?" Larrie huffed. She put her hands on her hips and jutted out her chin. Her eyes shot silver sparks at Jo. "Then why didn't you ask me to help you?" She paused and Jo said nothing. "You see, you have no answer. Since contrary to your opinion, I do *think* about things, I can tell *you* the reason! You don't want me to know what you're doing. What's the big secret? What are you hiding, Jo Trelawny? I know you're hiding something." She folded her arms and narrowed her eyes in Jo's direction. "I wasn't born yesterday, you know."

Jo had been watching Larrie delivering her tirade. His expression transformed from stubbornly opposi- tional to thoroughly amused. As she spoke, the corners of his mouth began to twitch. His eyes started to twinkle. He pressed his lips together as if suppressing the merri- ment bubbling up inside him, but finally he threw back his head and let loose with laughter.

Larrie stared at the genie. "You're laughing at me? I cannot believe you have the audacity to laugh at me! What is so funny!"

Jo took a deep breath and tried to gain control. "You have soap in your hair—" He pointed and continued laughing. "Your clothes are drenched. I can see—see every curve. You have your hands on your hips like a scullery maid while you fire accusations at me like a bar- rister at a witness in the dock. 'What are you hiding, Jo Trelawny. I know you're hiding something.' " He mim- icked her voice perfectly. "Then you said—" He had to stop for a minute to try to suck in a breath because he couldn't speak for laughing. "You said, 'I wasn't—' " He had to stop and gasp. " 'Born *yesterday*.' And that—is— so funny—because you aren't born at all yet!"

Larrie gaped in astonishment at the man in front of her. He was laughing at her. *How dare he?* she thought.

She looked down at herself. Her yellow shirt had plastered against her chest and become transparent. Only the strategically placed embroidery kept her at all decent. Her hair hung in wet strings. Soapsuds sat like cotton puffs on her hair. She felt soap on one ear. She must look like an urchin. Then she thought of his imita- tion of her. He had captured her movements precisely. Her own mouth began to twitch.

Just then her eyes caught Jo's. They held. A current passed between them that was hotter than the sum- mer wind, and strong enough to stop Larrie's breath. She stared. He stared back. Neither of them seemed to breathe. The world around them blurred and faded. Larrie saw only the genie named Jo and the heavy-lidded dark eyes that were looking at her with a naked passion.

Jo stepped toward her and whispered tenderly, "Lady Larissa, I cannot help myself," as his lips came down on hers. And this time Larrie didn't push him away.

Jo's kiss was demanding, hard against her lips, and delightfully exciting. Lights seemed to be shooting through the darkness behind Larrie's closed eyes. She parted her lips and his tongue darted inside her mouth. He explored her and possessed her. He wove his fingers through her hair and held her head still in his strong hands.

They kissed for a long time. When they stopped, Larrie's knees were weak. She hoped she'd have the will to resist him if he wanted to go further. Then she realized she rather hoped he would, and so when he lifted her chemise over her head and caressed her breasts, she let him. She had stars in her eyes and they were dazzling her.

He told her she was beautiful. He whispered that he wanted her more than any other woman he had ever known. He touched her. He stroked her. He made her mew like a kitten. Her nipples were hard and erect, little pink top hats just begging to be kissed. He did kiss them for just the briefest of kisses, before he abruptly pulled away. He stepped back. "We must stop," he announced.

Larrie's eyes, which had been closed, flew open. "What? Why?"

He picked up her chemise and tenderly slipped it over her head, dressing her as if she were a child. "We must stop, but not because I don't want you—I do want you. I desire you immensely. But it's the wrong place. The servants can walk in at any moment."

Larrie felt confused. "So let's go to your bedroom—"

Jo folded his arms across his chest and regarded her

with a serious face. "We could. But you accused me a few minutes ago of hiding a secret. You don't trust me. I fear you'd regret our lovemaking."

Now clothed again, Larrie found her reason returning. Her face turned flaming red. She had suggested they slip away to bed, and he had said no. She felt terribly embarrassed. What had she been thinking? Obviously she hadn't been thinking about what she was doing or where it was leading. Her words were stiff and dry, but her heart was still racing. "I probably would have regrets. It's true. I don't trust you."

Jo Trelawny didn't seem perturbed by her sudden withdrawal. He just watched her with a very satisfied look on his face. "I underestimated you once more, Ms. Smith. I should have asked your help. I should have told you everything. I am hiding something."

"I knew it!" Larrie said.

"You're much too smart for me." Jo's voice might have held a hint of sarcasm but Larrie wasn't quite sure it did.

Chapter 18

"Let me get this straight. You want to go looking for the old guru who enchanted you to find out how to break the spell? Then you can become a man again. What's the big secret? Why not just tell me that's what you wanted to do in the first place?"

Larrie was sitting primly next to Jo on a velvet-covered maroon settee, a Victorian camelback with wooden armrests carved like lion's paws. The house's furniture, all very British looking, had no doubt been imported. It would have been perfect in a fashionable town house in London's Belgravia, but it looked out of place in Asia. Evidently Jo's "going native" had been highly selective and didn't extend to his living accommodations. He certainly hadn't opted for a village hut.

Larrie noticed that Jo was regarding her carefully before he answered. She wondered if he was trying to decide how much of the truth he could, or should, reveal. Finally he looked away—a sure sign he was about to evade the truth—and started to speak.

"I didn't tell you in the first place for many reasons. First of all, you have no motive to help me and a strong one not to."

Larrie was taken aback. "Motive? I don't have any motives at all in this, except to get back home."

"Exactly. If I break the spell, you might be, as you pointed out, stranded in a century and country not your own. But surely you see your motives go beyond that."

"I told you, I have no motives. I'm not that kind of person." Mentally she added, *But I wonder if you are.*

After a long pause, Jo finally looked her in the eyes with naked honesty. "Are you really that innocent? Haven't you thought this through? You possess a genie. You can use me to wish for anything your heart desires. The wishes I can grant are, as I explained, ones that can change your life. You can become wealthy beyond imagining. You can acquire power. You can be 'discovered' by a Hollywood producer and become a famous movie star. I think that's the most popular of wishes. I've fulfilled it several times over the years, and I'm only one genie of many.

"And like the suddenly famous actors, you can completely transform your life in a blink of an eye. You can even—in a modest way, since my powers aren't unlimited; I cannot raise the dead, for instance, or stop a war—transform the world."

Larrie hadn't considered any of those wishes. It wasn't so much her innocence as her not being truly convinced she had a genie. She had assumed that all the strange things since Ms. Ydoboni's phone call had occurred because she was having some sort of nervous breakdown. She was hallucinating. She was out of touch with reality, even though she didn't feel delusional in the least. The wish she had made came from her heart, from her deepest yearnings, not her head. To buy into this whole genie scenario and wish to become the first woman president or to be running an antiques store empire, she would have to be mad.

She really didn't know if she was truly crazy now, and if this was all an illusion. Her logic told her it must be, but her emotions more and more were insisting it was all real.

As was her style, Larrie made the decision right then and there to go with her feelings as the one true thing she should believe in. This India was real. This genie was real. And this genie, or the man he had been, was basically good. She saw Singh's devotion to him, and such loyalty had to be earned, not bought. She recognized that even though Jo yelled and acted put-upon, he had brought the children into his house and told the servants to get them whatever Larrie requested. She didn't believe he had done that because she was the mistress of the lamp. She suspected he wanted to please her. She suspected he just needed a small push to do the right thing.

That he had been put under a spell and locked up, without due process or trial or conviction, in a tiny lamp for more than a hundred years enraged her sense of decency, now that she began to believe it. His imprisonment was morally wrong.

Her heart filled with pity. She moved her head ever so slightly. She reached over and gently took Jo's hand. "Listen to me. I do come from a very different time and place than you do. I can only guess you've never known many Americans, especially rural Americans like the people who live on the farms in my part of the country. But in my Pennsylvania we help people who need our help.

"It's true not many of us have big dreams. Mostly we appreciate what we have, love our land, and celebrate our families. So no, Jo Trelawny, none of the things a genie can do occurred to me." She took a deep breath and plunged on. "And although I know you *could* strand me here, I would ask you not to. I will believe that you wouldn't *if* that's what you promise—since a man is as good as his word. That's why I would gladly help find a way to free you."

She sighed.

"That's the kind of person I am. I don't know what kind of person you are—I think at heart you're a good man. But I think you could be a far better one. Maybe the guru was right that you needed to learn a lesson— but he had no right to do what he did."

The genie gave Larrie's slender fingers a squeeze. "Thank you for thinking that. But surely you have something you'd wish for. Everyone does."

Larrie's answer was a series of sighs and no words for a minute. Then with infinitely sad eyes, she said in a soft, kind voice, "Jo, what I would wish for, as you said a few minutes ago, isn't within a genie's power to provide. Many times I wished for Ryan to return. But in my heart I knew the dead are gone from this earth and cannot come back to the living. Nor should they. I accept that truth as much as it hurts.

"As for other 'life-altering' wishes, the ones I might consider making, they would be for others, not myself. I might wish for all my family to live long and happy lives. Yet I would never do it. Why? Although I want a long and happy life for each and every one of them, I have no right to make it happen by magic. It wouldn't work in the long run, you see? I don't know what they are supposed to learn through their mistakes, or through their grieving, or during their periods of unhappiness.

"I've come to understand that only a fool is happy all the time. And if my wish kept a loved one from dying young, magically stopping the tragedy of a shortened life, how can I know if my interference eliminated a heroic act that saved a dozen other people or was noble in some other fashion? I don't know what roads the people I love are supposed to walk. I don't know where my own path will go. But I have to travel it, with no shortcuts, with my choices directing me to wherever I'm going. Do you understand?"

Jo Trelawny's face changed as he looked at her. "I've lived more than a hundred years and I never thought it out like that. How did you get so wise?"

Larrie's eyes were wet now. "By suffering, Jo. By loving someone so much that losing him felt as if it would kill me, but when it didn't I had to figure out why."

Jo reached over and pushed a strand of hair from Larrie's cheek, dampened now by a single tear. "You're a good woman, Larrie. I'm not such a good man. And I have never loved like you have. I don't suppose I ever will."

Larrie gave Jo a gentle smile. "Another thing I've discovered the hard way, when all my dreams died one terrible night, is never assume you know the future. Nobody, not even a genie, does."

As if uncomfortable all of sudden, Jo Trelawny dropped Larrie's hand, without explanation, and stopped looking at her. He strode back to the brandy decanter. "So does all that mean you'll help me find the guru?"

Feeling a little puzzled, Larrie repeated that of course that's what she meant.

Jo poured brandy in a tall glass and took a long drink of the amber fluid. While he drank, he stared at his grandfather's portrait on the wall and not at Larrie when he answered. "Since you now desire it, we'll take the magic carpet tomorrow and go north. The guru is headed back to Baltistan, or so my sources tell me. We should find him within a day or two."

"A day or two. I didn't think it would be—" She was quiet for a moment. "I must ask you to change your plans."

Jo whirled around, his eyebrows rising. "Change my plans? Are you backing out?"

"No, but I must be honest with you. I'm not convinced you can get us back to Pennsylvania a few hours after we left. You landed here in India a week after your enchantment and I'm not so foolish as to think *that* was planned. If I'm absent very long, my friends and family will be worried sick."

"So you want to go back? Now?" Jo looked stricken, his lips pressed together so tightly they were turning white.

"No, I'll stay here until we find out what you need to know, except first—I want to call home."

"Call home?"

"Yes. People do have telephones in 1906, don't they? They must have them in India too. I assume you can find one I can use."

"India has had telephone service since 1882. There is an exchange in the governor's palace in the city of Lahore. It's not thirty miles from here. But there is no service to America."

Larrie rose off the settee. She noticed that her yellow chemise was nearly dry and no longer transparent. She decided her clothes looked presentable if just a bit wrinkled. Her voice held a cool matter-of-factness when she replied to Jo. "There is no service to the twenty-first century either. But you can arrange the connection, can't you?"

Jo barked a laugh and put down his brandy glass. "If your calling home is what it takes for you to help me search for my guru, then I'll make it happen. When do you want to make the call?"

"Right now. It isn't so late yet. Barely seven in the evening. I wish to call tonight."

British companies, encouraged by Lord Curzon, the former viceroy of India, had, by 1906, crisscrossed British India with thousands of miles of railways. The Indian trains were highly efficient and ran with regularity even in the farthest reaches of the Punjab. So Jo and Larrie easily caught a seven o'clock train to Lahore.

Larrie became as excited as a child when she saw the train coming down the tracks into the small rail station in the village. Grinning broadly, she climbed aboard a quaint wooden passenger car pulled by a chuffing steam engine. There was no first-class carriage, and she sat on a rattan bench seat amid families traveling with piles of luggage, a few crates of squawking chickens, and quite a number of bicycles. Jo stood nearby, having given up his seat to a woman with three small children tugging at her skirts. He boosted one of her toddlers into his strong arms. Larrie put another on her lap, and the grateful woman held an infant to her breast.

After barely a half hour, the little puffing engine pulled into the main Lahore railroad station. Built by the British of a ruddy red brick, it boasted pointed arches, clock towers, and turrets so impressive that the grand structure had Larrie gaping at its magnificence. And after they left the train, a cab—horse drawn, not motorized—took them to the Mughal-Gothic style governor's mansion in minutes.

Although the governor himself, Sir Lancelot Hare, had gone to Calcutta earlier in the day, Jo Trelawny and his pretty American friend, Ms. Larissa Smith, got a warm welcome from the governor's wife. In fact the avid curiosity of Lady Madeleine Hare, called Bunny by her friends, had been ignited by the appearance of John Trelawny, the Punjab's most eligible bachelor—and, as everyone knew, a bit of a rake—with this unescorted young woman whose hair had been bobbed exceptionally short. The surprise visit reeked of intrigue and a touch of scandal.

Lady "Bunny" Hare, whose overbite and weak chin gave her an appropriately rabbity look, fluttered about the couple, talking very rapidly without waiting for Larrie to answer.

"Ms. Smith of Pennsylvania? Are you one of the

Philadelphia Smiths? No? Now I remember, they were Smythes, weren't they? But it's the same thing, isn't it? I suppose there are a great many Smiths in America. Are you here on a spiritual quest? Are you one of those Theosophists? We've had so many Americans come to India, following Madame Blavatsky. When she was alive, that is. She's been dead a long time. But that Annie Besant is down in their Madras ashram, isn't she? She wears native clothes like you, that's why I'm asking. I'm not a Theosophist myself. I'm Church of England. I don't understand all this trying to talk to the dead and those dreadful séances they're always holding."

Larrie didn't know what to say, so she stayed silent and let Jo do the talking for them both. He was glib and charming, and Larrie had to work very hard to keep the surprise off her face while he spun the most amazing lies.

Jo walked up to the chattering Lady Hare and put his strong arm around her bony shoulders. He spoke in an intimate way, taking her into his confidence. "Bunny, my dear dear Bunny, you are as sharp as a tack. No one can get by you with anything. You've seen everything at a glance.

"I must tell you the whole story. It all started when I was in the Bengal Lancers with Ms. Smith's cousin. He's a Barnstable, one of the Cornwall Barnstables. You remember good old Rollie Barnstable, don't you? He's a crack shot and wicked with a saber. That's how Ms. Smith and I became acquainted. Through Rollie. We met last year. In Paris. Oh, yes, I went to Paris. Don't you remember? No? It was in April. Perhaps you had gone to London that month?

"Ms. Smith and I met, and it was love at first sight. We're engaged, but it's a secret. I know I can rely on you keeping that in strict confidence. Oh, good, I see I can. Now here's the thing. Ms. Smith absolutely has to put in

a call to break the news to Rollie. He's stationed in Am-
ritsar. He's likely to call me out as a cad if she doesn't!
Would it absolutely be too much trouble for her to use
your telephone?"

The excitement of being part of a clandestine romance lit up Lady Hare like a candle. She giggled. She
twittered. She rang a bell for a servant. She whispered
to Jo, "You know you can rely on me. Lord Hare and I
eloped, you know. His mother didn't approve of me. I
had aspirations to be on the stage. It was the talk of the
season. You won't remember. You were just a child."

An elderly servant in a *dhoti* entered the room. Lady
Hare motioned to him. "Rama will take you to Lord
Hare's study. Make the call. I would never forgive myself if Ms. Smith's cousin shot you!" She giggled again
as Rama dutifully led the gentleman and his "fiancée"
across a courtyard to a room, no doubt Lord Hare's
study, which had a telephone affixed to one wall.

"You can ring the exchange from here, sahib," old
Rama said and left.

Larrie hoped the genie could make the connection.
Now that she was about to make the call, she felt impossibly far away and very homesick. Her heart began to
pound as Jo picked up the receiver and turned the crank
on the side of the box.

Chapter 19

"Mom! Why are you answering Aunt Lolly's phone? Is there something wrong?"

"Larrie! Where are you? Are you all right?"

"Of course I'm all right. Why are you asking? I called to tell Aunt Lolly I might not be back tonight and not to worry if I don't show up."

"Tonight? Where were you last night? Why didn't you call then?" Her mother's voice sounded strained and anxious.

"Last night? What day is this?" *This isn't good*, she thought. *The genie must have already messed something up.*

"It's *Tuesday* night, Larrie. Have you been in an accident? Are you hurt?"

Larrie had to think fast and spewed out the first lies that came to her. "No, I'm absolutely fine, Mother. I had to take care of some business in—in New York City. It had to do with that estate I just bought. I've been holed up in the library and meeting with some researchers, that's all. Lost track of time." She decided to change the topic. "Why are you at Aunt Lolly's? Has something happened to *her*?"

"Hold on a minute, Larrie. I'll take this into the other room and tell you." Larrie could hear her mother call out to someone, "It's Larrie. Yes, she's fine. She went into New York City, that's all. You want to talk with her? Give me a few minutes, and I'll put her on."

A moment later, her mother was speaking into the phone again, her voice low. "Larrie, I didn't want Aunt Lolly to overhear. I know you've been fighting this, but your father and I are taking her in for a competency examination tomorrow."

"What? Why?" Larrie's temper was instantly climbing. She hadn't been gone forty-eight hours, and they were trying to put Aunt Lolly in a home. "There is absolutely no reason for that!"

"You have to listen to me, dear. She's really gone around the bend this time. Ticky told us about the garage door—"

"That could happen to anyone! It doesn't mean she's incompetent."

"It's not just that. She's hallucinating."

"What do you mean she's hallucinating?"

"She's insisting she saw you and some man come through your kitchen window sitting on a throw rug and fly off. In her exact words, Larrie, she told me herself, 'They ascended until they were above the clouds, then headed east. The young man blew me a kiss.' She says she also spoke to your 'new boyfriend' the previous evening. She says he's from India and was in the Bengal Lancers or something. She also says he's a duke's son and he's 'top drawer.' Larrie, she's completely mad."

"No, she's not! She absolutely is not. You can't do this!"

"We can and we will. It's for her own good. She's completely lost touch with reality."

"But I do have a new boyfriend! He's British. He—he did live in India."

"Larrie, stop lying to me. We know the whole story. You were right here having a picnic dinner with that

New York art dealer at the same time Aunt Lolly insists she was conversing with your boyfriend in your living room. You certainly didn't fly out of here on a rug. I know you think you're protecting your aunt, but she's a danger to herself. And since she insists on driving, she's become a danger to others. Now when are you coming home?"

"Ahhh—soon. I'm not exactly sure, but sometime tomorrow I think. Who's there? Who wants to speak to me?"

"Your friend Melanie is here. She's been here all day, worried sick about you. And that nice Van Killborn has stayed right with her. He's waiting for you. He says it's urgent to speak to you. And poor Melanie—she's waving to me at this very moment—she's gesturing that it's urgent for her too."

By now, Larrie saw that Jo was signaling to her to hurry up and finish the call.

"Mother, I don't have time to talk to either of them. I have to go. But please, I'm begging you, wait until I get home and explain the situation before you do anything with Aunt Lolly. She's not crazy, I swear it."

"We've already made the appointment. Nothing *you* can say is going to make any difference. We need to hear what a *doctor* determines about her sanity."

"Mother, no!" Larrie cried out—but the line had gone dead.

Larrie's face had become terribly pale when Jo took the black earpiece from her hand and hung it up next to the box on the wall.

"Bad news, I take it," Jo remarked.

Larrie nodded. "I really have to go back to Pennsylvania. They're trying to put Aunt Lolly away in a home." Her voice was weak and dispirited.

Jo glared at her, his feelings naked. "So you *are* backing out! So much for your pretty speech about you Pennsylvanians helping people." His handsome face was carved out of marble, hard and cold as stone.

"No." Larrie shook her head. "I'm not backing out." She suddenly grabbed Jo's arm forcefully, her fingers clutching his bicep. "But once we find your guru, you have to get me back—and no later in time than the Wednesday after we left."

"Wednesday? What day is it now in the future?"

"It's Tuesday night! We must have spent a whole day and night traveling into the past. Jo, you can't screw up our return. Swear to me you won't!"

Hearing that Larrie didn't intend to leave, not immediately anyway, Jo seemed to have recovered his devil-may-care attitude. "You have nothing to worry about. Everything will work out. As far as your aunt's situation goes, you do have that third wish. Use it for her! Magic caused her situation, so use magic to get her out of it. You said you didn't need a wish for anything else, so there you are."

Larrie thought Jo was a little too glib, but he might have a point. "All right, that's a possibility. I'll consider it, *if* it turns out to be necessary. But seriously, Jo, I need to be home by tomorrow, future time. Aunt Lolly would be devastated if she was forced into a retirement home. She might lose her will to live. I'm not going to take that chance. I need to get back to the future. Do you understand?" She lifted her chin and glared at him.

Jo got a funny look on his face. Before Larrie knew what was happening, he had pulled her into his arms again and was kissing her hard. "Oh!" she managed to say before his lips possessed her and she was swept away. If she were able to think, which she wasn't at the moment, she'd have to admit that no man had ever affected her sexually like Jo did. His touch set her on fire. She couldn't resist him, and she didn't want to resist him. His kisses felt so good, she wanted them to go on and on.

And because she liked it so much, she kissed him back and melted into his arms, her breath already coming fast. Somewhere in the recesses of her mind, a little voice started to tell her, *Larrie, you're falling for this guy. Be careful—*

Then another little voice said, "Oh, that's so romantic!" Bunny Hare's words brought Larrie back to her senses. She jumped back, her face flaming hot from embarrassment.

Flustered, she stammered, "Lady Hare! I didn't hear you coming. Excuse us, please."

Bunny Hare wore a great smile. "No need! There isn't a woman in the world who can resist Jo Trelawny. I think it's marvelous that he's finally found a woman to clip his wings. Quite a few fathers with pretty daughters are going to heave a sigh of relief, I'll tell you. And, Jo, my dear boy, I know this is a secret and all, but now that Ms. Smith has told her cousin, we simply must write up an announcement for the *Times.*"

The words flew out of Larrie's mouth. "Oh, no! I don't think we should!" Then she went completely still. Her body froze unmoving while her mind whirled, trying to figure out what the implications might be of intruding on the records of the historical past with a make-believe engagement. She had begun to believe she shouldn't leave any trace of having been there. But then she had already interfered in history, hadn't she? With the children.

Lady Hare had bent over and begun searching through Lord Hare's desk drawers for a pen and paper. "Now, Ms. Smith, I won't hear any arguments." She glanced over at Jo. "And not from you either, John Trelawny. The lady's reputation will be in tatters if someone besides me sees you *in flagrante delicto.* It's obvious you can't keep your hands off each other."

She straightened up, ready to write. "Jo, I owe this to your grandmother Trelawny. After your mother's scandalous, er, well—we won't talk about that. But *you* must do your family proud, so the *Times* it is." She stamped her foot and looked extremely determined. "Now tell me what to put in the announcement."

Larrie hadn't glanced at Jo since she tore herself from his arms. When she looked at him as Lady Hare waited for him to speak, he appeared stricken for the briefest of seconds, then covered his discomfort with a wide, insouciant grin. "The *Times*. Absolutely fabulous. It's a wonderful idea! You know what to say, all the usual drivel. I went to Harrow, of course. And Sandhurst. Served in the Forty-first. But you know all that. Ms. Smith—her first name is L-A-R-I-S-S-A—is the only daughter of a wealthy landowner in Pennsylvania. She is twenty-five years old. What else shall I say, Larrie? Have you done anything horsey? That always impresses."

"I rode my pony in the gymkhanas put on by the 4-H."

"Perfect. Put in she's an accomplished equestrienne. A fall wedding is planned. Here in Lahore. Will that do?"

Bunny Hare's little round eyes sparkled. "That's splendid! You must be wed right here, in the governor's mansion. No, no, don't protest. You don't know how dreary life in the colonies can be. An absolute bore. I shall be thrilled to put on a wedding." She bounced in excitement, clapping her hands, and to Larrie, the small woman actually seemed to hop.

Larrie moved close to the genie and hissed at him, "This is very cruel. There isn't going to be a wedding!"

Jo gave Larrie a wink and moved even closer. When his breath stirred her hair, she felt a thrill race through her. He whispered in her ear, "Think of the excitement it will cause when the bride scarpers and disappears. You'll be the talk of Lahore for weeks."

Larrie didn't know why she should care, but she jerked away. Jo's words bothered her a great deal. She gave him an angry look and spoke in a quiet, icy voice. "As I said, Jo Trelawny, nobody can see the future. And I don't like this one bit."

Chapter 20

"Larrie hung up? It can't be. Can you call her back? No? This is disastrous. I needed to talk with her. I must have that furniture." Van Killborn sank into a wooden chair next to Aunt Lolly's kitchen table and put his head in his hands.

Melanie awkwardly patted him on the shoulder. "She'll sell to you. You'll see. You just have to wait until tomorrow, when she comes home. I'm certain of it."

Van raised his head. "You don't understand. Oh, God, if she doesn't sell—" The fear clenched in his stomach. He turned anguished eyes toward Melanie. She smiled at him. She had been so kind to him all day long. They had really been getting to know each other. He felt she was on his side, and he hoped she didn't hate him when she found out the truth.

He wrenched his glance from hers, looked around the small, warmly lit kitchen and saw that Larrie's mother wanted to say something to him.

"I really didn't mean to cut off the phone call, Mr. Killborn. Larrie was talking one minute, then there was this awful buzzing sound, and she was gone. I know you wanted to get in a word with her."

"It was terribly important." His voice sounded thin and strained.

Melanie nodded. "Yes, and I really needed to talk with Larrie too. Exactly where is she? Why didn't she come home last night?"

"Business. She says she's in New York talking to some people about that estate she just bought. She said something about research."

Van jumped up, his eyes filled with anxiety. "What! She's in New York? Who's she talking to? Did she say? Ohmygod, this can't be happening." He started to pace up and down.

Then he noticed that Melanie was watching him with questioning eyes. He didn't want her to get suspicious. He came close to her. "I'm under a lot of pressure." He kept his voice low and intimate. He saw how she reacted to him. She liked him, and that was a good thing. He liked her too, and he needed an ally. And there was this sexual attraction that had sprung up between them. She'd help him if she could, he was sure of it.

"My client is calling me constantly about the items Ms. Smith has." He moved his head close to hers so he could feel the heat from her skin. He was nearly whispering. "She told me she needed two days. Two days and she was sure we could make a deal. I'm upset she hasn't come back, that's all. Are you sure she isn't with some guy?"

When Melanie answered him, her lips were only inches from his. He had done that deliberately, but not maliciously. He liked being close to her.

"Larrie is not with a boyfriend," Melanie said sotto voce. "If she met someone, she would have told me. She has me worried though. I have a couple of things to say to her about just leaving without a word. But the main thing is, she's fine. I'm sorry if you're upset though, really."

Van took Melanie's hand and gave it a squeeze. "I know you are." The touch of her soft flesh excited him.

She was a magnificent woman. He stood there staring at her, and for a minute he forgot his anxiety over the Ydoboni estate and thought about getting her alone where he could kiss her.

Melanie could barely keep breathing as Van's eyes bore into hers. Her nerves were dancing along her skin. She could see his desire for her. She wasn't imagining it. But she also could see Van was in some kind of trouble, she could sense it. She'd ask him later, when they were alone.

A delicious tremor ran through Melanie. *Alone.* She wanted to be alone with Van Killborn more than anything she had ever wanted in her life. She knew she had to play it cool, to back off and not let her feelings show, but she was so nuts for him. Since the first sight of him, Melanie O'Casey had lost her heart.

And Van seemed to like her, she felt it in the way he behaved with her. When he looked at her, there was no disgust or ridicule. His eyes roamed her body as if she were a goddess. He seemed to appreciate her ample curves and substance. Yes, that's what she had, *substance.*

She regarded the gorgeous young man in front of her. With a breathtaking realization, she knew she would do anything to make this relationship happen. She had to be very careful. She needed to do everything exactly right.

Having made up her mind, she murmured another reassurance that Larrie would be back soon, but she herself had major qualms about Larrie's absence and had a host of unanswered questions. For one thing, how did Larrie get to New York? She didn't drive her truck to the bus station, and Ticky hadn't taken her. Something about the situation bothered her, she just wasn't sure what.

Larrie's mother was holding up a pitcher, asking if anyone wanted some iced tea. Melanie realized her throat was dry and said she'd like a glass. Van declined. When Melanie walked over to get her drink from Larrie's mother, she glanced over at Aunt Lolly, who had a Latin book open in her lap and seemed oblivious to the people crowded into her kitchen and their conversation. Melanie lowered her voice and said to Larrie's mother, "It's a shame, about, you know—"

"I'm not deaf, Melanie O'Casey." Lolly snapped the book shut. "Or crazy. Larissa *is* with a man. I don't know why she's lying to you, but I don't blame her, really. She's been through enough, the poor girl. If she wants to have a secret affair, that's her business. I only wish she had taken me into her confidence. I wouldn't have said a word to any of *you*."

Larrie's mother shook her head. "Larrie isn't with a man, Lolly. She's at some library in New York. You know she's been in a terrible state since Ryan's death. There have been times I feared we'd lost her, she cared so little about living. I don't know if she'll ever be emotionally whole. She may never fall in love again. And certainly not yet!"

Lolly made a disgusted sound. "A lot you know about your own daughter. I'm not saying she didn't grieve, because I've never seen anyone grieve that hard and at my age, I've see a lot of hearts broken by death. But she was a teenaged girl when she fell in love with Ryan. She's a woman now. She'll love again, don't you worry about that. And this new boyfriend, he's the one. He's special, this one is. A duke's son too!"

She put down her book and stood up. She was still wearing her wrinkled lilac ball gown and white go-go boots. "I must go find Ticky. We have matters of grave importance to discuss."

Melanie and Larrie's mother exchanged looks communicating that they both agreed about poor old Great-aunt Lolly. She was totally out of her mind.

Making the tactical decision to leave before Van, so as not to seem as if she were hanging around waiting for him, Melanie made her way down the driveway toward the road where she had left her car on the berm. She saw Ticky looking in her direction.

Melanie didn't really want to talk with him. Ticky Blackstone tried her patience. He got on her nerves. A couple of years ago, he had handed her an ad for Weight Watchers. "It worked for my brother's woman, and she was twice as fat as you," he said. Melanie could barely tolerate Ticky after that.

She was strolling along slowly, hoping Van would catch up and Ticky would disappear. Instead, when she reached the Old Highway, Ticky stepped in her path. He told her he was staying at the antiques shop that night. He explained he intended to "work security" until Larrie came back and told him different. He had his gun too. Nobody was going to get nothing without going through him first and he'd just as soon shoot those New York thugs as say howdy. And, whether Melanie had thought of it or not, old Lolly was up in that apartment all alone. Ticky was going to call Shem and Shaun to patrol the grounds and take over guarding the shop when he had to sleep.

Glancing back up toward the garage apartment and wondering why Van hadn't come out right after she did, Melanie didn't pay close attention to anything Ticky said. She offhandedly replied, "Do you honestly think all that is necessary? Larrie didn't say anything about you needing to stand guard. I think you're taking this too far."

"Ms. O'Casey, I don't like what's going on. I feel it in my gut." He patted his stomach. "Something ain't right.

Look at it logically. Larrie's not acting normal. I feel it in the air. Trouble. Trouble's coming. Mark my words. But it's not going to happen on my watch."

Just then Van came striding down through the yard. Ticky studied him. "You like that city guy?"

"Yes, I think I do."

"Well, I don't. He's up to something. You behave yourself, Ms. O'Casey. You don't have a lot of experience around men. No offense, but you ain't dated much."

Melanie bristled at that remark. It was true, of course, and everybody knew it, but she didn't like Ticky saying it. "*No offense,* Ticky, but you're one to talk. The way I heard it, you came home one night last week and your girlfriend was gone. So was all your furniture."

Ticky spat onto the road. He had taken off the ASS-HOLE TODAY T-shirt he had worn all weekend and now sported one with TWELVE REASONS BEER IS BETTER'N WOMEN written across the back.

"That's just my point. Sex makes you stupid. But that's nothing compared to love. Man, you're dumber than dirt when you're in love. I see the way you light up around that city guy. You know how it is. You're going to be acting like you don't have a brain in your head. Don't say I didn't tell you so either."

Ticky walked off just as Van reached them. He headed toward Lolly's apartment, and he didn't look back.

Van gave Melanie a white-toothed smile. "I guess there's no point in hanging around here any longer if Ms. Smith's not coming home until tomorrow. But you know what? It's dinnertime. You want to get something to eat? I heard there's a Ruth's Chris Steak House up at Mohegan Sun, the new casino that's opened up. We can get a decent meal there."

"Oh, yes! I'd love to," Melanie answered too fast. She caught herself just in time before she squealed in delight.

"Great! You know, there's no sense taking both our cars. Let's go in mine, and I'll drop you back here later. Okay?"

Melanie just nodded, struck dumb by this wonderful turn of events. Her brain seemed mired in some kind of sticky morass of gooey happiness. She couldn't think straight. She had never felt so excited in her entire life.

Melanie's daze continued through a pleasant dinner during which she and Van talked books. They liked the same authors, and both of them were worried that John Grisham might be burning out. His last books were disappointing. Then they moved on to movies. Melanie didn't even notice she and Van had managed to drink two bottles of Pinot Noir along with their porterhouse and steak fries. She was too busy trying to convince Van that a classic Bergman film really was worth sitting through, depressing as it might be. And he was annoying her a little by extolling the beauty of petite Li Gong, the Chinese actress who starred in *Raise the Red Lantern* and nearly all of director Zhang's other films.

Just then the dessert menu appeared in her hands. "I really shouldn't—" she started to say.

"Don't be ridiculous, Melanie. You're tall. You can afford the calories. Eat! Have the cheesecake."

"Well, if you think I should—"

"Absolutely. And bring us both brandies," Van told the waiter.

Melanie's cheeks were already rosy from the wine and she had an unfamiliar light, airy feeling. "A brandy? Do you think we should have another drink? You have to drive me back to Larrie's, then I have to drive home, you know."

Van appeared to give that situation some thought. Then he grinned at her. "I have the solution to that! Come back to my room. Oh, don't get the wrong idea.

I have a suite. We can sit in the living room and order a movie on the television. Maybe there will be a good foreign one on the list. The TV's a big flat-screen. By the time the movie's finished, we'll both be sober as a judge."

Melanie could barely breathe. This sophisticated, Greek-god handsome man was asking her back to his room, or at least his sitting room. Plus, they had been together all day, and he still wanted her to stick around late into the night. She couldn't believe this was happening to her.

"That sounds nice," she murmured and ducked her head shyly, the rose of her cheeks now deep and beautiful against her skin the color of cream.

It was probably the brandy that did it. By the time Melanie entered Van's penthouse suite, she was more than a little tipsy. They sat down on the couch and tried to order a movie from the instructions on the hotel's network. They were both giggling because they couldn't figure out what to do and kept pushing the TV remote control's buttons at random. Their hands touched as they fumbled with the clicker. Their faces came close together. Suddenly Van's lips were on Melanie's in a long, awkward first kiss.

They broke apart when the movie started. Although Melanie had no idea how it happened, they had ordered a film about werewolves called *Los Lobos in Love and Heat.*

Melanie blushed when she saw what the heroine was doing with some furry beast in the very first scene. "This isn't an art film," she stammered, but she stared at the actors doing the most astonishing things on the screen until Van turned her head and started kissing her again.

Later Melanie swore she didn't remember getting up and walking into Van's bedroom. She didn't remember how she ended up without her clothes in his bed. But she would never forget how he looked naked and how it felt to have him touch her in places she had never been touched before.

She remembered the very nice things he said to her about how much he liked her breasts. And he spent a long time showing her how much he did like them in ways that took a great deal of imagination and felt extremely fine.

Melanie would also never forget when Van asked her if she'd make love to him and she breathed her answer. "Yes. Yes, I will. Please yes." She remembered vividly him sliding into her because it was, after all, her very first time. Then her head starting spinning and she called out his name. A sky of whirling suns filled her mind and blocked out all reason.

Van made noises too that made Melanie think he had a fine tenor voice.

But she didn't remember falling sleep afterward, and snoring gently, a smile on her face. Soon she slept so soundly, she didn't know when Van slipped out of bed, got dressed, and quietly left the room.

Chapter 21

"I want to look in on the children," Larrie told Jo when they returned from Lahore and walked into his sprawling, one-story house on the outskirts of the village.

"They'll be asleep. It's late," he said.

"That's all right. I'll rest better knowing they're safe."

Larrie quietly slipped onto the back veranda. Because of the bright moonlight—for the night was clear and the moon was full—she could see the children sleeping on the blankets Tara had given them. She walked around them, listening to them breathe, and happy to see them looking so peaceful in their slumber.

When she got to the little girl named Mayree, she stooped down and stroked the child's soft cheek with her finger. The child's eyes fluttered open and she smiled when she saw Larrie.

"Sleep well, little one," Larrie said. "I just wanted to say good night."

"Good night, memsahib," Mayree whispered. She reached up and took Larrie's finger in her tiny hand. "Memsahib?" she said.

"Yes, Mayree?"

"You my mama now."

Larrie wanted to protest that *no* she couldn't be

her mother. She had to leave India soon. She couldn't stay. But the tiny girl's eyes had fallen shut, even as she fiercely clung to Larrie's finger and didn't let go for a very long time.

Jo was sitting in a leather-covered club chair, sipping a brandy again when Larrie finally returned to the parlor. "If you're ready," he said, setting down his glass and the newspaper he had been reading, "we should get to bed. We need to start early in the morning."

Larrie didn't answer right away. She couldn't get Mayree's sweet face from her mind. "I want to make sure the children get a good breakfast before we go."

Jo waved away her objection. "Tara Singh will do it."

"It's not right to keep asking Tara to take on extra work. Can you get someone from the village to come here and act as a nanny?"

Jo rose from his chair. "A nanny? You can't be serious about me continuing to have these children living here."

Larrie's nostrils flared. This time Jo saw her temper starting to build. He held up his hand. "Okay, we'll talk about it. I can afford another servant, I suppose. But you're not going to be in this village much longer. What do you want me to do with them when you're gone?"

Larrie's chin lifted. "I've been thinking about that. I have a plan, and I hope you'll agree."

Jo walked over to her. He put his hand under that chin that showed such a pretty neck every time she lifted it and kept it tipped up, so her lips were close to his. "Are they that important to you? These orphans nobody has ever cared about before?"

"Yes, Jo, they are. I want them fed and clothed. I want them watched over and protected. I want them to have a home."

Jo kissed the tip of Larrie's nose. "If that's what you

want so badly, it's not a very big thing to ask of me, when I'm asking such a huge thing from you." His mouth slipped from her nose to her lips.

Neither of them heard Tara quietly walking in the hall outside the parlor. He muttered to himself, "I knew I shouldn't have bothered to prepare separate rooms."

Larrie did intend to sleep alone in her own bed. Although she and Jo went into the hall together toward the sleeping quarters, she disengaged herself from Jo's arms when they came to the door he said was hers.

"I'm right next door," he whispered. "If you get scared or lonely, my bed is big enough for both of us."

"I'm sure I'll be safe and content in this room, but thank you for the offer." She opened the door and slipped inside. Becoming intimate with Jo would be very easy to do. She only had to let herself keep kissing him and nature would take its course. But it wouldn't be wise. She already had strong feelings for him, and that could only lead to heartbreak.

She found a white nightgown laid out on the pink bedspread of a bed so high off the floor that it had a step stool for her to use to get into it. Mosquito netting had been draped all around it making a pretty and practical canopy. She picked up the filmy, finely stitched nightgown but didn't put it on. She had noticed a basin of water and soap on a washstand. A soft towel hung over the rack above it.

Larrie stood in front of the washbasin and wiped the cool water over her skin with the cloth, slowly cleaning the sweat and dirt of the day from her body. A breeze coming through the open window further cooled her wet skin. She smelled the scent of jasmine coming through the window too, for its shutters were unlatched and thrown wide, since this room looked out at an inner courtyard, not the world at large.

After she was dry, she put the nightgown on. She felt tired. She had had a very long day, which in fact was two days. No wonder she was weary. She looked down at her wrists. She still wore her own wristwatch on her left one and Ryan's on the right. Neither one of them was running.

She stood there for a long moment. Then she slowly unfastened her own watch and put it on the washstand. She heaved a great sigh. She unbuckled the leather band of Ryan's watch. She had nearly made love to another man today. She hadn't gone that far, but she needed to take Ryan's watch off her wrist. And so she did, gently putting it beside her own.

As she climbed up into the bed, its sheets clean and sweet smelling, she thought again about the reasons she was sleeping alone. First of all, Jo was purportedly a genie, and if he wasn't a figment of her imagination, he was a man from a different century and a different world. As soon as they found the means to break the spell that kept him enchanted, he would be gone, as she would be gone too, back to her farm and her animals and the people she loved.

Larrie put her head down on a wonderfully soft goose-down pillow. It was too hot to pull the covers over her so she pushed them aside. Her mind went back to Jo. There was something more important than the temporary nature of their relationship. He had been very honest with her. No matter what feelings she ever had for him, he wouldn't return them. He didn't know how to love, and after hearing about his childhood, she understood why.

She had no doubt he'd happily have sex with her. He'd like her, as he said about the girl he had abandoned, a great deal. But his emotions would never match his momentary passion. Once the desire had waned and died, Jo Trelawny, as was his style, would be gone too.

Then a little smile began to play around Larrie's lips. According to an announcement soon to appear in the *Times*, she and Jo Trelawny were engaged. A fall wedding was planned in the governor's mansion of Lahore. *It would serve him right if it really happened*, she thought, then caught herself. What a strange thing to think. Larrie had no intention of ever marrying John "Jo" Trelawny, whether he was a magical genie or a red-blooded, normal man.

The smell of jasmine came wafting through the window again. Larrie's eyes felt very heavy. She fell fast asleep.

Far into the night, at the hour when only predators prowl the world, the nightmare started for Larrie. She was trapped in a dream state unable to escape something terrible chasing her. Her legs wouldn't run. She wanted to scream. She couldn't cry out. She felt very frightened. Her life was in danger. She tried with all her might to yell for help.

"Larrie! Larrie! Wake up. You're having a nightmare."

The being-caught-in-cement sensation vanished. Larrie opened her eyes. Jo, his bare chest pale in the moonlight, stood next to her bed.

"You're shaking all over. Are you okay?"

In fact Larrie's teeth were chattering and she was trembling like an aspen leaf caught in a mountain wind. Unbidden, tears began to course down her cheeks. She didn't even know why she was crying, except she had been so scared and she was in a strange bed in an unfamiliar place in a faraway land.

Jo sat down next to her and gathered her in his arms, stroking her hair as if she were a child. While he murmured reassurances, Larrie buried her face against his chest and held him tight until the fear began to subside.

And as the fear left, she became aware that it was not only Jo's chest that was bare.

She also became conscious that they were alone together in the dark. They were together on the clean,
sweet sheets of a lovely big bed. She noticed that Jo had
stopped talking and was breathing quite heavily as he
held Larrie in his arms. As for herself, she could barely
breathe.

All her rationalizations about why she shouldn't make
love with Jo Trelawny seemed bogus. Seen in this light,
which of course was the white-gray monochrome of pure
moonlight, the very fact that their romance couldn't last
was the very best reason to enjoy each other now. Now
was all they had. Why deny the desire that was stealing
over her, moving from her toes upward, making her skin
tingle, making her breath catch in her throat, making her
heart beat faster?

Larrie couldn't think of one good reason not to lie
down and let Jo Trelawny have his way with her. So she
lifted her head from his chest and put her arms around
his neck. Their lips met. His hand slipped under her
nightgown. She sighed into his mouth and he groaned
into hers.

He gently turned her onto her back and covered her
body with his own. They fit perfectly. They were two
halves becoming one whole being. The bed began to
rock in an ageless rhythm. It rocked for quite a while
before it stopped and Jo and Larrie lay together in each
other's arms.

Then after a little while, when the stars had wheeled
quite a distance across the small patch of sky above the
courtyard, the bed started rocking and rocking all over
again.

The sunlight streaming through the window woke
Larrie. She felt something heavy atop her. She pried
open her sleepy eyes and exclaimed, "Oh!"

A dark mop of hair lay on the pillow next to hers.

A brawny, tanned arm lay possessively across her bare breasts. A large, muscular leg had entwined with one of hers. A loud male snore came from the direction of the dark hair.

"Ohhhh no!" Larrie said again, and began to mull over the situation in her mind while she absentmindedly ran her fingers up and down Jo's arm. *I've really done it now. I've given myself to this person, this duke's son, without asking anything in return. We've enjoyed a roll in the hay, as they say. And yes, I thoroughly enjoyed it—I admit it. But now, in the bright light of day, I know it's a mistake because I'm beginning to care for this man. I'm beginning to love him, or maybe I did all along. And he can't return my love.*

As Larrie lay there trailing her fingers up and down Jo's arm and thinking about him, his snores stopped. He stirred. He turned his head so the dark mop of hair was replaced by a handsome face.

"Good morning, Lady Larissa," he whispered and gave her a languid smile. "How is my lady today? Well bedded and satisfied, I hope."

Larrie couldn't help herself. She smiled back. "And how is my lord? Well bedded and satisfied, I hope?"

The arm across her chest suddenly moved downward and the hand at the end of the arm landed on a part of her body and did something that made Larrie's eyes open very wide. "*Oh!*" she said as the fingers at the end of the hand started moving and probing and tickling and teasing.

"I am never satisfied, my lady," Jo said.

With that, the big, handsome genie shifted, turning toward Larrie and lifting himself up on his free arm so that the long length of his well-muscled body stretched out next to her.

"You can see now that I am still not sated, my lady."

With a little blush, Larrie glanced over at Jo. The sun

was up and a weak light filtered into the courtyard and through the window. She could see Jo's entire body and his unmistakable maleness for the first time. "You and your . . . your little man, look hungry, I agree," she murmured and gasped as Jo grinned and his probing fingers, now between her legs, suddenly pushed right into her.

"You know," she said, her eyes closing in desire, her thighs spreading wide, "I think I'm still hungry too."

"Then let's dine," Jo suggested. He covered her with his body and positioned himself between her soft thighs. Then the bed moved, endlessly rocking, slowly at first, then faster, until it thumped and thumped against the floor, making quite a noise.

Outside the closed bedroom door, Tara stopped with a tray in his hands. "Humph," he snorted. "Separate rooms! Separate rooms indeed." He silently moved away, deciding he'd return with the lady's tea at another time.

Chapter 22

The children had big smiles and jam-smeared faces when Larrie, with Jo in tow, entered the back veranda in the middle of Tara's serving breakfast.

"Mama! Mama!" Mayree began shouting, a chant that was soon echoed by the other nine orphans. Larrie's heart lurched. She'd have to explain, or have Tara explain, that she couldn't be their mama, but not right now, when they all looked so happy. With snowy white napkins tied around their necks, their dark hair brushed—and all the girls had ribbons in theirs—their shirts laundered, and their hands freshly washed, they looked healthier too, at least to Larrie, although that might have been wishful thinking.

She thanked Tara profusely for all he had done and told him he should seek out a nanny from the village as soon as he could. "Make sure she's an older woman, Tara, one whose children have grown up. Question her neighbors and make sure she's kind. Find out if she has a dog or bird because a person who loves pets will be gentle and responsible. And the pets must come along too. I wouldn't make her leave them behind." She stopped for a moment, then plunged ahead with a new thought. "A widow would be perfect, because she will probably welcome the income and wouldn't mind spending time away from her home."

Jo interrupted. "I'm sure Tara Singh knows how to hire a nanny. He was an accomplished sergeant major in the Lancers. But he's used to a life of men. I'm afraid he's tiring of household duties like serving tea and breakfast to children."

"I'm content, sahib," the Sikh said.

"You are not, but you are loyal and won't say so. Don't worry, Tara, we'll be done with this domestic life soon enough!"

What does that mean? Larrie wondered in the brief second before she said out loud, "Do I hear bells?"

Tara Singh broke into a broad grin. "Come, look!" he instructed and she followed him outside.

When she stepped into the sunlight, she was welcomed by a chorus of distinctive voices that seemed to be complaining about their state as they sang in a Caruso-like tenor, "Baaa, baaaa." Larrie clapped her hands in delight, for there in the yard behind the veranda a dozen brown goats with floppy ears were eating the bougainvillea. Each nannie goat had a little tinkling bell on a collar around her throat. Only the massive billy did not. He had a large bell on his leather collar and it clinked as he shook his head and eyed Larrie with suspicion.

"You found goats! And they're Nubians too! How wonderful. Of course Nubians are awfully stubborn, but this breed gives milk with the highest protein and butterfat content. You are a paragon, Tara Singh. Where on earth did you get them?"

"Not so far away, memsahib. A shepherd was driving his animals to a high pasture in the mountains for the summer. He was happy to part with some of them, especially for the price I offered him."

"Bought with my money," Jo groused, but if Larrie had looked closely she would have seen he was trying not to smile.

"Still a bargain, sahib!" Tara assured him with a grin

and exchanged a conspiratorial look with Jo that Larrie turned her head and saw but didn't quite understand.

Meanwhile Larrie had waded into the herd and was rubbing necks and patting noses. "Now we must locate a flock of laying hens and a rooster or two. And before I forget, Jo, we need sacks of lentils as soon as possible."

Jo stood some ways off, as if not enamored of the smell issuing from the yard. "Goats, lentils, chickens. We've become farmers, have we?" Then he gave a hearty laugh. "I shouldn't complain! I suppose you might have been a woman who demanded I buy her rubies and diamonds. I should count myself lucky."

"Sahib Trelawny is a very lucky man!" Tara Singh said loudly. "Lady Larissa will make a fine wife, or so it said in this morning's *Times of India*."

Jo burst out with an even bigger laugh. "What! It made the morning edition! Bunny must have a great deal of influence with the press. I imagine all England will be reading about my coming nuptials in the *London Times* tomorrow. That news should shake up my mater and pater."

Larrie didn't find the engagement announcement at all funny. "Don't you think the written record might complicate things? Historically, I mean," she said stiffly.

Jo brushed her worries aside and seemed terribly pleased with himself. "I have no bloody idea. At any rate, it's already done. As Caesar said as he crossed the Rubicon, '*Jacta alea est,*' the die is cast."

I've heard that said before, Larrie thought. Aunt Lolly had taught the Latin passage to her years ago. It meant there was no turning back. Caesar was going to invade Gaul no matter what the consequences. The decision was irrevocable.

An ominous feeling stole over Larrie. Aunt Lolly! There might be real trouble if Larrie didn't get back home in time to stop the competency hearing. And one thing Larrie knew, for better or worse—even if she did get back to Beaumont PA as planned and in one piece, she had no chance of ever getting back to being the person she had been just a few days earlier.

"Taking off on a magic carpet might attract attention, you know," Jo said thoughtfully when they returned to the parlor for tea and toast. "Look what happened when we sailed past Aunt Lolly." He stopped at the tea cart and poured them both a cup.

"What are you suggesting, that we go by horseback?" Larrie stood before a wall mirror and took a long look at herself. She had found a new *salwar kameez* in a parcel outside the bedroom door when she and Jo finally decided it was time to stop pleasuring each other and get out of bed. The shirt was a lovely mint green and the trousers were white. She thought the Punjabi style suited her, and the light cotton shirt and pants were extraordinarily comfortable to wear.

"Do you like this?" She pirouetted to show Jo the new clothes.

He glanced over. "The color sets off your hair. Come have your tea. It's getting cold."

Their lovemaking had the consequence of making them behave in a much nicer way to each other now. They spoke like a loving couple rather than like battling adversaries. The change was striking, and Larrie rather liked it. She liked it so much that if anyone had seen her at that moment, they would have said she glowed.

She walked over to the tea cart and picked up her cup. Jo had already put in milk and sugar, just the way she liked it. He was getting to know many of her preferences and he took care to please her. She unwittingly looked at him with adoration and took no caution to disguise her feelings.

"Now, about our journey." She picked up the thread of the earlier conversation. "What have you decided?"

"I gave the matter some thought. How do you feel about hiring an elephant and a *mahout*, a driver? We can take the carpet along. As soon as we're away from the village and people who might see us, we can use magic to reconnoiter from the air. Hopefully we'll find the guru before the day is through."

"An elephant ride! I'd love it. But what about the *mahout*? He'll see us flying, won't he?"

"I thought about that too. We'll wait until he naps in the heat of the afternoon. Even if he wakes up, the thick forest will keep him from seeing the sky and spotting us flittering about."

Larrie sipped her tea and regarded Jo over the brim. He was back in his leather club chair holding a pair of scissors. He seemed to be cutting out the announcement of their engagement from the *Times of India*.

"Why are you doing that?" she asked him.

Jo held up the article he had clipped from the society page. "No picture of you, of course, but they've found a dandy one of me in my uniform. 'The Hon. John Trelawny to Wed American Heiress.' That's the headline. I'm keeping this! No one will believe it's true if I can't show them the very story, printed with the date." He put it carefully inside a book lying on a table next to the chair. "I'm a confirmed bachelor. Don't suppose I'll ever take the plunge—unless some girl's father holds a gun to my head." He laughed.

A terrible, unexpected pain squeezed Larrie's heart. She tried not to let it show in her face. "You don't seem to have learned any lesson at all from your enchantment. Isn't that attitude precisely the reason for your punishment?"

Jo flung himself out of the chair. "It can't be helped, can it? I can't will myself to love a woman. And from what I've seen of marriage—" He shook his head. "It's a bitter imprisonment."

Larrie turned away and directed her words in the direction of the portraits hanging on the dark-paneled wall. "Your grandparents seem to have fared well enough. Your parents never loved each other to begin with. I don't think you can generalize that *all* marriages are unhappy."

At that point Larrie realized that Jo had crossed the room and was standing behind her, his body pressed against her back, his lips leaving trails of kisses along her neck. "And why would I ever need to wed, when this arrangement is so much nicer?"

Larrie pulled away, feeling put out and not knowing why. "We don't have any 'arrangement,' as you put it. What we did was just a—just a *fling*. Or as the young people in my time put it, we *hooked up*. It hasn't reached the level of an *arrangement*."

Jo gave her a steady look, noting how she carried herself. He couldn't have missed the tone of her voice either, which had risen in pitch and sounded aggrieved. He spoke gently, coming close to her again and folding his arms around her.

"Perhaps we should *arrange* something, Larrie. I know we'll be parting soon, but it was more than a *fling* for me. I think you're aces. A wonderful girl. Just because we aren't really going to marry doesn't mean I think of you lightly. I care a great deal about you, in my own way, of course."

Larrie sighed. "I know that." She leaned against him and enjoyed the way he smelled and felt. "I think you're *aces* too. I'll never forget you, Jo."

Although Larrie couldn't see it, a shadow dimmed the genie's face. "I hope you don't lose your good opinion of me before this is all over," he said into her hair.

"Whyever would you say that?" Larrie felt an alarm go off inside her.

"No reason. But as you told me yourself, even a genie can't see the future."

Larrie sat comfortably upon cushions in the *howdah*, which was a wooden carriage on top of a huge bull Indian elephant's back. A colorful canopy shielded her and Jo from the burning sunbeams. The *mahout*, who sat on the elephant's neck with his legs dangling behind the great beast's ears, held a *thotti*, a thick wooden pole with a wicked iron hook on the end. He urged the beast forward with it, a bit cruelly, Larrie thought. He had a sharp nose and thin lips, and his forehead didn't even have a sweat. The *mahout* looked comfortable in the heat of the day and unfazed by the thick humid air.

They had left Jo's home village by midmorning. Taking a venerable trade route, they headed north toward the highest mountains in the world. It cut through miles and miles of cultivated fields and stands of mango trees. It passed by groups of roadside houses that made up small settlements. And sometimes it took them into sizeable towns where the *mahout* called out when he saw a man or woman to ask if anyone had seen a guru named Harkrishnan ji.

"Very old man, very old," a man or woman would always answer. "He walks slowly toward Baltistan. You will find him if you keep going straight ahead."

So the elephant and its passengers traveled on. As the hours passed, the houses became fewer and fewer. The road narrowed into a rutted track before it entered a thick woods and became nothing more than a well-trodden path.

But even in the shadows under the sheltering leaves of tree boughs above them, Larrie found it no cooler in the forest. The heat of day sapped her strength. She felt relieved when the *mahout* said he must stop to water the elephant and rest a while.

Jo gave Larrie a meaningful glance and gathered up the Persian carpet in his arms. After they had climbed down from the *howdah*, he told the *mahout* that he and the lady would return in a while. They'd either continue the journey north or perhaps be heading home.

The *mahout* looked surprised, but he just nodded and said, "As you wish, sahib."

The carpet ascended rapidly above the forest. Crisp, cool air slapped Larrie's face and stung her cheeks as they flew at a breathtaking speed toward the snowy peaks of the Himalayas.

"I don't know how we'll ever see an old man," she called out to Jo, her voice straining to be heard over the wind. "We can't see the ground because of the trees."

Jo pointed to the north and Larrie followed his pointing finger to discover that the trees thinned and the landscape stretched out brown and stony for miles.

"We'll find him there, I'm sure of it," he said with his lips very close to her ear.

"I hope so," Larrie answered, clutching the sides of the rug tightly with her hands. They were flying very high, the rug was small, the air currents had begun to shake them fiercely, and she'd be glad to return to earth.

"There!" Jo cried after some minutes. "Do you see him?"

Larrie shaded her eyes with her hand and squinted. She could barely discern that far, far below them a figure walked toward the mountains, a staff in his hand.

She nodded. Her heart speeded up. She stifled a scream as the carpet began to rapidly descend.

By the time they had landed, the guru had halted. He leaned heavily on his staff. Jo stood quickly and leapt off the rug. "You! It's you! Guru Harkrishnan. I've found you at last."

"At last?" The old man's voice was gruff. "It's been barely a week since I made you a genie."

"A week and a century have passed and you know it! It is a horrible fate you've given me, old man!"

"Still proud, still haughty, I see," the old man muttered, shaking his head. "But that was not your sin. It's only foolish pride, ha! Have it while you can."

"You're wrong! I *am* a humble man now. I have suffered, old man. I need to be free. You were once willing to tell me how to break the spell. I need to know. I desperately need to know." Jo sank down on his knees. Then he prostrated himself before the guru with his forehead to the ground.

Jo Trelawny kept his face in the dirt while his weight shifted onto his forearms and knees in a posture of submission. The old man ignored him. Instead he turned his rheumy eyes toward Larrie. "So it's all coming to pass. Are you Larry?"

Larrie's eyes widened in surprise. "My name is Larissa Smith, Mr. Harkrishnan. I'm called Larrie. I'm the genie's current mistress." A blush crept up her neck when she said that, so she stammered, "I mean his mistress in the sense of owning the lamp. I agreed to help him find you." She paused and studied the old man again. The way the ancient guru was gripping his staff with both gnarled hands and leaning on it so heavily, she was overcome with pity. "But you look so tired, sir. Have you far to walk to get home?"

The old man nodded. "Very far, child."

"That will never do! We'll be glad to give you a lift, won't we, Jo?"

Jo lifted his head slightly and glared at Larrie with one eye. "A lift?"

"Why, yes, we have a magic carpet, don't we, Jo?"

She turned to Harkrishnan. "We can have you home in no time. But first, if you wouldn't mind, Jo has been so anxious to hear what you have to say. Won't you tell him how to break the spell that imprisoned him in the lamp? Once he knows, I can go back to my own home. In America, a century from now."

Harkrishnan made a long, slow, steady appraisal of Larrie. He glanced down at the prostrate genie. Then he looked back at Larrie. "Come, let us sit down together and talk."

Jo raised his head.

"Not you, genie. Stay where you are. I don't think you are humble enough."

In a few steps Larrie had joined the guru and they both sat cross-legged on the ground.

"Do you believe in genies and magic?" he asked her gravely.

Larrie studied the lined, wrinkled face of this very old man. He smelled of sweat and smoke. His robes, gray with age and frequently mended, were far from clean. His hands trembled a little when he tried to keep them still. The guru was no dream. He was an old man sitting on the cold ground next to her, of that she was absolutely certain, so she answered as honestly as she could.

"In the beginning, when Jo first appeared, I didn't believe in him. Not at all. I thought I had gone mad. But now, after—" She lowered her eyes to look at her hands, which fidgeted in her lap. "Well, after everything that has happened—I do believe in genies and magic. I've witnessed it myself." She stopped. She lifted her head and peered into the genie's withered face. "It's hard to throw out everything you've assumed to be true all your life. It shakes you up. It changes everything. But I'm glad I know. The modern world insists on proof and science and facts. Knowing that there is magic makes the world bigger somehow. And better, I think."

The guru reached out one of his calloused bare feet and kicked Jo in the head, quite hard.

"Hey!" Jo yelled. "Why did you do that?"

The old man ignored the question. "So, Sahib Trelawny, you've succeeded in one thing you needed to do to break the spell. She believes in you."

"Thank God," Jo murmured toward the stony ground. Then he cautiously rose enough to look at the guru. "What else must I do? What words followed 'You must—'? I've tried to figure them out for the past hundred years."

Harkrishnan turned his attention back to Larrie. "He's a very stupid genie, don't you think? A hundred years and he's not come up with the obvious answer. You are a bright young woman; I see that. I'm sure you know. You tell me. Or rather, why don't you tell this lowly, pathetic, enchanted creature at my feet how he can become a man."

Larrie looked at Jo's wildly curling, unruly brown hair, the slope of his broad back, his shapely behind sticking up in the air. Just then, Jo lifted his head again. "*She* doesn't know. How could she?"

"Silence, genie," the guru barked. He kept his old eyes on Larrie's solemn face with her serious gray eyes and the plucky spray of freckles across her nose. "Tell him, my child, the answer he seeks. Tell him how he can leave the lamp forever and take his place back in this world as a man."

Larrie did know. She had suspected it from the first, when Jo told her the whole story of his plight. "He needs to fall in love," she said.

Chapter 23

Hearing this, Jo the genie collapsed flat to the ground as a terrible howl ripped from his throat. "Nooooo! Nooooo! I'm doomed. I cannot love!" He rolled around on the hard earth, moaning with great drama. "Can a man with no legs walk? Can a man with no eyes see? I cannot make myself love! It's not in me."

Finally he lay still, flat on his back, his eyes staring sightlessly toward the clear blue sky.

The old guru shook his head slowly, a look of utter disgust on his weathered face as he watched this performance. He spoke quietly to Larrie. "So wrapped up in himself he can't see beyond his nose. How can you, such a smart woman, love a man like that?"

Larrie started with surprise a second time at the guru's perspicacity. "You think I love him?"

"It's a pity, but I see you have lost your heart to him. You have a lot of work to do on that one. In a hundred years my plan to teach him a lesson doesn't seem to have worked. It is time for a different approach."

Larrie raised her eyebrows. "What chance have I to succeed if you, with all your powers, didn't?"

Harkrishnan laughed softly. "I think you have powers over him I do not. But I can't promise you he'll learn to love. He seems determined not to."

"You think he's capable of it then?" Larrie whispered as she watched Jo dramatically pounding the ground with his fists.

"It's in him. He never was an unfeeling man. But all his life, he's locked up his heart. That Sigmund Freud fellow might have an explanation." The guru patted Larrie's hand. "Let's hope you can find the key."

Larrie sat thoughtfully still next to the guru while a depressed and dour-faced Jo listlessly piloted them on their magic carpet into Baltistan. They traveled far up above the tree line into the remote Himalayas. Although it was summer in the valleys below, winter lingered here. Larrie shivered as they swooped down at the edge of an icy glacier and the Persian rug settled to the rocky ground.

"I can walk from here," the ancient man said as he pulled himself to his feet with his staff. "The village isn't far up this path, over a bridge, and onto a high plateau. I'm sure you remember that, Jo Trelawny."

Jo's eyes looked hurt. "I remember the way. I can fly you there directly. I would very much like to see my son. I've been wanting to see him for over a hundred years."

The old man shook his white head in the negative.

Larrie saw the anger flash across Jo's face. "He's *my* son."

Harkrishnan shrugged. "Perhaps some other time. You wouldn't be welcome, not with another woman at your side and no contrition in your heart." The guru turned his back and started walking slowly toward a pass between two sheer rock walls.

Jo called after him, "I have contrition! I'm terribly sorry Rani is dead. You're a hard old man."

"There is hard and there is hard. It is well to know the difference." The guru's voice faded into an echo and like the setting of the evening sun, his figure diminished, became indistinct, and then was gone.

"Well, I'm knackered," Jo griped, looking at the empty space where the guru had been. "It's all done. You might as well get used to me, Larrie. I'm going to be your genie for some time. If you'll allow me to return to my home to settle my affairs, I'd appreciate it. Then you might as well wish yourself and me—enslaved forever—back to your own time." He sighed heavily and his head hung down.

Larrie patted Jo's shoulder absentmindedly to comfort him, but her attention was focused on the blue ice of the glacier. "Jo? Do you have a pocketknife?"

"Huh? Yes. Why do you ask?"

"I want to take a chunk of this glacier back with us. A rather large chunk. If we pack it in the elephant's hay and wrap the carpet around it once we land, we can prevent its melting."

"Whatever for? Do you crave an iced tea so much?"

Larrie stared thoughtfully at the huge glacier and all its lovely ice. "We have goat's milk. We have mangoes. We have sugar at the house, do we not?"

"We have lots of sugar in the kitchen pantry. Bags of it."

"And salt. You do have salt, right?"

"Boxes of the stuff. Why?"

"We're going to make ice cream!"

In the twinkling of an eye, since the carpet was magic after all, Jo and Larrie returned to the *mahout* and his elephant. The thin, cruel-lipped elephant handler looked startled at the sahib and memsahib's sudden return. He looked curiously at the heavy piece of ice, a phenomenon he had seen but once in his entire life. He helped Sahib Trelawny pack it in hay and wrap it in a carpet, but he was not told where they had gotten it.

"Drive your fellow home, *mahout*," Jo ordered as he helped Larrie into the *howdah*, then climbed in himself.

Once inside, he threw himself down on the cushions and groaned. He covered his eyes with his forearm. His own miserable existence filled his consciousness and he seemed to see nothing else.

The *mahout* turned the elephant south and began the trek back. It wasn't more than a few minutes before they heard the sound of shouting and sticks hitting the underbrush. Jo immediately sat up. "A tiger hunt. Those are the beaters. We're right in their path."

The *mahout* too had become alert. He looked frantically around, trying to guess where a tiger might spring from the forest followed by the elephants of the hunters. It was a dangerous situation. His large bull elephant might bolt, or worse, decide to charge the oncoming beasts. He and his passengers would surely be tossed to the ground and trampled if that happened, but the *mahout* didn't know what direction to take. The beaters seemed all around them.

Jo prepared to grab Larrie and remove her from the elephant by magic, but he never got the chance before a terrible buzzing began. A colony of bees had been disturbed by beaters and now swarmed toward them in a threatening dark cloud. The insects numbered in the thousands and their stings could kill a man.

The *mahout* didn't hesitate. He slid off the elephant and began to run. Jo realized his and Larrie's only chance was to deflect the swarm by his magic, so he stood up in the *howdah* to wave his hand.

At that very moment a tiger burst from the forest onto the path. The elephant trumpeted and reared up on its hind legs. The *howdah* rocked, then slid gracefully with its passengers to the ground, where both Jo and Larrie rolled out and into the path of the great snarling cat.

The tiger, startled, then enraged, charged as Larrie screamed. Jo grabbed her and threw her with all his might to safety, turned, and took the full weight of the tiger on his back. Meanwhile the air had become black with bees, and their buzzing drowned out even the tiger's growls.

Maddened by the appearance of the tiger and full of fight, the bull elephant now swung its great bulk around. It raised its huge foot to bring down on the spitting, fighting cat, which was unfortunately on top of Jo. Meanwhile, in the underbrush, Larrie, the breath knocked out of her, was trying to stand, horror-struck at what she saw.

And suddenly Jo was gone. The elephant's foot came down, barely catching the tiger by the tail. The great cat screeched loudly before pulling free and running off. The elephant reared up again into the midst of the swarming bees. They circled the great beast; its thick hide protected it from the stings but it reacted to their noise with wild eyes.

At that moment there was the loud bang of a hunting rifle. The insects rose in a dark cloud. Then they flew away in a long gray line, fleeing a second bang from a rifle.

Larrie slowly got to her feet and saw that the elephant had remained wild-eyed with fear. It had begun pawing the ground and bellowing as if to charge at Larrie. She froze. She spotted Jo picking up the *thotti* and expertly hooking the frantic beast's trunk, using all his strength to take control of the panicked creature. The elephant forgot Larrie and focused on its new *mahout*. It could charge or obey—

The elephant, perhaps remembering the *thotti*'s iron hook, obeyed, then began to rock back and forth in a mindless way. Jo had the beast under as much control as he was going to get, so he mounted the elephant's trunk and climbed up into the *mahout*'s seat. Once there, he removed his tattered shirt and tucked it into the headpiece across the animal's forehead, covering its eyes. Unable to see, the elephant immediately stopped its nervous rocking and stood still.

Larrie saw Jo's shoulders sag in relief. She crept out of the brush. Seeing her, Jo beckoned her to come on. She went as far as the *howdah,* lying in pieces on the forest path. "I'm not leaving without my ice," she called out.

Uttering a string of colorful oaths, Jo slipped down off the elephant's neck and retrieved the carpet-wrapped ice from the smashed wood of the *howdah.* Then he had the elephant pick it up with its trunk and place the package on its own back. After that Jo managed to lash the bundle down with the remaining straps that had held the *howdah.* Then, his voice insistent, he called to Larrie to join him. The shouts of the beaters and the rifle fire had moved away, but Jo told Larrie he'd feel easier if they got out of the forest entirely.

"What about the *mahout*?" Larrie asked after Jo had taken her hand and pulled her up to sit behind him.

"That coward! Let him find his own way home. I should pummel him senseless when I meet him again."

Larrie straddled Jo from behind and put her arms around his waist. "He was afraid of the bees, Jo. You can't blame him."

"Can't blame him! He left us, and his animal, to our fates. I have no sympathy for that man. He abandoned his post. He deserted in battle. If he were a soldier, I'd have him hanged." Jo used the staff of the *thotti* to urge the elephant on.

Larrie felt something wet against her cheek. She pulled back. "What's this? Your shoulder is slippery with— Jo! You're bleeding! It's a terrible cut. And here's another. The tiger's claws have gashed you deeply. You're wounded. How bad is it?"

Jo answered through gritted teeth, "It hurts like hell if you must know. But I'm grateful the cat didn't get his teeth into my scalp. I'll be okay. Tara will tend to it when we get back."

Larrie's heart to thump wildly. "Jo! That's hours from now. You could bleed to death before then."

Jo looked over his shoulder at Larrie, his mouth now stretched into a jaunty grin despite his pain. "We'll be home before you know it. I'm still a genie, and if you'll assist with the request, this situation definitely calls for magic!"

"Just like old times, sahib," Tara Singh said as he bandaged Jo's back. "You tried to wrestle a tiger with your bare hands."

Larrie had seen that no major blood vessels had been damaged, and the bleeding had slowed by the time the elephant vanished from the forest and materialized in the yard behind Jo's house. The goats made a tremendous racket, and Tara had come rushing from the veranda just in time to keep Jo from tumbling off the elephant's back and onto the ground.

Tara put his arm around Jo's waist and half carried him into the house with Larrie right behind them. Larrie directed Tara to keep Jo in the kitchen while she boiled the water to clean out Jo's wounds. She had a servant bring some good lye soap as well, and only then did she let Tara begin his doctoring of the wounds. Once she was satisfied no debris from the tiger's claws or the forest floor remained, she instructed Tara to take Jo's best brandy and pour it over the gashes.

"Are you certain, memsahib?" Tara asked doubtfully.

"I am certain."

Jo swore loudly when the alcohol burned into his flesh, but he went along with it. In the forest he had demonstrated to Larrie that he was a brave man, and now she saw he was one who didn't flinch from pain.

After the alcohol had dried a bit, she allowed Tara to apply the bandages—freshly laundered sheets cut into strips. And as Larrie supervised Tara's nursing, she tried to keep her fears from showing. She knew how easily infection could set in. She had treated many abscesses in her pets. But there were no antibiotics to be had in this era. If the wound became septic, there wasn't much she, or anyone, could do.

Larrie wondered if a genie could die. Obviously he could be badly hurt. She hovered. She kept asking Jo how he felt.

"For God's sake, Larrie, I'm not going to die! Let Tara do his job. I've been hurt worse than this before. Haven't I, Tara?"

"Yes, sahib. You had a bad habit of running into the enemy's sword."

"I didn't ask for you to insult me! At least I met the enemy and held my ground."

"Yes, sahib. We fought like wolves. You just got bitten more than I."

Jo threw his head back and laughed. "You were always a lucky devil, Tara. But we did have our fun."

"Fun! Nearly getting killed is not fun." Larrie had been on the verge of tears to see Jo so hurt and now he behaved like it was nothing more than a game.

Jo hopped off the table where Larrie had insisted he sit. "Are you done, Tara Singh? I would like to get some of that brandy in me, if there's any left."

"Plenty left, sahib," Tara said, grinning as he poured Jo a full tumbler of the stuff. Jo took a huge swallow, wiped his mouth with his hand and turned to Larrie, who was still hovering.

"Ms. Smith, I believe you have some ice melting in that carpet still on top of the great elephant bellowing and stamping in the yard. Weren't you going to teach Tara how to make what you Americans call ice cream?"

His words had the desired effect of distracting her. Larrie immediately remembered her grand plan to make ice cream for the children. "Oh, yes! And

I've not even said a word to any of them since we've returned."

"Then why don't you tend to the orphans and the ice-cream making. I've had enough mothering."

Larrie bristled. "Some thanks! I will go and see the children. At least they appreciate me!"

She didn't see Jo wink at Tara as she hurried off to find the children, the mangoes, the milk, the sugar, and the salt. "I need a large barrel and a smaller one, Tara Singh," she yelled back over her shoulder. "And an ice pick, please!"

Although in Larrie's opinion the results could have been better—not quite smooth enough, she thought, but then she had never used the cream from goats' milk before—the ice cream caused a commotion. Not only the children had to try it, but so did all the servants. Even Jo, seeming none the worse for his injuries, insisted on a bowl.

Larrie watched them devour the entire batch and then she had to make another. And another. Each time she felt she improved the results. She made the first batch with mangoes, but the second time she decided to use pods of vanilla which everybody loved, and in the third batch she used almonds.

And by the third batch, they had run out of bowls. Her eyes sparkling, having more fun than she'd had in years, Larrie had Amita bake round flat breads on a hot griddle. Larrie sprinkled each one with cinnamon and sugar before she rolled them into cones and plopped the ice cream inside with a spoon.

After that, everyone wanted an ice-cream cone. One of the servants was so overcome with amazement, he had run home to tell his wife. She told a neighbor and now villagers were lining up by the back door. The praise got louder and everyone's bellies got fuller.

At last the glacier's blue ice was all used up and the feast was done. But another idea had formed in Larrie's brain.

"Tara!" she said with the tone of voice that brought an instant wrinkle to his forehead. "If we bring big blocks of ice here from the mountains, is there a cave where it can be stored?"

"Yes, memsahib, but won't it melt before it arrives?"

"Not if we bring it by train packed in sawdust. That's what people did in Pennsylvania before we had refrigerators."

Tara looked puzzled. "What's a refrigerator, memsahib?"

Larrie gasped at her mistake. She stammered and didn't know what to say, but Jo just laughed. "It's an American kitchen device, Tara. But more to the point, why do you want freight cars full of ice, Larrie?"

"I think we shall begin to make and sell ice cream. I think I can find a way we can make it here, take it into Lahore, and sell it from carts. We'll make tons of money! We can give everyone in the village a job! It will provide an income for my orphans, maybe for the rest of their lives."

The room became absolutely silent. Larrie had expected some resistance, but no one was saying a thing.

Finally Tara Singh coughed and spoke not to Larrie, but to Jo. "This ice cream is delicious, sahib. And a very original sweet. But going into trade? Do you think it's possible to do as Lady Larissa suggests?"

Jo just laughed, but quietly. He had one of the orphans on his lap, and the child, sated by a bellyful of ice cream, had fallen asleep with the genie's arms around him. "I think Lady Larissa will do the impossible if she puts her mind to it. What will you call your ice cream, Larrie? Have you come up with a name?"

Larrie stood there for a moment, trying to think of

something. It had to be exactly right. She wanted it painted on all the carts, which would be white boxes mounted on bicycle wheels so they could be pushed. She thought and thought. "Ah, I have it," she said at last.

"And what is it?"

"Trelawny's Tastee Ice-Cream Cones!"

That evening, after being again assured by Jo that she could land back in the future no later than Wednesday afternoon, Larrie, with some trepidation, put off making the wish to return to Pennsylvania.

But she wrestled with her decision. She was deeply worried about Aunt Lolly and what might be happening in her absence. She was afraid Jo wouldn't get them back exactly when he thought he could, but in the end she made up her mind that the best thing to do was spend another entire day in India. She reasoned that Jo needed to rest for a day and get his strength back. She also had a great deal to do, such as arranging to manufacture and distribute ice cream, setting up a classroom, and making sure the new nanny, whose name was Bibi, was going to work out. She refused to even think about leaving the children. She pushed that eventuality into the back of her mind.

Besides all that, to accomplish everything she decided she needed to do, she needed to get a good night's sleep first. She discussed her decision with Jo as they sank down into his bed—it seemed foolish for her to go to her own room now. They would spend the next day getting everything in order and putting Tara Singh in charge.

Jo agreed he should rest a little, but he needed as much time as possible to tend to transferring deeds and bank accounts. He looked strained and sad when he said it.

"I have to go back home, Jo. I know it's hard for you to leave," Larrie whispered, "but please don't give up hope. Maybe you can come back to your life here someday—"

Jo gave a deep sigh. "The spell will *never* be broken, Larrie." He rolled over carefully to avoid his bandaged shoulder and gathered her into his arms. "If I was ever going to fall in love, I know I would love you."

"But you don't?" Larrie's voice sounded hollow.

Jo shook his head and kissed her forehead. "I desire you so much I don't care how much my shoulder pains. I intend to couple with you all night if I can. I admire you more than any woman I have ever met. And I am terribly fond of you, I truly am. But—"

"But?" Larrie said and turned her head away when Jo's lips sought hers. She stared at the white wall beyond the mosquito netting.

"But do I love you? Am I walking on air? Am I feeling all those things I am supposed to feel if I am in love? I'm sorry, Larrie, more than you can ever guess, but no, I don't. I'm not in love with you. I'm sure of that."

Chapter 24

Melanie O'Casey was jolted into consciousness by the pop song on the bedside clock radio. It wasn't Sarah McLachlan's moaning about having fallen that sent a wave of remorse crashing down on her. It was the knowledge that she had made all the wrong moves with Van Killborn. She had slept with him on their first date.

She opened her eyes and checked the time. It was after eight. She stared at the acoustic ceiling of the hotel room and realized lifting her head would require an application of mind over matter. Finally she groaned and climbed out of bed on wobbly legs. Jackhammers pounded inside her brain. Her stomach rolled and heaved. She could barely see out of her swollen eyes— but she had good enough vision to know that Van was not there.

Clutching her temples, she made her way into the bathroom to search for a painkiller. She spotted the brown leather satchel that was Van's toiletry kit sitting next to the sink. It seemed the most likely place for a bottle of ibuprofen. She really wasn't snooping when she found an open box of condoms—*Thank goodness he brought them*, she thought—a blister pack of Pepcid, and a bottle of Lactaid pills for lactose intolerance. She mentally filed away the information.

Then, still searching for a painkiller, she found a little brown bottle of pills nestled in the bottom of the kit, squirreled away inside a wad of tissues. The prescription had been filled for Van by a pharmacy on Madison Avenue in New York City. The instructions said, "Take one to two tablets as needed for insomnia." The drug was a generic, flunitrazepam. A notation indicated, "No refills."

Melanie's first thought was that Van must be under a lot of stress. He had stomach problems and couldn't sleep. The man definitely had something on his mind. Her second thought hit her like a violent swipe with the hammer working away inside her skull. She took another look at the drug name: flunitrazepam. She knew what it was. She had been a big Nirvana fan when she was in junior high. The trade name was Rohypnol, and the street name was a "roofie." Kurt Cobain had overdosed on roofies and champagne in the weeks before he died. A lot of rockers with cocaine and heroin habits took them.

But roofies had another use. They were the leading date-rape drug.

Melanie carefully rewrapped the pill bottle in the tissues and returned it to its exact position in the bottom of the leather carrier. Once she was satisfied he wouldn't know she had touched it, she raised her head. Her own white face caught her attention in the mirror. Her mascara had run. Her creamy skin was blotchy, and her eyes revealed how upset she now was.

She remembered Aunt Lolly's warning about Van, that he had a rottenness at the core. By going through his personal things, she had seen beyond the handsome face to the reality within. She found out he was a man with worries. He had heartburn, stomach problems, and insomnia.

But that was a best-case scenario. The drug in the pill

bottle suggested he could also have a drug abuse problem. She squeezed her eyes shut. There was an even worse explanation for his having Rohypnol. She didn't even want to think it, but considering how much she couldn't remember, she had to face the possibility: Van might have used a roofie last night, on her.

A taxi took Melanie from the hotel in Wilkes-Barre to Larrie's, where she had left her car. She hadn't bothered to leave Van a note. After all, he hadn't left her one. She was heartsick and miserable. *How could I have been so dumb?* she thought over and over again.

When the taxi pulled away, Ticky Blackstone came ambling out of the barn door that led to the Sparrow's Nest. He took one look at Melanie and shook his head. "Don't suppose it will do any good to say 'I tole you so,' now would it?"

Melanie gave him a dirty look and didn't answer. Trying not to jolt her still aching head, she gingerly went up the driveway to her PT Cruiser and opened the car door.

"I tole you so!" Ticky called after her. "And you might be wanting to know we had some company here last night."

Melanie stopped, carefully turned her head toward Ticky, and squinted her eyes. "What do you mean by 'company'?"

Ticky spat in the dirt. "A silver Mercedes drove past here twice. It stopped the second time. Somebody tried the door. Another minute more and I would have shot the sumofabitch. But whoever it was—and I know who it was and I bet dollars to doughnuts you know who it was—got back in his car and drove off.

"Little while after that happened, that big old black truck of Killborn's came past. It slowed way down. But Shem and Shaun were out on patrol and the driver must have seen their flashlights. Makes you wonder why they was out here, seeing that nobody was selling nothing at two or three in the a.m."

"Are you sure?" Melanie felt sick.

"I ain't blind, now am I? I said me and the twins were going to stand guard. That's just what we did and a good thing too."

"I guess I better find out what's going on," Melanie murmured more to herself than to Ticky.

She stood there and thought for a moment. "No word from Larrie?" she finally asked.

"Not a peep."

Melanie wasn't one to cry over spilled milk. She pulled herself up tall. Whatever had happened between her and Van, well, it had happened. To paraphrase Scarlett O'Hara, she'd worry about that tomorrow. What she had to act on right now was Larrie. She gave Ticky a steely-eyed look and said, "Something is really, really wrong. I'm going to take a look around. I'll start with her office. Maybe I can find a clue to where she's gone. You keep watch."

Melanie sank down at Larrie's desk. Her friend wasn't neat. She shoved aside crumpled Peppermint Pattie wrappers and started picking up notes scribbled on backs of envelopes and scraps of paper. Barn Kitty hopped up on the desk and insisted on attention. Melanie rubbed the cat's ears and spoke her own thoughts out loud. "Larrie wouldn't go off and leave you, Kitty. She wouldn't walk out on her dogs either. She's somewhere she shouldn't be. In trouble. I'm never going to forgive myself if Van had anything to do with it."

After pulling Kitty onto her lap so she could look through the rest of the papers on the desk, she admitted she had found nothing. She nudged the cat onto the floor and heaved herself to her feet. She walked outside. Ticky was smoking a cigarette and staring off into space, his face blank. The three dogs lay at his feet. They looked depressed.

"Is the house open, Ticky?"

"Always is." He took a deep drag and exhaled a cloud of smoke.

"I'm going to look around. Make some kind of noise if you need to get my attention, okay?"

"You got it, Miss Melanie."

At first, Melanie had no idea what she was even looking for. She tried to recall what Miss Marple would do, or Hercule Poirot. She exercised her little gray cells. Then it came to her: *An anomaly. Something unusual. Something odd. Something that wasn't here a week ago. That's what I'm looking for.*

The first unusual thing she spotted was the snitz pie, half consumed, in the refrigerator. Would Larrie eat half a pie and leave it uncovered? But it wasn't much of a clue and Melanie continued searching. She found a tin of brass polish and a cloth on the mantel, but nothing brass to polish. Another oddity, but again not very helpful.

Then Melanie went upstairs. She looked in the bathroom. Larrie's toothbrush and deodorant sat forlornly on the sink. Then she went into Larrie's bedroom. She flung open Larrie's closet. She knew every item of clothing in her best friend's wardrobe—not a difficult accomplishment since Larrie, once an avid mall goer, hadn't shopped over the past year.

Melanie moved around some hangers and determined nothing was missing. An empty overnight case sat on the floor. That convinced her that Larrie hadn't packed a bag. She crossed the room to Larrie's dresser. All of a sudden, Melanie's heart started fluttering like a hummingbird's wings. She knew right away she had found it. The anomaly. The thing that didn't fit. It was only a white business card, but it was so out of character for Larrie to have, it had to mean something. It said:

MADAME LOUISA

☾ Intuitive Interpreter of the Hands

☾ Tarot Card Reader

☾ Reiki Master

Psychic life counseling by appointment

(570) 555 1212

Melanie didn't hesitate. She pulled out her cell phone and dialed the number.

Madame Louisa clearly remembered Larrie when Melanie described her. She also squealed in alarm. "What's wrong? What's happened to her?"

"I—I don't know. She seems to have disappeared. I found your card. You're a psychic. Can you tell me anything?"

"I warned her!"

"About what?" Melanie was becoming nearly sick with worry.

"The antiques. I warned her about danger in the antiques. Did she obtain any new items after Saturday?"

Melanie's fingers tightened on the cell phone. "Yes, yes. She bought out an old man's estate."

Melanie heard a sharp intake of breath from Madame Louisa. "She must have brought something—a spirit of some kind—into her life with them. Something powerful. She should have called me. I could have detected it."

"Are you sure? How could a spirit have made her disappear?"

"Can you hold on a minute? I want to get my tarot

cards. I need to channel this information so I can understand it."

Melanie waited, her fingers getting sweaty holding the
phone, her arm beginning to shake. "Do you see anything
yet? Are you reading the cards?" she finally asked.

"Shhh. You're breaking my concentration."

Melanie fell silent. She thought this was crazy on one
level; on another she had a gut feeling Madame Louisa
really did know something. Finally the woman's voice
came through the phone.

"It's not as bad as I thought, but it may be worse than
you expect."

"What does that mean?"

"Your friend is following her destiny. She's far away.
She'll be back, but she'll be gone. What she seeks lies in
something old. The antiques probably. But you—"

"Me?" Melanie squeaked.

"You have met a man."

The blood rushed from Melanie's head, making her
feel faint. "Yes," she stammered.

"He's troubled."

"I suppose he is."

"Listen to me, young woman. He's caught between
two opposing forces, one dark, one light. He tells lies."

"No!"

"Yes. His only hope is love. But I warn you, you are
taking a risk with him. You have to be the Earth Mother.
You have to be his conscience. He's always going to have
an internal weakness. Are you strong enough to handle
this?"

"I don't know. What lies has he told?"

"I can't answer that. Look, I usually charge thirty-five
dollars for a reading. Your friend was somebody very
special, so I don't mind a freebie. But you? If you need
help with your love life, call me back with a credit card
number."

"Uhhh, okay—" Melanie murmured, nonplussed. Just then, from outside the window, Melanie heard what she at first thought was a squealing pig. Then she realized an out-of-tune voice was singing an old Eagles song. Ticky was bellowing out the lyrics, badly remembered, of "Hotel California."

Somebody must be coming. "Thanks, but I gotta go now," Melanie said and ended the call.

"Well, lookee lookee at what's coming up the road. A silver Mercedes." Ticky spat again into the dirt.

Melanie had rushed out of the house and now stood next to her PT Cruiser. She didn't know whether to get into her car and drive away or confront Van. She was held immobile by indecision long enough that Van Killborn made the choice for her. His car turned into Larrie's driveway spitting stones. He slammed on the brakes and skidded to a halt.

Before Melanie could move, Van was out of the car and yelling at her, "Why the hell did you leave? I've been worried out of my mind."

Melanie squared her shoulders and dramatically opened the driver's door as if to get in and leave. "I could ask you the same thing. You weren't there when I got up this morning."

Van strode over and stood on the other side of the open car door. "What is the matter with you? I went to Starbucks to get us some good coffee. I bought us apple crumb cake too. When I got back to the room, you were gone. You didn't even leave me a note. Why?"

Melanie didn't have any answer she wanted to voice. Instead, in an icy tone, she took the offense. "Why? Why did you leave the hotel room last night and drive out here?"

"I thought—I thought—I thought you were asleep," Van stuttered.

"That's interesting. Why? Did you drug me?"

"Huh?" His face looked genuinely puzzled at her accusation; then he seemed to get it. "Do you mean the brandies? Okay, I admit that I wanted you to drink too much."

"Why did you want that, Van Killborn?" Melanie snapped.

Van's face turned instantly red. "I wanted you to sleep with me. I didn't think you would unless you were drunk."

It was Melanie's turn to look puzzled. "Why would you think that?"

Van looked at her with puppy-dog eyes. "Because you're not like the women I usually date. None of them was ever a virgin. You're too good for me, Melanie. We both know that."

"We do?" Melanie said, melting under his gaze.

"I wanted you so badly," Van went on. "I was wrong to get you drunk. I knew I should take it slow and wait, but, Mel, I couldn't help myself. I can't help myself now." He leaned over the top of the car door and took her face in his hands and kissed her soundly.

Melanie's knees went weak. She kissed him back.

"Jesus, Mary, and Joseph, will you get a look at this!" Ticky's voice cut into the romantic moment like a buzz saw.

Van broke the kiss. Melanie shot Ticky an annoyed look.

"What do you want?" Van griped. "Can't you see we're busy?"

"Yeah, well, you were real busy last night. Driving out here. The lady asked you why. You might be getting over on her, but all that lovey-dovey stuff don't mean nothing to me. I want some damned answers."

Van made some inarticulate noises. "Um, er, I, you know—"

Melanie hit him square in the chest with the heel of her hand. "Stop that, Van. Just tell us why you were here. And don't you dare lie about it."

Van rubbed his chest. "Okay, I was here. I wanted to make sure nobody broke in and stole the furniture."

Ticky snorted. "Seems to me the only person who wants that furniture bad enough to steal it is you."

Van gave Ticky a withering look. "If I came out here to steal the furniture, how was I going to take it? Put it in the trunk of my Mercedes?"

Ticky wore his anger like a badge. He stuck out his chest. "Do you think I'm a dumb hick? You had that big black truck coming out here right behind you."

The color drained out of Van's face. "My truck was here last night?"

"Like you didn't know that," Ticky sneered. "If me and the twins hadn't been here, I bet you would have stole Miss Larrie blind."

"I didn't know. Oh, shit. That's not a good thing. Oh, shit." He ran his hands nervously through his blond hair.

Melanie gave Van another smack with the heel of her hand to get his attention. "Van Killborn! It's time you told me what's going on."

"Me too," Ticky said, planting his legs apart and reaching behind his back to pull out his gun.

"Ticky!" Melanie yelled. "Put that thing away! Van will talk to me, won't you, Van?"

Van nodded. "Maybe it's time I do. Let's go get some coffee and I'll tell you everything."

Ticky didn't put the gun away. He kept it aimed right at Van's heart. "I don't think so. Look at it logically, Ms. O'Casey. I may be only the hired hand, but I'm representing my boss here. Somebody's got to look out for her interests. I'm not meaning to insult you or anything, but you have something besides Miss Larrie's business on your mind."

He gestured with the gun. "How about both of you come into the shop. I got some coffee brewed up in the Mr. Coffee machine. It's only a couple of hours old. Got a jar of Cremora too. You can have a cup while this city fellow tells us what's really going on."

Ticky held a styrofoam cup of thick black coffee in his left hand and his gun in his right after the three of them sat down in the tack room at the back of the barn that Larrie used as an office.

Melanie noticed that Van had started perspiring, and it wasn't at all hot in there. She folded her arms across her ample chest. She admitted she was infatuated with Van, but she wasn't totally blind, as Ticky suggested. If Van was going to become husband material, he had to clean up his act. She used her best librarian voice on him. "You'd better start talking, Van. I'm starting to doubt every word you've ever said."

Van let out a deep breath. He turned the full wattage of his baby blues on her. "Mel, I'm in a lot of trouble. I'm going to be in a lot more if Ms. Smith doesn't come back today and sell me those pieces from the estate."

Melanie had to fight her impulse to help him convince Larrie to make the deal. She was not going to try to earn Van's love by getting him what he wanted. And she wasn't going to be an enabler either. "What kind of trouble?" she insisted.

"Just as I told Ms. Smith, the antiques and antiquities business has been hit hard by the downturn in the economy. My family's business is hurting, although we deal in big-ticket items and our clientele is generally very wealthy. Even the rich have cut back on spending. We now depend on just a few major customers for most of our income. One of those customers wants the items from the Ydoboni estate. I promised him I'd get them. If

I disappoint him and we lose his patronage, we'll probably have to close down."

"Seems to me you're leaving something out of this here story," Ticky said, disgust written on his face. "Like the '*I'm* in a lot of trouble' part."

"That's just it. This customer, you don't break your promises to him. You've heard about him. John Ga— No, I shouldn't say. But the guys who came up here in my moving truck work for him, not me. I told Ms. Smith that."

"So if you don't deliver the furniture, this guy is going to beat you up?" Ticky's face was filled with doubt.

"Worse than beat me up. If I go home empty-handed, I could end up with a bullet behind my ear."

"My God, no!" Melanie cried out before she could stop herself.

"I'm afraid so," Van said. "It's a bad situation, Mel. Mr.—let me call him Mr. G.—is getting impatient. I thought he might tell Tony and Sammy to just grab the furniture. That's why I drove out here during the night. I've been worried sick."

Ticky rubbed the side of his nose with the barrel of the gun. "I bet the 'worried sick' part is true. Not sure if the rest of your story is. Tell me, Mr. Killingbird—"

"Killborn." .

"Whatever. Anyways, what were you going to do if Miss Larrie decided not to sell to you?"

"She all but promised me she'd sell. I haven't thought about what I'd do if she doesn't."

"Bullshit, Mr. Killingbird. You know exactly what you was gonna do. You'd have to steal it then, now wouldn't you. Or force Miss Larrie to sell. What would you do, kidnap her dogs?"

"I would not! Our firm has a spotless reputation. I don't have to defend myself to you, you cretin."

"Who you calling a creep-in?" Ticky's face turned mean, and he still had the gun in his hand.

"Stop this!" Melanie yelled and shut the two men up. "I'm not sitting here to witness a pissing contest. Ticky, you have a point. Van, you're in a helluva mess. If your story is true, your options are limited. But there's something not sitting right with me about what you've said. I'm not saying it's all a lie, but Van, you're still hiding something."

The sweat had beaded up on Van's upper lip. "I don't know what you mean."

Melanie studied him—the beauty of his eyes, the refinement of his aquiline nose, the guilt written clearly on his face. "I admit I haven't done a whole lot of thinking about this furniture deal."

"Yeah, furniture isn't what *you've* been thinking about," Ticky muttered.

Melanie shot him a filthy look and turned her attention back to Van. "Larrie told me that you offered her a huge sum for four items in the estate."

"Absolutely true. I did. I told her I was willing to take a loss just to keep Mr. G. happy."

"No, no no, no no," Melanie muttered mostly to herself. "That does not compute." She kept her pretty eyes on Van. "You just said your firm is in financial trouble. But you dress like a prince. You drive an obscenely expensive car. Now you've traveled to Pennsylvania to broker a deal where you stand to lose a lot of money? I don't think so."

"You don't?" Van looked depressed.

"No, I don't. I think you intend to make a lot of money from this furniture. I don't doubt you're being pressured by a mobster. You're certainly scared about something. But what's really at stake here? We're not dealing with a painting by Van Gogh. We're dealing with what? Twenty, twenty-five thousand dollars' worth of hundred-year-old stuff? Larrie said you wanted a tea caddy, a desk and a couple of other things. Uh-uh, I don't think so. You're not going to get a bullet in the head for not bringing that back to Mr. G."

Van avoided her eyes. He didn't answer. He hung his head and looked miserable.

Ticky might not think fast, but he figured things out. He waved the gun at Van. "Ask him about the paper. You know, the one he dropped."

Van's head popped up. "I dropped it here? That's why I couldn't find it. Oh, shit. Oh, shit."

"'Oh shit' is right, Van Killborn," Melanie said. She rummaged around in her purse and pulled the piece of paper out of the billfold part of her wallet. She took care not to rip it along its fragile folds when she opened it up. Then she read:

> Small places in big things
> You have to look for wings
> Near a rose in the middle
> Use the key to fiddle
> And the treasure you look for
> will spring

"So what is this treasure, Van? And where are you supposed to find it?"

Chapter 25

Van's whole world was crashing down around him. He had screwed up badly. Now his mistakes were like falling dominoes, taking all his hopes and plans down with them.

The worst mistake had been the first—bringing Mr. G. in on the deal. But with the antiques business hemorrhaging red ink, he didn't have the funds to keep running down leads and taking trips to India. Once he had used up his own money, he had to find a backer. He quickly spent every penny Mr. G. advanced, getting himself in deep with the mob boss. And when he finally got the call from the old Ydoboni woman, he didn't have the cash, not even the lousy twenty-five thousand dollars, to pay for the estate. He had to go back to the well that was Mr. G. once more.

It was at that point that Mr. G. stopped being the smiling, naïve treasure hunter he had seemed to be. Instead, he insisted on sending his enforcers along with Van. Van realized too late that Mr. G. wouldn't be satisfied with the fifty-fifty split of their original agreement. Mr. G. had saddled him with two thugs and explained his "new terms." Van could either hand over the treasure and smile while he did it, or his family's business would be burned to the ground. That Van wouldn't be alive to tell about it was a real possibility as well.

It was as simple as that. And as complicated as that.

Van looked over at the Valkyrie who had come into his life less than twenty-four hours ago. He had fallen for her immediately. Just like in the film *Jerry Maguire*, she had him at hello. Now she was going to hate him. He supposed if he was dead it wouldn't really matter anyway.

He cleared his throat and announced, "I guess I've got nothing left to lose." He turned forlorn eyes to Melanie. *My God, the woman is beautiful*, he thought. "Everything Ticky suspected about me is true. For half a century, my family has been hunting for the treasure that belonged to the Mughal Aurangzeb. It was taken by the pirate Henry Every in August, 1694, from a ship called the *Fetah Muhammad* that he attacked with his own ship, the *Fancy*, off the coast of India.

"The treasure hunt began when my grandfather obtained the original of the poem you just read, at an auction of items from a remote village in the Himalayas. That's a copy I made of it. Legend suggested that this particular Balti village was the home of a famous Sikh guru. The Mughal's treasure had once been in the village too, but had been moved from there and ended up farther south, in an Indian settlement near Lahore."

Ticky gave an exaggerated yawn. "This is a long yarn, Killingbird. Cut to the chase, will you?"

Van gave Melanie a desperate look.

"You can give me the whole story later, Van. Just tell us where the treasure is now."

Van nodded. "Okay. Josiah Ydoboni took possession of the treasure when he purchased the contents of a warehouse filled with furniture and old records in the Punjab. Your friend Larissa Smith bought that furniture this past weekend, right out from under my nose. From everything my family has found out, I've been led to believe the treasure is hidden in the teak and mahogany armoire."

"The treasure must be rather small. How much can it possibly be worth?" Melanie asked.

"Small?" Van's lips turned up in a quavering smile. "I suppose so. It's a single gem encircled by diamonds. It's called the Eye of the Snow Leopard. It's the largest flawless ruby known to exist in the world. By a conservative estimate, it's worth over a hundred million dollars."

Ticky looked at Melanie. Melanie looked at Van. Van nodded. "Shall we go look for it?"

Van had envisioned this moment in his mind hundreds of times. He led the way to the massive armoire. He asked Melanie to read the first line of the poem as if he didn't know it by heart, which he did.

"'Small places in big things, you have to look for wings,'" she read.

Van pointed to the top of the piece of furniture. "We're looking at an armoire or clothespress. This one is probably Dutch in origin, not British. The marquetry inlay of mahogany was probably added later, as was that crest—"

"I don't need no lesson in furniture," Ticky interrupted.

"You need a lesson in manners," Van barked back.

"Maybe you could tell me all the details later." Melanie tried to play the diplomat.

"The point is," Van huffed, "that crest. It's called a swan neck pediment, only here the swans' necks that arch up toward the center are actually wings. So there are the wings of the poem. What comes next?"

"'Near a rose in the middle, use the key to fiddle.'"

Van pointed to the finial between the wings. It was a carving of a single rose. He reached up and turned it. It unscrewed easily and he handed it to Melanie. His hand was trembling a little when he felt with his fingers inside the cavity where the finial had rested.

"I've got it." He brought out a small brass key. He handed it over to Melanie.

Melanie looked at it. It was only an inch long and had a cloverleaf filigree on one end. "But what does it open? The poem said, 'Near a rose in the middle, use the key to fiddle, and the treasure you look for will spring.'"

"Therefore we should discover a hidden keyhole somewhere near the rose." Van ran his long fingers expertly over the carving on the pediment. Nothing slid. Nothing moved. He moved to the top of the clothes-press itself, which was ornately carved in the French, not the Dutch style—a fact he relayed to Ticky and Melanie, although no one else cared.

He hesitated. "This cockerel-head escutcheon is interesting."

"You want to repeat that in English?" Ticky griped.

"A rooster head carved on a shield."

"Why didn't you say that in the first place?"

Van ignored Ticky and wiggled the shield. It moved, stuck, moved again. Van's heart started to race. He had found it. He had really found it. He blinked tears of joy back from his eyes. He pushed a little harder on the carved wood shield and it slid to the side, exposing a keyhole inserted into the front of a small drawer.

"The key, please." He extended his hand to Melanie, who set the key in his palm.

He took the key, put it carefully in the lock, and turned. There was a loud click and the drawer sprang forward. Van pulled it out of the armoire entirely and held it in his hands. It had a carefully fitted wood cover with a ring for lifting it off. The long drawer measured perhaps six inches wide, four inches high, and well over a foot in length.

It was heavy, and by this time Van's hands were clearly shaking. He was afraid he might drop it. "Let's go where there's a safe place for me to set this down and good light to see what's inside."

"Take it back to Miss Larrie's office and put it on the desk," Ticky told him.

Van stood in front of the drawer, now safely resting on Larrie's desk. Melanie leaned forward on his left, and Ticky, still clutching his gun, crowded in on the right. Van would have preferred to savor this moment alone, but he didn't have that option.

"Okay. Here goes." He took a deep breath and put one finger in the ring. He lifted.

"What's that?" Melanie asked. A black cloth lay folded inside.

Van grinned. "I bet I know."

He picked it up and revealed a green velvet presentation box underneath. He unfolded the cloth which turned out to be a flag, a Jolly Roger, but not the most familiar kind. Against a black field sat a white skull in profile, with a kerchief tied on its head and an earring peeking out below the kerchief, although the skull naturally had no ear. Two bones formed an X and the skull was at the point they crossed.

"It's Henry Every's own flag. This *is* the Mughal treasure. I've found the Eye of the Snow Leopard!"

He snatched up the green velvet box and lifted the lid.

"Oh, my," Melanie breathed.

"Well, well, well," Ticky muttered. "That's real purty."

Van just stared. His heart didn't leap. It plummeted. He studied the open box, which was filled with magnificent emeralds and cut diamonds, most of them well over two carets and in such quantity that they filled the box to the brim. But Van didn't see a huge ruby among them.

So intense was his frustration, he could barely keep from dumping the precious stones out onto the desk. But he didn't dare risk losing even one of the exquisite gems. He carefully put the box down and picked up a pencil to cautiously probe through the jewels. He methodically poked the eraser end of the yellow Ticonderoga into every square inch. His hands now trembled as if he had palsy. Finally he put the pencil down. He wished he could just collapse onto the chair and weep. Instead he turned to Melanie with a face turned gray and ashen. "The Eye of the Snow Leopard isn't here."

Chapter 26

The day after the tiger fight and their return from finding the guru in the mountains, Larrie did something extraordinary. She stayed in India under the British Raj and did not make a wish to return to the twenty-first century as originally planned. She had several good reasons to delay going back to modern times. Her constant anxiety over Aunt Lolly pushed her to return, but Jo swore to her that no matter how long they tarried in India, they would arrive back at Larrie's farm shortly after noon on Wednesday, two days after she and Jo flew off into the blue beyond.

People believe what they want to. Larrie took Jo at his word.

Larrie thought, or more likely rationalized, that the major reason for delaying her departure was the ice cream. The factory and pushcart enterprise that she had envisioned with such enthusiasm was a grand scheme. But it was proving as difficult to make a reality as most grand schemes and wild million-dollar ideas. Larrie plunged into the overwhelming number of tasks required when setting up a new business.

It was to be a one-woman venture. While Jo stayed in his study dealing with accounts and business matters, Larrie, not allowed to travel alone and therefore accompanied by a rail-thin, nervous, middle-aged male servant named Bachint Singh, took the train into Lahore.

Very near the main railway station in the center of Lahore, Larrie quickly found a rail agent who gladly negotiated the cutting and transporting of ice from the northern mountains. The price had Larrie mentally tallying up that a mountain of ice cream would have to be sold to make a profit, but she was sure it would be.

Once they left the rail agent's office with the ice problem solved, Larrie had Bachint locate an experienced cooper to construct large hand-cranked buckets to churn the ice cream, for it had been very tedious to shake the buckets by hand. After that, they went to Bachint's cousin, Lavindeep Singh. Larrie had figured out that Sikh men have the last name Singh while women have Kaur, which made everyone seem related, even though they weren't.

Lavindeep was a cabinetmaker, and it was he who would build the insulated boxes for the pushcarts. Being a real cousin of Bachint's, Lavindeep insisted they join him for tea, and to be polite they did.

From the cabinetmaker's woodshop they took a horse-drawn taxi to the other side of the city to purchase the bicycle wheels the boxes would be mounted on. Each stop was especially tedious because, with the exception of the rail agent who was English, Bachint Singh had to convey Larrie's specifications to the Urdu-speaking men and bargain for the best price. Being an antiques dealer by trade, Larrie bargained by nature, and her opinion that she could have done better made her irritable and impatient.

Finally, all was finished. With her feet aching and her stomach growling after many hours in Lahore, Larrie realized that since the single cup of tea with the cabinet-maker, neither she nor Bachint Singh had eaten a thing. Acting out of impulse, as she so frequently did, Larrie stopped in at the governor's mansion to see Lady Bunny Hare, who promptly invited Larrie into the parlor for a high tea and sent Bachint Singh to the kitchens for his.

Larrie explained why she was in Lahore as Lady Hare filled the cups.

"How do you like your tea? Milk and sugar? Here you go. Now, you were telling me you're going to manufacture ice-cream cones! Quite a challenge in this beastly climate, but what a wonderful idea. Let me see, I distinctly remember that ice-cream cones were invented a few years ago at that World's Fair you had in St. Louis. They made a waffle cone from a batter, I seem to remember."

Bunny paused for the briefest moment and passed a plate of small sandwiches. "Do have one. Or two. On the left are cucumber and watercress. On the right are potted meat."

While Larrie nibbled on a cucumber sandwich, Bunny rattled on. "I've had ice cream a few times, always in France. It's a rare treat on the Continent. But you say you've invented a new cone with cinnamon and sugar! That's your stroke of genius. And selling it from a pushcart is smashing too."

Bunny Hare chattered constantly, but she seemed like a kind and good woman, Larrie thought. Larrie gratefully sipped her sweet tea and said, "I think making the product locally will give an economic boost to the village. It will help them move away from subsistence farming, teach the benefits of a cottage industry, and promote entrepreneurship."

Bunny tilted her head in a rabbitlike way. "You have such an odd manner of speaking, Ms. Smith. I suppose that's because you're an American. Everyone seems so business-minded over there. All those Rotarians. By what day do you think you will actually be making the ice cream and have perhaps twenty or thirty gallons?"

The terrifying monster called time reared up before Larrie again. It filled her with anxiety. She worried about disturbing the future, of changing history, but yet she couldn't be sure that was even possible. Anything she did in 1906 would have already happened, she assumed. Her head spun when she thought about it and tried to be logical. She could make no sense of it, but she knew it would be wise to get back to her own century and the world she knew.

She sighed deeply and her eyes looked far away before she answered Lady Hare. "The railway agent promised the first delivery of ice to the little station in the village by early next week—Monday, I hope. The hand-cranked ice-cream makers are being assembled by a barrel maker right here in Lahore. I paid extra, and the first two ten-gallon buckets will be delivered within two days, or so I was promised.

"Our flock of goats is producing well, but I'm hoping to buy another twenty or so of the Nubians. We need only the cream, so the skimmed milk can be sold or used. I have sugar and salt being sent back to Jo's warehouse right now. I'm not sure when the pushcarts will be operational, but all in all, I think that in a week or so, we'll have a supply of premium ice cream in four flavors: Mango Madness, Almond Joyful, Very Vanilla, and Bingo Berry. I would like to add chocolate but the cacao beans must be imported, so perhaps at some later date."

Bunny, her eyes luminous and round, looked at Larrie with wonder. "My goodness, that's extraordinary. And your names are so fanciful. I'm not sure what a Bingo is but perhaps from the Bing cherry? They come from America too, now don't they? It doesn't matter. All your flavors sound luscious. Now here's my idea! I should like to host an ice-cream cone party to introduce your enterprise. Since you'll have a supply by then, we can hold it next Friday night. If all the colonials put in orders, you'll be making pots of money in no time. You haven't said anything. Isn't it a splendid idea?"

Larrie's mouth was suddenly dry. Next Friday? She wouldn't be here next Friday. Yet Lady Hare was being so kind—and her party would be a great product launch. She gulped down some tea. "Yes, it's a splendid idea and very generous. Except, you see, Jo and I are planning to travel to America. I would like him to meet my parents. I think we are going to leave after the coming weekend, on Monday, Tuesday at the latest."

"You *think*! That means you still don't have firm travel plans. Next Friday is just a few days more. You can postpone your departure, can you not? You can just as easily leave right after the party. I've talked about you to all the other English in Lahore. I've told them all about your spiritual quest, following Madame Blavatsky and all, and your fateful meeting with Jo in Paris. But they want to hear the whole romantic story from *you*. You must stay for the party!"

"I suppose," Larrie agreed, her voice tentative. "It sounds like a plan."

"'It sounds like a plan'! You have such a charming way of phrasing things. I'll have to remember that. 'Sounds like a plan.' " Then Bunny Hare clapped her hands. "I know, we'll make it an ice cream–engagement– bon voyage party! Oh, what fun it will be.

"You've livened up my entire summer, Ms. Smith. We're going to be the best of friends, I just know it. And you still haven't met my Lancelot. He'd be crushed, simply crushed, if you and Jo left before his return. He's telephoned. He saw your announcement in the *Times*. He says he can't believe it!"

Larrie whispered under her breath, "Neither can I."

In the end Larrie accepted that she would be in India for at least a week and a half. She thought about home:

about Aunt Lolly, the antiques shop, and the dogs. She worried terribly about her aunt, but she felt confident that Ticky could handle the dogs and the shop. She gave little thought to Van and the Ydoboni estate, except to decide that she would just make the sale to him as soon as she returned. Sticking to her self-imposed rules didn't seem very important to her anymore.

On the trip back from Lahore, she put her head back on the rattan seat. The wheels went *clack clack clack.* The cinders and smoke billowed past the windows. The engine chugged and chuffed and blew its whistle. It was a short ride, but Larrie thought for a long time. *Really, no one but Lolly needs me to come home. Why am I worried? What could possibly go wrong in sleepy Beaumont, Pennsylvania, while I'm gone?*

Jo brightened when Larrie told him that Bunny Hare was planning an ice-cream party the following Friday and they must stay to attend it. He pushed the chair back from his desk and threw down a pen on the green blotter. "To tell the truth, I feel too exhausted to time travel right now. I've been writing for hours. The delay is a good idea all around."

All of Larrie's doubts about lingering in the past fled. "You feel exhausted? Do you have a fever? Has Tara changed the bandages today? Is there any sign of sepsis? You must stay in bed!"

Jo reached out a strong, tanned hand and grabbed Larrie, pulling her into his lap. He nuzzled her neck. "Relax, mother hen, I'm fine. I'll stay in bed if you come with me, although I won't get any rest if you do."

Larrie laughed, but pressed the back of her hand against his forehead. He did seem warm. "Maybe you should lie down."

"Come with me and I will," Jo said, kissing her.

Larrie's heart skipped. A tingling started deep inside

her. She put her cheek next to Jo's. "Maybe just for a short nap. I'm awfully tired too. But we'll have to sneak to the bedroom. I'll never get there if Mayree sees me. She doesn't know I'm home yet."

Later, as Jo napped, Larrie thought how, in the short time since she had brought the children into Jo's great house, Mayree had become her shadow. The little girl insisted that "Mama" sit with her at breakfast each morning, and little by little Larrie had learned the sad tale of the little girl's past. Mayree's mother had done the laundry in a colonial judge's home, and that's how the child had come by her knowledge of English. But her mother had died—of a terrible pain in her belly, according to Mayree—and Mayree had been left to fend for herself. No one looked after her except the other children on the streets.

Now, crawling as often as possible onto Larrie's lap, the little girl seemed to constantly soak up more words, and chattered like a squirrel.

Larrie tried not to show favoritism and gathered all the children around her, but she had to admit Mayree was special. She had tied the yellow ribbons in Mayree's hair herself that morning before leaving for Lahore, while Bibi, the new nanny and the mother of six grown children, expertly brushed hair and made sure everyone had clean clothes.

But it was Larrie who tenderly washed the jam off Mayree's face. She noticed that the child's cheeks were filling out and her eyes looked brighter—and those eyes never let Larrie out of their sight.

During the impromptu subtraction lesson Larrie had given after breakfast, before setting out on the ten o'clock train to Lahore, Mayree stayed at her feet. When it was over Mayree clung to Larrie, crying piteously, when she and Bachint Singh had to leave. Bibi picked up the inconsolable child and held her in her arms. Finally Jo himself came out of the house and asked what was wrong.

Seeing that Larrie looked more distraught than the child, he had put the little girl up on his shoulders and marched around singing "The British Grenadiers." After three or four choruses of "Sing tow, row, row, row, row, row, the British Grenadiers!" Mayree stopped crying and began to giggle. But later, when Larrie stood on the train platform, waiting for the train to Lahore, the memory of the little girl's sobs tore at her heart.

The afternoon nap, broken only by an hour dinner, stretched into a good night's rest with Jo—until a rooster began crowing at dawn. Larrie sat upright in bed. An abundance of sleep had left her ready to leap out of bed. She nudged a still-snoring Jo.

"The chickens are here! Let's go see them!"

Jo groaned and put a pillow over his head. His voice was muffled by the goose down. "I'm not a farmer. Never wanted to be one. You go."

Tara Singh had a kettle boiling on the modern coal stove in the kitchen. "You're awake, memsahib?" He poured the hot water over a sieve filled with tea leaves to make the tea and handed her a cup.

I do miss my morning coffee, Larrie thought, and drank the hot liquid. "I heard the rooster. How many chickens have we gotten?"

"A great many. Two dozen? Bachint Singh is trying to keep them from leaving the yard. I've heard him cursing at one particular hen for some time."

Larrie peeked out the open door, but it was barely after dawn and too dark to see anything. She heard Bachint Singh's agitated voice though. "We must fence in a chicken yard today and get to work on a coop. The hens need laying boxes, and there should be a watering trough."

Tara Singh nodded in agreement. "The *Times* said your father had a great estate in America. Did you have chickens there?"

"Yes, we had a little bit of everything. But until the big cooperatives took over, we had mostly dairy cows. And I always had a horse or a pony. My parents live in a condo now."

"Cooperatives? Condo? There are many things in America I do not know about, memsahib. But I too know a little about chickens."

"Then we shall be fine, Tara Singh."

"Mama?" a sleepy voice said.

Larrie glanced toward the hallway to see Mayree standing in her nightshirt, her tiny hand rubbing her eyes. Larrie went over and swooped the child into her arms. "We have chickens, baby girl! Would you like to see them?"

The child nodded and Larrie carried her through the veranda into the dirt yard beyond. A corral had already been built for the goats. They began bleating when Larrie stepped outside, thinking they were about to get breakfast, she supposed. Larrie set Mayree down. "I'm afraid Sahib Trelawny is not going to be able to sleep much longer," she said and then called to Bachint Singh.

"Go inside and get your tea, Bachint Singh. Mayree and I will chase the hens for a while." Bachint Singh nodded gratefully and trotted toward the house.

"Just keep the chickens from straying too far, Mayree. We don't want any to get lost. I'm going into the little shed at the back of the yard for just a minute to see what we have to help us build a fence."

Larrie could barely see inside the shed, which held a rake and shovel and some other gardening tools. On a high shelf she spotted a hatchet that could be used to cut brush. She thought a fence of twigs would have to do. She didn't believe chicken wire had been invented yet, though it would be easy enough to weave wire together like that—if she could get some wire. She noticed that the goats had gotten quiet, but soon she was lost in thought, contemplating how to quickly construct a chicken coop.

Then she heard Mayree scream.

Larrie rushed from the shed and looked around for the child. She spotted her not more than twenty feet away, where the open fields spread out from the edge of the yard. The little girl was standing very still. A cobra had reared up in front of her, nearly as tall as the child, its hood spread. Larrie knew at once that the snake must have smelled the chickens and come in search of eggs.

In a very calm voice, much calmer than she felt, Larrie called softly to Mayree. "That's a good girl. Don't move. I'm going to go behind the snake and keep it from biting you."

Larrie rushed inside the shed and grabbed the rake. She raced back outside and then, moving as quietly as she could, her heart pounding loudly in her ears, she circled behind the great serpent whose poison would kill a grown man in under an hour.

Despite Larrie's efforts to walk silently, the snake sensed her coming. It swayed and started to swing around in the direction of the new threat. Larrie didn't hesitate. She sprang forward, bringing the rake down to catch the snake right behind its hood. She drove it to the ground, its neck imprisoned between the tines of the rake. It thrashed hard, hissing, its tail flailing. It took all of Larrie's strength to keep its head pinned down.

"Run, Mayree!" she yelled. "Get help!"

Mayree sprinted away as fast as her little legs could carry her toward the veranda and the kitchen beyond. Larrie felt relieved that the little girl was out of danger. As for herself, she thought there was a good chance she'd be bitten. By this time, the snake was twisting around with all its might. Larrie put as much pressure as she could on the rake to keep the serpent from getting free.

But the rake wasn't very long, her own feet were bare, and the cobra's tail had smacked into her shins a few times. And now, to her dismay, that tail was curling around her ankle and the cobra was using her for leverage. It was just a matter of time before the snake would wriggle free.

Larrie mentally steeled herself to accept her death, here in the Punjab, a hundred years before her time.

Chapter 27

Jo Trelawny heard the goats bleating first, then a strange quietness before he heard the child scream. He jumped out of bed and pulled on some trousers. He ran into the kitchen at the same moment Mayree came running through the back door.

"Mama said get help. A big snake tried to bite me!" Then she burst into tears.

Jo bolted through the back door and into the yard. He saw Larrie straining with all her strength to hold down a huge cobra with a garden rake.

She called out, "Jo, there's a hatchet in the shed. Hurry! No! Wait! Use magic."

Jo stopped and raised his hand. He pointed at the snake. "Be gone!" There was a bright flash of light and the snake vanished. Larrie, now off balance, toppled over the rake and landed like a fallen tree on the ground.

Suddenly Jo was lifting her up. His face was pale and his hands cold as ice. "Were you bitten?"

"No. I'm fine."

Jo held her tightly against him. "You scared me."

"The cobra scared me! Is Mayree okay?"

Gripping her hard, as if he'd never let her go, Jo said, "She's got a fine set of lungs, that one. She wasn't hurt that I could see."

"You're holding me so hard I can't breathe, Jo. I'm okay. You know, we need a dog, or a mongoose. They'll keep the snakes away."

Jo looked at her with narrowed eyes. "Ten children. A nanny. Goats. Chickens. Now you want me to get a dog. Or a mongoose. And that's just in three days. I'm going to need a bigger house. We'll probably have an elephant before Friday comes and—" He stopped all of a sudden.

"And we leave, isn't that what you were going to say?"

Jo coughed to cover the catch in his voice. "Yes, when you go home."

Neither of them spoke. The sky was getting brighter in the east. A bird began to sing in a nearby tree. Chickens were pecking around their bare feet. And they saw none of it, heard none of it. They had eyes only for each other.

Finally Larrie pushed a lock of Jo's curly dark hair off his forehead with a gentle hand. "You're going with me, Jo. How bad can it be? You'll have to leave India and your life here. But we'll still be together."

Jo practically groaned. "We *won't* still be together. It doesn't matter if we're in your time or mine. I'll be a genie captured in a bottle, enslaved to do your bidding. I won't feel like a man. And when you make the third wish, it will be over. Completely over. I'll be gone."

"What are you talking about? Where can you go? I own the lamp. Ms. Ydoboni said I must keep it forever."

"She didn't understand. She didn't know what happens. Her brother never made a wish. He kept the lamp locked away in a cabinet with me inside it. But once the person who rubs the lamp wishes, and the wishes are used up, the lamp disappears. Most of the time, it is set adrift in the sea to wash up on shore. Sometimes I get caught in a current and float in the ocean for years."

Larrie's teeth had begun to chatter. She shivered, and it had nothing to do with the cool morning air. "You mean I wouldn't be able to find you? I wouldn't even know where you'd gone?"

Jo let go of her and his arms hung at his sides. He looked carefully into her face. "That's it. I'm temporary. I'm not going to be able to stick around. Are you sorry we went this far?"

"Oh, Jo! I'm not sorry. I'll just never make the third wish. We'll cope somehow. We can go on as we are. I'd never treat you like a slave. You'd feel like a man, I promise."

Jo laughed without mirth. "It's not in your hands, Larrie. And it's not in mine. You'll never make another wish? It will happen, I'm sure. But if not, you'll get older. I will not. You'll die. I'll live on. Surely you can see that as long as I'm enchanted, I'll be a genie, not a lover. Not a real man."

Chapter 28

Melanie sat with Van on Larrie's front stoop in the afternoon shade. Earlier she had suggested they search through the rest of the things from the Josiah Ydoboni estate to see if the Eye of the Snow Leopard was hidden somewhere else.

Van shook his head. "It would be a waste of time. The poem told us where the gem had been hidden. Somebody's already taken it, maybe years ago. I don't know what to do. I'm going to end up in the trunk of some mobster's Cadillac with a bullet in my head and my feet in cement." He moaned. "I suppose I could run away."

Melanie tried not to feel exasperated with Van. She realized he was in a terrible situation and probably wasn't thinking clearly. However, she preferred to focus on finding a solution rather than wringing her hands over the problem. She made her voice sound upbeat.

"Running away wouldn't solve anything. Mr. G. would still burn down your family's business. And where would you go? You'd be looking over your shoulder for the rest of your life thinking somebody had a contract on you. Why don't you just tell Mr. G. the Eye of the Snow Leopard wasn't there?"

Van looked at her with haunted eyes. "Then what? He's not going to pat me on the back and say, 'Better luck next time, Van. Here's some more money to keep looking.' I don't think so. There's no way out of this." Van put his head in his hands, his shoulders sagging.

"Offer him the other gems to make up for the lost ruby."

Van lifted his face. It held genuine surprise at Melanie's suggestion. "Mel, I found the Mughal treasure, but it's not mine. The gems belong to Ms. Smith. I couldn't take them even if I wanted to. Ticky's down there in the tack room guarding them with that old gun of his. He's just looking for an excuse to shoot me. He doesn't like me. You might have noticed."

"For heaven's sake, Van, I wasn't suggesting you *steal* the jewels. I know Larrie. I think you can go on the assumption that she'll offer you a share of them because that's fair. You found them. She'll want to share them with the old lady too, because her brother owned them, even if he didn't know it."

"I can't count on that, Melanie. You can't offer them to me, and Larrie is under no legal obligation to offer me anything."

"I tell you, I *know* Larrie. We've been friends our whole life. I would give her anything I had. She feels the same about me. I know what she will do. Morally, she'll feel you deserve a share. Your portion of those emeralds and diamonds will still be worth a fortune. Negotiate with Mr. G."

Slumped in depression, fear clearly gnawing away at his insides, Van sighed and said, "I know you're trying to be helpful, but the stones aren't worth anywhere near a hundred million dollars. That's not even it. With Mr. G. it's not so much about the money. It's about having something nobody else does. He's not going to negotiate."

Melanie wasn't about to admit failure. "He will negotiate if it's the emeralds and diamonds or nothing. He's a businessman. Convince him he's still coming out ahead on this. He'll still have part of the lost Mughal treasure that Killborn and Sons located. You'll both get great press. It's a win-win deal."

Van reconsidered. "It's worth a shot, I guess." There was the sound of a car on gravel. His head whipped around nervously. "Whose white Toyota is that pulling in the driveway?"

"Relax, it's probably Larrie's mom and dad's." Melanie stood up for a better view. "It looks like Aunt Lolly's in the backseat. They picked her up early this morning to take her to the competency exam."

Larrie's dad waved from the driver's window, but he didn't get out of the car. Aunt Lolly emerged from the backseat. She was wearing an Indian print dress decorated with beads and mirrors. She had put a plastic flower in her hair, which she had braided in a coronet around her head. She wore Birkenstocks on her feet. The first thing she did was to extract a pack of cigarettes from her macramé purse and tap one out. She lit it up and inhaled.

"Looks like Aunt Lolly's really agitated. She never buys her own cigarettes."

Larrie's mother, Anna Maria, exited from the other side of the Toyota and walked up to Melanie. "Isn't Larrie back yet? It's after four."

Melanie shrugged. "She hasn't shown up. She did say she would be back today, didn't she?"

"That's what she told me. But if she doesn't make it back, it's her business, I guess. She's an adult. She told us where she was. She's probably wrapped up in something and lost track of time."

Melanie glanced over at Aunt Lolly. "So what's the verdict?"

"It's so exasperating," Anna Maria Smith said. "We all know that Aunt Lolly is one can short of a six-pack.

I asked the psychiatrist if we should put her in a home. The way I phrased it was 'in a supervised care facility.'

"He said, 'You could do that, or you could buy her a condo in Venice, California. She'd fit right in and it costs about the same.' I asked him what his professional opinion was. He said he'd write up his report but Aunt Lolly was 'borderline,' and while she had some 'harmless delusions' her memory was extraordinary, her intellect was as good as his, and as far as he could tell she could dress and bathe herself, although he wasn't going to comment on her fashion sense."

Melanie fought back a smile. "So what are you going to do?"

Anna Maria sniffed. "You know and I know she has her good days and her bad days. He saw her on a good day. She's in her eighties. She ran her car through a closed garage door. Next she'll be leaving the gas on and burning down the house."

Since Melanie had just been in Aunt Lolly's kitchen, she tried to remember what it looked like. "I think she has an electric stove."

"She can still start a fire with it, Melanie. Don't be a smart-mouth. We're taking Aunt Lolly for a second opinion. Then we're going to court to get power of attorney."

"I thought she was going to turn over control of her affairs to Larrie."

"Larrie isn't even here, now is she? And why should my daughter have that kind of a responsibility? At this stage in her life she doesn't need to be tied down looking after an old lady. Aunt Lolly has plenty of money to pay to live in a beautiful facility. I'm not talking about putting her in a snake pit. It's for Larrie's own good as much as it is for Lolly's."

Suddenly Melanie had a much clearer understanding of why Larrie's mother had been pushing for Aunt Lolly to enter a nursing home. Anna Maria was afraid Larrie would use caring for Aunt Lolly as a reason to avoid going on with her life. Anna Maria Smith might be right about that, and she was definitely right about Aunt Lolly. Melanie had seen it herself. The woman not only marched to a different drummer, she marched in a different world.

"He doesn't believe me," Van announced when he walked back to where Melanie sat looking out over the shadows lengthening across the lawn. Van had gone to sit in his Mercedes while he called Mr. G. on his mobile phone. Melanie assumed that Van wanted privacy, which didn't sit all that well with her. On the other hand, she recognized they were practically strangers even though they had been intimate last night. But all things considered, she had trust issues with him, and she felt she had reason to.

Van put one leg up on the step and leaned on his knee. "I'm finished, Mel. He says I'm holding out on him. He wants the emeralds and diamonds, no question about it. You were right about that. But he wants everything, he says. I have until tonight to get that armoire in the truck—with the Eye of the Snow Leopard inside it—and back to New York City. Or else."

"Or else what?"

"I didn't ask, but the answer is obvious."

"What are you going to do?"

"Be damned if I know. If I go back to the city and confront him, I'll be driving to my own funeral. I can see it now. I'll say, 'Mr. G., here are the diamonds and emeralds. They're all I have.' And he'll say, 'Here's all I have.' Then *bang bang bang* and I'll be dead."

Melanie tried to remember the *Godfather* films. *How do you deal with a boss of bosses?* she wondered. The best she could do right for Van at this moment was offer hope. "Maybe I'll think of something."

"I doubt it," Van said dismissively. "Let's go down to see Ticky. When I don't arrange for Sammy and Tony to come over and get the armoire, Mr. G. will. One way or another there's going to be trouble."

Melanie and Van started to walk across the lawn toward the barn. Van reached out and took Melanie's hand and pulled her to a halt. "I'm really sorry, Mel. I brought this situation here. I don't want you to get hurt. It would be safer if you go home."

Melanie's heart melted. Van wasn't perfect. He was a flawed gem, but he was a diamond in her eyes. She'd stand by her man. "I'll stick around. I can't believe those guys would show up and start shooting. I mean, this is real life, not the movies."

Van let out a deep breath. "These guys are from *New York*, Mel. They work for the G—uh, the family. These are the real people those movies were based on."

Chapter 29

For Larrie, her time in India was bittersweet. She was accomplishing almost everything she wanted to do. Despite some setbacks, Trelawny's Tastee Ice-Cream Cone Company was up and running. Gallons of ice cream had been made and stored in the cave filled with ice, ready to be taken into Lahore for the party. The entire village had gotten "ice-cream fever" for the food and the business opportunity, and everyone who wanted a job had been promised one.

Busy from dawn to dusk every day, Larrie barely found time to visit Lady Hare's dressmaker to have a ball gown made for the party. When she finally met with the fussy little man who ran a shop filled with Indian women bent over Singer sewing machines, she found that the wasp waist of the Edwardian style was made for an hourglass figure, not her long, lean body. She rejected every dress sample he showed her.

Finally, after the dressmaker brought out issues of the *Ladies' Home Journal* in an attempt to convince her that he made fashions that were all the rage, Larrie told him she'd design something of her own. She sketched out a flapper-era chemise with a dropped waist and a handkerchief hem. She told him she wanted it made from yellow China silk and decorated with bugle beads—as many as possible in the short time they had to create it.

Larrie was well aware that her style was twenty years ahead of its fashion debut, but she didn't care. The shorter, unstructured dresses of the 1920s suited her. She was quite pleased with the gown she created, although her appearance at the ice-cream party would probably raise eyebrows and cause whispers.

Let them blame it on my being an American, she decided.

While Larrie scooted around dealing with ice cream and goats and ball gowns and children, Jo spent most of the time moody and distant in his study. One day he took to his horse and rode out toward the mountains alone for an entire afternoon. Another day, he shut the study door and talked to Tara Singh for hours.

Once Larrie spied him out in the yard behind the house. He was with the orphans, teaching them how to milk the goats. He was squirting them with the warm milk from the teats and making them laugh. The boys climbed on his back and hung on his arms.

Larrie nearly called out to the boys to be careful of Jo's bandaged shoulder. But she thought better of it, and tiptoed away, pretending she had never been there and had never seen Jo—who said he never wanted to be a farmer—milking a goat and treating the children he once said he didn't care about with such kindness.

Although Larrie understood Jo's deepening depression, she would have liked to savor the precious time they still had together. Now, during the days of the Raj, his life was nearly as it had been before his enchantment. She could see what he had lost when it all vanished, when he vanished into the lamp.

In the quietest hours, especially those when the rooster woke her up at dawn, Larrie slipped quietly out

of bed and pondered what the guru had told her. All
Jo had to do to break the spell was to fall in love. He
couldn't do that because, as the guru said, he had locked
up his heart.

"Let's hope you can find the key," Harkrishnan had
told her. But Larrie didn't feel any closer to discovering
the key now than she did when she was sitting on the
cold ground in Baltistan.

As for her own feelings for Jo—they were different
than those she had had for Ryan.

Sitting in the Punjabi kitchen, a warm cup of tea in her
hand, Larrie found she could now remember Ryan without breaking down. She had wrapped up the watches in
a velvet cloth that Amita had found for her. She never
felt like wearing either one again. And she had gotten to
a point where she thought about Ryan with a little sadness and a lot of smiles. When she looked back, or rather
forward, from here, so far away in every sense, she saw
that her love for Ryan had been innocent, undemanding, and simply always present, always there.

She reminisced, while she sat in that silent kitchen
with the sky just beginning to lighten and the birds starting to sing, about how she and Ryan met. The summer
before she went off to college, she had been just seven-
teen. She had rejected taking a waitress job or working
in McDonald's, and found she could make more money
working in a dress factory in the Wyoming Valley. It was
hard, backbreaking, tedious labor.

But Zane, the shop foreman, knew her dad, and so he
always looked out for her. Sometimes she and the older
man talked during her coffee breaks, and once in a while
he said hi during lunch too.

One day he asked if Larrie had a photograph of herself she could give him.

The only photo Larrie had was one of those hideous
school pictures taken during senior year for the year-

book. Her red hair looked Day-Glo orange against the blue background and her freckles danced across her face like spots—or zits.

She asked Zane why he wanted it.

Zane gave her a broad smile. "I am going to give it to my son. You're perfect for him. I think he should marry you."

And Zane was right.

The very first time Larrie ever saw Ryan was one Friday night when Zane convinced her father to drive Larrie over to their house on some flimsy pretext. Larrie suspected the real purpose of the visit was for her to meet Zane's son, so she had dressed carefully in clean jeans and a cute halter top.

When she got there, Zane told her Ryan was in the family's garage working on a car. She shyly went to the open garage door. A tall, skinny twenty-year-old in a torn white T-shirt was half leaning, half lying across a fender, trying to reach something inside the engine of an old car. He looked up at her. His face was black with grease, his hair stuck up all over the place, he was wearing pants that didn't fit right, and he couldn't seem to utter a word, even to say hello.

Larrie thought, *Sorry, Zane, your son is not for me!*

But a half hour later, after Ryan had run upstairs and showered, changed his clothes, and reappeared in the kitchen where Zane was still talking to Larrie's dad while Larrie wondered why they couldn't go home, the grease-covered geek in the garage had been transformed. He was gorgeous. He was sexy. He was the man for her. She fell in love, not at first, but at second sight.

Later Ryan told her he fell in love with her the minute he looked at her picture.

That's how their love was—easy, complete, and forever. They never doubted each other, never even had a fight. All they needed to be happy was each other. And they were happy, ridiculously happy, until the war in the Middle East and death tore them apart.

John "Jo" Trelawny was not easy like Ryan. He was infuriating. He was argumentative. He was demanding. He was complex, troubled, brave, strong, generous, loyal, very kind to animals and children, and a man's man whom women watched with hungry eyes. Larrie knew she loved him. She wanted to love him for the rest of her days. But that couldn't happen because he was a genie, as insane and impossible as it seemed.

As long as he was a genie, he couldn't be more than an interlude in her life: someone who had been there and then would be gone. That fact was a torment to Larrie, but she wouldn't have changed a minute of their time together. It had been better than the best of all possible dreams.

Funny enough too, although it signaled an ending to her adventure in the Punjab, she found herself looking forward to Lady Bunny Hare's fabulous ice cream–engagement–bon voyage party. She realized what an amazing experience it would be to experience a history and meet people she had only read about.

For one thing, Bunny had assured Larrie she would meet the British viceroy of India, Lord Minto. For another, Bunny, being under the mistaken impression that Larrie was a Theosophist, had gone to a tremendous amount of trouble to invite the feminist and occultist Annie Besant to the affair. Besant had to travel all the way from Madras, but she accepted the invitation, lured by the promise of a generous donation from Lord Hare for the Theosophist ashram there.

Yet the very best part of the evening would be the company of the dashing Jo Trelawny, her escort, her genie, and in the eyes of the Raj, her husband-to-be. She wanted him to show her off, and she relished the thought of being seen with him. For a few hours, lanky, freckled, nonglamorous Larrie would be Cinderella at the ball, with Prince Charming at her side.

She had an unacknowledged, niggling worry that all wouldn't happen as she hoped. She knew Charlotte Brontë's words, "Life is so constructed that an event does not, cannot, will not match the expectation," since Melanie—who loved to memorize quotations—said them often enough. But Larrie could not imagine what could possibly go wrong.

Then, at the end, when the party was over, she would make a wish to go back home.

She and Jo had come up with a plan for their departure from India and the early twentieth century. First Jo informed the servants, as well as his colonial friends, that he and his new fiancée would be traveling to America for a prenuptial visit with Larrie's parents. As their fabricated story further explained, directly after Lady Hare's party, they would take the night train to Bombay and from that port, a ship would sail them east to America's California shore.

By Thursday night, the servants might have wondered about the absence of packing and amassing of any luggage, except for a single satchel which, although none of them knew it, contained just one item, a Persian rug. But whatever Jo had told Tara Singh during their long morning discussion kept the subject of packing trunks from being broached by anyone.

Jo told everyone he and Larrie would be back in time for their grand wedding in the fall.

No one had reason to doubt them. An item even appeared in the *Times of India* about Lieutenant John Trelawny's trip to Pennsylvania to meet the parents of his intended bride. But no fabrication or carefully constructed lie could alleviate Larrie's concern for the orphans she had taken in, particularly Mayree. Jo, with a generosity far beyond anything Larrie expected, had arranged their financial support. They would have this home for their own and be cared for by Bibi or another nanny until each was sent off to boarding school in England.

"You said you didn't have a farthing from your parents," Larrie reminded Jo when he told her he had met with a lawyer the day he rode out on his horse and set up a trust fund for the orphans' security. "And you said you began an exporting business to raise cash for your adventuring. Where has this money come from?"

"My grandfather left me something in his will. He and my father didn't get along, and he thought my older brothers were rotters too. My inheritance is enough to live on. I'm not rich by some standards, but as I once told you, I was an officer and a gentleman."

Reading between the lines, Larrie concluded that John "Jo" Trelawny was more than wealthy enough.

Yet the knowledge that she had given the orphans far better lives than they would have had without her didn't stop Larrie from feeling miserable to the point of tears when she thought of leaving. Worst of all, the thought of never again seeing Mayree and the thought of how the child would grieve at her absence brought a searing pain that almost drove Larrie to her knees.

She had even asked Jo about the possibility of taking Mayree with her into the future. But as resilient as any child is, Jo felt that to take a five-year-old from her culture—and the life she was meant to lead in her own time—might be disastrous and would certainly be wrong.

Larrie understood; she even agreed, in principle. But she couldn't make her emotions go along with it. She knew she was going away forever. That precious little girl might spend her entire childhood waiting for Larrie to come back. And when "Mama" didn't return, would the sense of abandonment scar Mayree too deeply to ever heal?

Tormented by these thoughts of Mayree and worried about Jo's fate in the future, where he predicted he would be thrown by a third wish onto the waters of fate and disappear, Larrie found she couldn't sleep a wink on their last night in the village house.

Jo stayed up too, with hollowed eyes and rigid jaw, his face like that of a man condemned to death. He paced. He drank brandy. He stared out into the night. And so it came to pass that Larrie and Jo didn't spend their last night in India as two lovers entwined in each other's arms. They spent it feeling miserable.

Over and over, Larrie kept asking herself the question, *What am I going back to the twenty-first century for?*

The only answers she had were *Aunt Lolly needs me* and *It is where I belong*.

Chapter 30

Larrie in her flapper dress of bugle beads and yellow silk, Jo in the impressive light blue uniform and black turban of the Forty-first Bengal Lancers, looked as handsome a couple as there had ever been. They walked arm in arm to the front door of Jo's Punjab home. Larrie managed a bright smile. Jo winked when he said good-bye.

The servants waved to them as they got into the governor's own black Ford Model N, sent by Bunny to get them and causing a great sensation as it pulled away from the house. The servants kept waving at Sahib and Memsahib all the way down the drive. Only Tara Singh looked ghastly—stone-faced and grim.

Even the children took their leaving well, with only a few sniffles from some of the girls and tears in the eyes of the boys. Mayree buried her face in Bibi's lap and refused to look at Larrie or give her one last kiss, no matter how much Larrie pleaded. Finally Jo pulled her away from the child and said, "Let well enough alone, Larrie. She's going to be fine."

In Lahore, a crowd of beautifully dressed young ladies chattering like sparrows gathered around the buffet table in the reception hall of the governor's mansion. After taking just a few steps into the room, Larrie heard a woman's voice whispering behind her: "Do you think she bobbed it herself? Red hair is gauche enough, but to have it cut that short! You'd think she wanted to be a man."

Another voice, nasal and aristocratic, responded, "If she paid someone to do *that*, she'd better get her money back. It's hideous. I cannot believe a woman of that caliber landed Jo Trelawny. Look at her strange gown. It's like a slip. Why, she has no bosoms or bum."

But on this occasion, when Larrie heard those unkind things, she just laughed. Those unimportant words couldn't hurt her anymore.

"What's so amusing, Larrie?" Jo asked, his face tense and his manner stiff.

"Something I overheard, that's all. Here comes Bunny, you better be nice."

Bunny was dressed in a fantastical gown of feathers in speckled grays and browns. She looked a bit like a stuffed owl. She pitter-pattered across the room with outstretched arms. She embraced Jo and hugged Larrie.

"We're serving the ice-cream cones in just a few minutes. I don't want to chance its melting. And you'll never guess. Annie Besant has brought that rabble-rouser Mr. Gandhi along—to talk about political reform. The Earl of Minto is about to have a seizure. It's going to be a scandal. I hope no one pulls a gun."

Her little nose twitched and she quivered with excitement.

Jo said reassuringly, "Gandhi preaches nonviolence, Lady Hare. He won't have a gun—and I don't think he's in danger here."

"He's already told me he won't eat the ice cream. He eats only a few very odd foods. But everyone else cannot wait to try it. Bingo Berry is on everyone's tongue. Oh, here it comes!"

"Lady Hare, how brilliant!" Larrie cried.

Instead of servants circulating with trays, Lady Hare had somehow obtained pushcarts replicating Larrie's own design, with TRELAWNY'S TASTEE ICE-CREAM CONES stenciled on the side. The servants positioned the carts around the room and dipped the ice cream into cones for the guests, who queued up and stood in lines.

And while everyone licked and got very cold mouths, a band on a raised platform played George M. Cohan's "Give My Regards to Broadway" in honor of Larrie's American home.

Larrie felt humbled at the kindness of her hosts, and then bowled over when she saw a wonderfully handsome man come weaving through the crowd of guests to greet them. Sir Lancelot Hare grabbed Jo's hand and thumped him on the back, saying things like "You old dog, you." Then he turned to Larrie. "The lovely Larissa Smith, I presume."

Larrie couldn't help herself—she stared. Then she stammered she was pleased to meet him. He could have stepped out of a storybook, he was so grand. Sir Lancelot turned to Jo and said he intended to announce their engagement to the guests—and how did Jo feel about that?

Larrie stole a look at Jo, who although he didn't smile, politely gave Lord Hare a little bow. "I would be honored, sir. I don't think most of your guests believe I really intend to wed. Perhaps if it comes from the proper authority, they will."

"After seeing your bride-to-be, I don't know how anyone would doubt it. You are a stunningly beautiful woman, Ms. Smith. And from what my wife tells me, an extremely intelligent one with quite a head for business."

"She flatters me, Lord Hare. But thank you for your kind words," Larrie responded, thinking that she could become quite fond of Lord and Lady Hare. She then realized she could come to love the ancient, mysterious, dangerous, colorful land of the Punjab too. Perhaps, like Jo, she had already "gone native," and with a stab of regret coursing through her, she knew she'd miss the Punjab and its people very much.

Meanwhile Lord Hare had taken Jo and Larrie by their elbows and steered them to the front of the room. "May I have everyone's attention please!"

The noise of the crowd abated first to a murmur and then to silence.

"As all of you know, my wife has hosted this party to launch a new Indian enterprise, the first ice cream company on the subcontinent. You have tasted its product. Can we have three cheers if you liked it?"

The room erupted in *"Hip hip, hooray! Hip hip, hooray! Hip hip, hooray!"*

Lord Hare's hearty laugh boomed out. "I take it that you do. But this party is also to honor a special man and the woman he has asked to be his wife. As all of you know, our own Lieutenant Jo Trelawny proved himself in the Battle of the Sikhs. He has received the Crown's highest award, the Victoria Cross, for valor in the face of the enemy. His only failing has been off the battlefield— on the playing field of love. He won many a lady's heart but never lost his own.

"Now I am happy to announce the engagement of John 'Jo' Trelawny to Ms. Larissa Smith of Pennsylvania, America!"

The band launched into "Yankee Doodle Boy."

Yelling over the sound of the music, Lord Hare concluded, "I congratulate them and wish them all the happiness in the world. Can I have three more cheers?"

Again the room rocked with *"Hip hip, hooray! Hip hip, hooray! Hip hip, hooray!"*

It was only when the final cheer faded away that the first bullet broke the window glass near where the odd little brown man named Gandhi had last been seen.

Women began screaming. Men shouted. To Larrie the noise sounded like emergency sirens rising and falling. People dropped to the ground or ran. She was aware of Jo pushing her down, then saying close to her ear, "I think it's time we got out of here."

More shots rang out. Glass broke. People kept screaming. Jo put his arm around Larrie and guided her out of the hall. He found the satchel where he had left it, hidden behind an ornamental stand. Holding Larrie's hand, he pulled her outside into a rapidly falling dusk, where Larrie could see people running out of the mansion and where Jo tugged her toward a wall where they wouldn't be seen. The moment they stepped behind it and into the shadows, Jo muttered something that Larrie swore sounded like abracadabra.

With a flash of light and rush of wind, Larrie felt the carpet leave the ground and sail toward the darkening sky. Up they went, up above the governor's mansion with people running from it in great confusion, up above the crowded streets of Lahore, up above the rail line leading toward the village, up above the Punjab soon to be forever gone.

Jo was again kneeling on the carpet at Larrie's back. She realized he no longer wore his uniform, but was in native garb, his chest bare, his skin tanned dark, and when he shifted his weight, she heard the bells around his ankles ring.

"You're going home, Larrie," he said in a voice rippled with pain. "And I am going back to my lamp for an eternity of servitude."

"It doesn't have to be that way," Larrie said, blinking away tears for Jo, for herself, for the children and land she was leaving in the past, for the astonishing world she had discovered far away from her own country and her own time.

Larrie could barely hear Jo's voice when he answered. "I see no escape from my enchantment. It is not that I will not, but I *cannot*, it seems, fall in love."

Larrie didn't respond. She remembered the guru's words. She wasn't about to give up searching for the key to unlocking Jo's heart. She didn't feel defeated. She was sure the answer lay before her.

Above the magic carpet the stars began to emerge, throwing diamonds across black velvet as they flew to the west. Larrie's mind stilled. She became very calm. Her resolve stiffened. She was not a quitter. She was not done. This adventure had all happened for a reason. What it was, she didn't yet know. But the answer would come.

She remembered one of her favorite poems, one Aunt Lolly taught her, telling Larrie that when you memorize a verse, you can carry it with you always. Poetry, Aunt Lolly went on to say, is the medicine that can bolster courage and give strength to a failing heart.

Larrie reached up and squeezed Jo's hand, which rested heavily on her shoulder. Then, looking out into the darkening sky as the carpet flew across the miles and years, she recited the final stanzas of Arthur Hugh Clough's "Say Not the Struggle Naught Availeth," the part she loved the best:

> For while the tired waves, vainly breaking,
> Seem here no painful inch to gain,
> Far back, through creeks and inlets making,
> Comes silent, flooding in, the main.
> And not by eastern windows only,
> When daylight comes, comes in the light;
> In front the sun climbs slow, how slowly!
> But westward, look! the land is bright.

Chapter 31

Ticky Blackstone did not flinch. His backbone straightened. His features hardened. His eyes glistened. He listened carefully as Van Killborn broke the news. Trouble was coming.

According to this guy—the same one who drove the fancy Mercedes, and who Ticky had pegged as being up to no-good since Day One—the Sparrow's Nest should expect an attack. It was coming by stealth or by frontal assault, sometime tonight, from those two thugs from New York in the hoity-toity black, gold-stenciled Killborn moving van.

Ticky checked the safety on his gun and listened without comment as the nervous New York dealer spilled his guts all over Larrie's tack room office. Ticky nodded and regarded the well-dressed, too-good-looking-to-have-to-try-very-hard fellow who had just learned the hard way that you don't shit where you eat.

At least he came clean in the end. It wasn't easy to admit it when you had been a low-down skunk and miserable sonofabitch. Ticky gave the guy points for doing the right thing—course he didn't seem to have any other option. But okay, Ticky would give credit where credit was due.

Ticky shook his head when he looked at Melanie

O'Casey. She held on to the fellow's arm with a grip that meant he wasn't going nowhere except with her, not that he seemed to be fighting the inevitable. The guy ogled her like she was a homecoming queen. Beauty in the eye of the beholder as they say. But one thing was for sure, the poor girl had it bad and there was no point in expecting a lick of sense from her now. She was dumber than dirt in love.

Ticky suggested to Melanie that she go on home and wait this thing out. Things might get rough. She'd only be in the way. She wouldn't have none of it. She was "standing by her man," she said. Ticky liked to have barfed.

Once the story was told, Ticky let the facts cogitate in his brain for a moment. Then he spoke. "We'll be waiting for 'em. We'll let 'em get what they're coming for. We'll catch 'em in the act. Then we'll bust 'em good. The only place those two knuckleheads will be traveling tonight is to the county jail."

The agitated blond guy, that Killingbird fellow, asked Ticky how could they possibly stop the perps. He said they'd be armed. They'd have a truck. They'd just drive off with the armoire and the jewels.

Ticky put a finger in his ear and found some pesky earwax. He flicked it off his nail into the wastebasket. "Don't you worry none. I have a plan."

Ticky picked up the office phone and called the twins. He told them that he had a Code Red down at the antiques barn. They should load their pickup with every hunting rifle they had. Maybe a couple tire irons and baseball bats too. Get over here *stat*, as they always said on *ER*. But once they got all the weaponry off their vehicle, they were to drive on down to the neighbor's place and park. This was an undercover operation. Did they understand that?

Their response—"Ya-hoo! We're going to kick some ass tonight!"—could be heard loud and clear by everybody. "Just high-spirited kids, that's all," Ticky said to the Van fellow, who looked about to faint.

Then Ticky called Wayne Smith and gave him a quick rundown of the problem. Wayne promised he'd get his biggest wrecker ready. The minute those Mafioso guys left their truck and entered the Sparrow's Nest, Wayne was going to come rumbling up the road. He'd ram those suckers if he had to, but they wouldn't be taking that moving van into town.

Feeling pretty damned good about his preparations, Ticky picked up the phone for the final time. It was introducing a wild card. But Ticky knew there was no better ally in a fight, no smarter field general, nobody who knew more about the tactics of battle, so he made the call.

"Ms. Lolly? Ticky here. We got a war on our hands. You got your digital camera with the infrared attachment, like you showed me? Good. Get down here to the barn and I'll tell you my plan."

Chapter 32

When Larrie found herself back in her own living room, the dogs barked and danced like whirling dervishes as they made circles on the couch, the chairs, the rugs, overwhelmed with joy at her return. She fell to her knees and wrapped her arms around them. At least her dogs were glad she had come home. Only after checking out each one, running her hands over their fur, and planting kisses with abundance, did Larrie look around. The first thing she noticed was the gathering darkness that lay outside the windows.

Jo was there, standing by the fireplace, staring at the Aladdin's lamp on the mantel. Larrie didn't have to read minds to know what he was thinking. No longer wearing a watch—both hers and Ryan's were wrapped in the velvet cloth and stashed in the little purse she had carried to the ball—she glanced over at the clock on the wall. It was nearly nine. She hoped it was still Wednesday, and, if so, they had only missed getting back on time by a few hours.

A wave of relief passed over her. She ran upstairs and changed into a pair of jeans and a Henley shirt after she hung her beautiful gown and beaded purse in her closet. She intended to go check on Aunt Lolly next. After that, she'd give Melanie and her mother a call, but everything seemed in order. She felt confident nothing could have gone wrong.

When she came back to the living room, her three dogs had started barking and running toward the front door. "Do you guys need to go out? Huh? Do you? Do you? Did Ticky lock you up in here before he went home? I need to stretch my legs a bit too. Come on, let's go."

She waded into their midst and threw open the front door. The dogs took off like racehorses out of the starting gate. Barking angrily, they sprinted down the front yard. Larrie followed them with her eyes. She quickly saw what had them riled.

"Hey! There are headlights down there! That's Van's truck. What's it doing parked in front of the barn? I think the barn door is open. Jo! Some guys are taking furniture from the shop. I don't believe this! I'm going down there. Who the hell do they think they are?"

She rushed outside and started running toward the van.

"Larrie! Stop! Wait!" Jo yelled and started after her.

"Hey! Hey, you!" Larrie screamed when she spotted the two thugs who had driven up with Van from New York City, the ones Larrie thought were carrying guns. The barn door had been pushed open although no lights were on inside. The two men were struggling to get the big mahogany and teak armoire up on the loading gate of the black box truck with KILLBORN & SONS written in gold on the side.

"Stop that! Hey! Stop!" Larrie screamed again. The men gave one last push to get the armoire in position; then they turned toward Larrie. One of them reached inside his jacket. Maybe he was going to pull out a gun, but Larrie's dogs got to him first.

Teddy, the sturdy Chow Chow, the most aggressive of Larrie's dogs, launched an attack at one man's leg with the other two dogs quickly joining in. Both men started yelling. One of them kicked Taco, and the little Chihuahua yelped.

My dogs! Larrie thought, and the inside of her mind turned cold. All rational thought fled and was replaced by rage. She had one purpose—to go after that monster with her bare hands.

She didn't hear Jo yelling "No!" behind her. She didn't hear Wayne's biggest wrecker backing with purposeful intent down the road. She didn't notice Shem and Shaun charging out of the barn with tire irons in their hands. She didn't see Aunt Lolly snapping away with her digital camera. She didn't see Ticky Blackstone taking a firing position and carefully aiming his gun.

Larrie reached the truck, and with a banshee's yell, she leapt at the man who had kicked her dog.

Right at that moment Wayne's wrecker tapped the front of the Killborn truck. The van jerked backward with a sickening jolt. The massive armoire, which the two muscular thugs could barely move even with the help of a dolly, rocked crazily on the loading gate, tipped, and began to fall.

Larrie saw the great bulk of it above her and screamed. Ticky got startled and squeezed the trigger. A blinding, burning pain filled Larrie's head. Then she was sliding down into blackness, down into oblivion, down into nothingness. She was falling fast into an eternal darkness—until someone grabbed her arm.

Larrie stopped falling. She turned her head to look behind her and see whom or what was there.

What she saw was a long tunnel, an ethereal light, and a familiar outline. She recognized immediately who it was. "Ryan! What—? What are you doing here?"

Ryan let go of her arm and stepped back. Larrie could see he was in his uniform. She scrambled onto her feet and found they both were standing in a green, grassy field filled with a strange shimmering light.

Ryan gave her a heart-melting smile. "The more important question, Larrie, is what are *you* doing here? You were leaping again before you looked, weren't you?"

Larrie felt confused. "I don't know. I don't remember." And she really didn't care. All she wanted to do was throw herself into Ryan's arms, but she couldn't seem to move. She put all her longing into her voice and said, "I never thought I'd see you again."

Ryan looked at her the way he always did, like somebody had given him a pony for Christmas. "Ah, Larrie, you were always going to see me again. When it was time."

Larrie had no difficulty hearing Ryan, she saw him whole and distinct in front of her, yet she could scarcely believe he was there. Happiness exploded inside her, followed by the wrenching understanding that he was dead, and perhaps so was she.

"Ryan," she cried out with anguish in her voice, "it was so hard for me, you being gone."

"I know that, sweetheart. I'm sorry about hurting you so. I didn't want to leave you. It was just my time. But I never did go, really. I've been watching out for you."

"You have? Then you know what happened. About the genie and all. About Jo." She paused. "Do you mind? About Jo?"

"Somebody had to make sure you didn't get in too much trouble, Larrie. Jo seemed like the right man to me. I sure wasn't going to let you get mixed up with that New York guy. He would have made a move on you if I let him. I made sure he didn't."

Suddenly Larrie began to laugh with a sudden understanding. "I should have known that was you, Ryan. Taking that battery cable off is something you'd do."

"I thought you'd figure it out sooner or later."

Larrie studied Ryan carefully. He had begun to fade. He was there but he wasn't there. She was afraid he was going to go, and she couldn't reach out, hold him fast, and make him stay. She needed to tell him what was in her heart. "Jo's not like you. He's a different kind of man. Nobody's like you, Ryan. Nobody ever will be."

"Larrie, stop worrying. I understand. I know how you feel. I'll always love you, but you have to go on. But you're wrong about John Trelawny. If you'd think about it, Larrie, we're more alike than not. He's just serving in a different battalion in another war in another time."

"Ryan, wait! You're fading away. I don't want to leave you!" Larrie felt as if her heart was going to shatter all over again.

"You have to go back now, Larrie. It's not your time. But don't worry. Even if you think that nobody's there, I am." Ryan blew her a kiss and was gone.

Larrie's head was pounding. It ached like somebody had clubbed her with a baseball bat. She could hear voices.

"It's okay! It's okay! She started breathing again!" It was Melanie O'Casey's voice.

Larrie moaned, tried not to move her aching head, and opened her eyes. Melanie knelt at her side. "Mel? What happened?"

"Don't move! Don't you dare try to get up. You might have internal injuries. The ambulance is on the way."

"What happened to me?" Larrie asked again.

Melanie fought tears. "Ticky shot you and that armoire fell over on top of you at the same time. We thought you were dead."

"I'm shot?" Larrie didn't feel that awful. She did have a loathsome headache, and she decided that her chest hurt when she took a breath. Maybe shock kept her from feeling the wound. "How bad is it?"

"Not bad. I don't think you're really shot. It looks like the bullet grazed your temple. You're not even bleeding much. That half-ton armoire is what just about killed you, I think."

Larrie irrationally felt like laughing but managed to just smile. "It's a fitting way for an antiques dealer to die. Crushed to death by a vintage clothespress." Then she carefully moved her head from side to side. "Where's Jo? Where did he go?"

"Who's Joe?" Melanie asked, following Larrie's gaze and not seeing anyone.

"He's my—never mind. He was running behind me. You couldn't miss him. Long dark hair. He didn't have a shirt on, or shoes. He wore white pants, and he had bells around his ankles."

Melanie shot an angry look at somebody behind Larrie. "Your frigging bullet gave her a concussion or worse, Ticky. She's delirious."

Aunt Lolly's voice cut in, angry and cold. "No, she is not delirious. You weren't even here when it happened, Melanie. You and Van were hiding inside the shop." Aunt Lolly's sweet, wrinkled face appeared behind Melanie. She shoved the young woman aside, crouched down, and took Larrie's hand.

"Aunt Lolly, where is he? Where is Jo?"

"I don't know, Larrie. He was here, but I saw something—I think he's gone."

"What happened? What did you see?" She squeezed Lolly's bony hand.

"The gun went off and the armoire fell on you. Jo was right behind you. He let out an awful yell. He grabbed that armoire with his bare hands and lifted it off you like it weighed nothing. He was yelling your name.

"Then he must have seen you weren't breathing and fell to his knees. He was screaming, 'Don't die. Don't you dare die on me.' Then he stared up at the sky as if he saw something there and yelled, 'Take me, not her, you bastard.'

"Your young man was distraught, nearly out of his mind. He leaned over and put his cheek next to yours but I could hear every word. He said, 'Larrie, I love you. Please don't die.' And that's when it happened."

"What happened, Aunt Lolly?"

"There was a flash, like a lightning strike without thunder. Your young man had vanished. One minute he was kneeling there right next to you. Then like magic, he was gone."

Melanie cut in. "Ms. Smith, that's not true. There wasn't anybody here, was there, Ticky?"

Ticky hung back, ashen-faced. He still clutched the gun in a shaking hand. "I don't know. When I thought I killed Larrie, I blacked out or something. I don't know if there was anybody here. But somebody pulled the armoire off her. Weren't the twins. They had tackled the two New York guys right before I shot."

Aunt Lolly stood up ramrod straight. "Of course somebody did. It was Larrie's young man. I can prove it."

"How can you prove it?" Melanie challenged her.

"I took pictures of the whole thing." She knelt down again next to Larrie and pushed the playback button on the camera. "I'll hold this for you. You go ahead and look."

Larrie did. Jo was there, big as life, just as her aunt had said. "Aunt Lolly," she whispered, "I don't want anybody to see these. Go up to your computer and get them off the card, please."

Lolly, always a good soldier, stood up and walked off, and did exactly as she was told.

Chapter 33

Larrie heard emergency sirens wailing through the night. They sounded like women screaming. A state police car pulled up along the berm of the Old Highway, another car right behind it. The Kunkle fire-department ambulance careened around them and drove onto the lawn.

Mel knelt down next to Larrie again, her eyes desperate. "The police! Larrie, you have to know that Van had nothing to do with this!"

Larrie was thinking about Jo and what might have happened to him. She hadn't even thought about the theft. "Huh? Van? You mean Van Killborn, the dealer? I didn't even know you knew him."

"I'm going to marry him," Mel said with a tremulous smile.

"I must be delirious. I can't make sense out of any of this," Larrie mumbled.

Two volunteer EMTs had pulled the stretcher out of the ambulance. One of them set it up next to Larrie while the other took her pulse and started asking her questions. Larrie kept telling them she felt fine, but they wouldn't let her get up.

Ticky was somewhere behind her saying over and over again that he was sorry, it was an accident. She managed to tell him to please shut up and stop worrying about it. She wasn't even hurt, not much anyway.

She heard one of the state police officers yelling at somebody. Red lights were flashing. A lot of people seemed to be running around. All of a sudden a reporter pushed a microphone into her face before the EMT told the toothy young woman to get her butt out of there.

Larrie just wanted to close her eyes and go to sleep. She felt jostled as the EMTs got her onto the stretcher. She glanced over toward Melanie just in time to see Van walk over and wrap her best friend in his arms. *Either I am dreaming or totally crazy*, Larrie thought as she was loaded into the ambulance and the EMT slammed the door.

"You're rich, Larrie. You'll never have to worry about money again." Melanie was talking. Larrie was in her own farmhouse and in her own bed. Her three dogs were on the bed too, pinning down her legs in a comforting way. She felt emotionally and physically drained. She had trouble focusing on Melanie's words.

She kept thinking that Jo must have broken the enchantment. He must have gone back to his life in India. The pain of knowing she had lost him was offset with the happiness that he had been set free. He would be home again. And even though she couldn't return, perhaps his presence would help soothe Mayree.

But she felt terribly unhappy. The first thing she had insisted on, after Melanie drove her back from the hospital and helped her into the house, was to go to the mantel. The old brass lamp was there. She grabbed it and rubbed it. She rubbed and rubbed. She demanded the genie appear. Nothing happened. She broke down in tears.

Melanie gently helped her upstairs to bed. Larrie didn't want Jo to be in the lamp, she really didn't.

But how devastating it felt when he didn't appear. She couldn't keep thinking about it without dissolving in tears. She told Melanie she wanted to go to sleep.

"You can't sleep. The doctor told me to keep you up for a little while longer. How's your vision? If you start seeing double let me know. You might have a skull fracture. You know you were really lucky. You only have a couple of bruised ribs."

"I don't feel lucky. How's Ticky? He didn't get arrested, did he?"

"Him! I told him to put that gun away. I thought he was going to shoot Van. Maybe he should be in jail."

"He was trying to protect my property, Mel. He was helping me. He didn't do anything wrong."

"He shot you in the head, didn't he! But no, he's not in jail. He had a license for the gun, and it accidentally discharged. The cops took a statement and let him go. The two New York guys got arrested for breaking and entering and theft. They had outstanding warrants too. They're locked up. Van's okay. They questioned him and let him go. I told you he didn't have anything to do with it."

Larrie pressed her lips together for a moment and made a face. "Technically he didn't. But he was being sneaky all along. Are you sure you're in love with him?" Larrie had some concerns about this budding romance. She had never seen Melanie so infatuated.

"Van was wrong, Larrie. He admits it. As for being in love with him—oh, yes, I am. And the best part of it is"—she paused dramatically—"he's in love with me. Who would have believed it, an Adonis like that goes gaga for a fat, small-town librarian."

Larrie put an arm over her eyes to block out the light that Melanie insisted on keeping lit. "Stop putting yourself down, Mel. You're beautiful. I'm glad some man finally appreciates you. I'm not so glad it's this one."

"Well, I am! I understand why you don't have such a high opinion of him right now, but he's learned his lesson. Men can change, you know."

Larrie peeked at Melanie from under her forearm. Melanie looked happy, happier than Larrie had ever seen her. She decided to keep her criticisms unsaid.

"Men *can* change. I agree. Now tell me everything all over again, from the beginning, about you and Van, the treasure hidden in the armoire, and how the Eye of the Snow Leopard seems to be gone."

Melanie began recounting the events of the last two days in excruciating detail, especially the episodes involving Van. By the time she had finished, despite her best efforts to keep Larrie awake, her best friend had fallen deeply asleep.

The next morning—after taking care of the dogs, seeing herself being loaded into an ambulance in a video clip aired on the local NBC news, and having her frantic mother and father show up on her doorstep at the crack of dawn—Larrie went over to Aunt Lolly's apartment. There were some photographs she needed to see.

Aunt Lolly had tea brewing in a Sadler teapot, and seeing it made Larrie's breath stop for a minute. Sunlight and shadows played hide-and-seek on the kitchen wall. Then Larrie didn't notice anything except Jo, now the screensaver on Lolly's computer screen.

Aunt Lolly had downloaded the digital pictures of him from the camera onto her hard drive. There weren't many, three or perhaps four all told. Larrie sat down at the computer and played back the photos one by one. She made Aunt Lolly repeat exactly what Jo was saying in each frame. Her hand started to tremble. Her chest got tight. She didn't know whether to laugh or cry.

"It took my death to unlock his heart," she whispered more to herself than Aunt Lolly. "He loves me."

"I would certainly think so! The man nearly went crazy when he saw you weren't breathing and he thought you had passed on. He said he loved you out loud. I heard him."

Larrie stretched out her hand and traced the lines of Jo's face with her forefinger. "He broke the spell. He's free. He's back in India as a man. I suppose I should just be happy, but it's killing me."

Aunt Lolly studied Larrie with wise old eyes. "Why don't you tell me what happened. I have a pretty good idea what he was. I talked to him. He told me when he was born and about his life in the Raj. I saw you two ride out of here on a flying carpet. Your mother wants to lock me up in a nursing home for crazies, you know that, don't you? But I know what I saw."

Finally turning away from Jo's pictures on the computer screen, Larrie took an offered cup of tea, feeling a catch in her throat when she remembered where and when she had her last cup of it. Sipping it and sighing now and then, Larrie told Aunt Lolly the whole story, or as much of it as was necessary. She made certain she didn't leave out anything the guru had said.

Lolly listened attentively. She took off her glasses. She rubbed her eyes. Finally, she said, "We need to have a meeting."

"A meeting? With who?"

"Whom," Aunt Lolly corrected reflexively. "Your friend Melanie. And that Van person."

"Why?" Larrie asked.

"The butterfly effect, that's why."

"Aunt Lolly, my head hurts enough. Don't talk in riddles."

"Quite frankly, it seems like riddles have a lot to do with this situation. But what I meant was, the butterfly effect, in chaos theory, is the idea that a small thing, like the movement of air from a butterfly's wings, can set off

a chain of events that end up as a tornado. We have our-
selves a tornado. I want to find the butterfly."

"Okay, I'll get everyone together, but I think Josiah
Ydoboni's sister needs to be here too. Her brother obtained the lamp in the first place. It would help to get
as many details of that as we can. Besides, some of the
treasure found in the armoire rightly belongs to her."

Larrie stood up. She had no dizziness. She felt steady
on her feet. "I feel well enough to drive. I have a little
headache, but otherwise I'm none the worse for wear.
I'm going over to the house in Centermoreland and see
if I can locate her."

Larrie turned off the highway and took the second-
ary road called Monkey Hollow Drive that led to Josiah
Ydoboni's little stone cottage. She quickly discovered
that in the brief time she had been gone, weeds and
brush had taken over the lawn and sprung up in the
driveway.

*There must have been a lot of rain for it to grow up
this much*, she thought, paying attention to the deep ruts
that had appeared where she had parked the last time.
She braked hard to avoid a rabbit that darted in front of
her. Only then did she look through the windshield.

She blinked once, twice. The house was gone. All
that remained of the fairylike cottage was a low wall
of tumbled-down stones and front steps that now led
nowhere.

People have no sense of history or respect for the past,
Larrie inwardly raged. It infuriated her that most people
would rather demolish an old house and build a cheap
new one on the lot rather than take the time to restore
the lovely craftsmanship and keep the fine wood of an
earlier era. Obviously the people who had bought this
property had wasted no time in bringing in the wrecking
crew.

Larrie got out of her red truck. The wind whistled through the trees with a lonesome sound. She saw there was nobody for her to talk to. The construction on this lot hadn't been started. The new owners were nowhere around.

She gazed to her left and to her right, hoping to find nearby houses and neighbors who might know where she could reach Ms. Ydoboni. If they couldn't tell her that, they might remember which realtor had sold the house, and Larrie could track the old lady down through the real estate office.

The only house in sight was a farmhouse across the road, its white paint badly peeling and a rusted-out pickup truck on cement blocks in the front yard. Laundry had been hung out to dry on a clothesline. *Somebody must be home there*, Larrie thought, and marched determinedly across Monkey Hollow Drive.

A tired-looking woman with brown hair hanging in greasy strings around her face appeared at the combination screen and storm door when Larrie knocked. Larrie could hear a television tuned to a daytime soap opera blaring somewhere inside.

"I'm sorry to bother you, but I'm trying to find the sister of the man who lived across the road from you. In that stone cottage."

"That old place? Let me get my husband. He's lived here all his life. Carl! Carl! Some lady wants to talk to you."

A balding man in a white T-shirt dirty with egg yolk and coffee stains appeared next to his wife at the door. He had a sour look on his face and suspicion in his voice. "You want to talk to me? What about?"

"I don't want to talk to you. I mean I don't want to talk about you. I'm trying to find the sister of the old man who lived across the street. He died, you probably know that."

"Lady, he died a long time ago. I have no idea in holy hell where his sister might be. Didn't even know he had a sister." The man looked impatient and ready to leave.

Larrie felt annoyed. "It wasn't all that long ago. Not more than a month. Are we talking about the same man? He lived in the stone cottage over there. His sister was just staying there to settle the estate." She pointed across the street.

The man shook his head. "You sure must be confused. That house's been gone since the 1970s. Nobody lives over there."

"Gone for thirty years? It can't be the same family I'm talking about. The man's name was Josiah Ydoboni."

"Ydoboni?" The man looked thoughtful for a moment; then his face went from hostile to sympathetic. "Lady, somebody's been playing a real mean joke on you."

Larrie felt confused. "Why do you think that?"

"Ydoboni. That's *I Nobody* spelled backwards. *Nobody* lives there. You get it now?"

Chapter 34

By the time Larrie returned to Aunt Lolly's, feeling shaken as if the world had shifted beneath her feet and changed a familiar landscape into a land strange and unrecognizable, she found Melanie and Van waiting for her in the kitchen. Her dogs were there too. She sat down and Taco jumped up on her lap, leaning into her. The other two dogs sat at her feet, as close to her as they could get.

Melanie and Van sat nearly glued together too, Melanie holding fiercely to Van's hand.

"My family's business was burned to the ground last night," Van said in a shaky voice. "Nobody was hurt, but everything's gone. Everything."

"I'm sorry to hear that. I really am. What are you going to do now?" Larrie knew that much of the antiquities inventory must have been irreplaceable. Van had learned a lesson, and it was a bitter one, it seemed.

Surprisingly, Van sat up straighter. "I was warned that's what Mr. G. intended to do. Cervantes said, 'If you play with cats, you should expect to be scratched.' It was my own fault all this happened. But I had some good news. You remember those fellows who were arrested up here?"

"The two thugs who tried to steal the armoire? Sure, why?"

"I have a friend who's a detective in the New York police department. A cousin, actually. He called me this morning. One of those thugs had an outstanding warrant in New York for something petty, receiving stolen goods or something like that. But the FBI had been watching him. He's linked to some nasty murders. The feds offered him a deal if he'd incriminate his boss. According to my cousin, this particular criminal is not what they call a stand-up guy. He's telling everything he knows.

"Mr. G. is going to be arrested later today. He's going to have more important things to worry about than me. Maybe I'll never stop looking over my shoulder, but I think I'm going to be okay."

Larrie nodded. She wished she was going to be okay. She felt as if her heart had been slammed with a sledgehammer. She had lost love, found it again, and now lost it again. If she had it to do over, she wouldn't have come back to this century. Aunt Lolly seemed to have survived just fine without her. Maybe remaining in the past wouldn't have worked out in the long run, but this—she looked around with hollow eyes—this just didn't have meaning for her anymore.

Van cleared his throat. "Your aunt took the liberty of telling us your story."

Larrie's eyes opened wide. "Really? Do you believe her?"

Van nodded. "Melanie here was harder to convince than I was. I know there are things that happen that can't be explained by science and reason. But even she couldn't argue with the pictures of your genie. He was there, running down the yard behind you. He was lifting that half-ton piece of furniture as if it weighed nothing at all. He was kneeling next to you—and I could barely look at that one, his grief was so terrible on his face. Then where he had been kneeling was nothing, but you can see Melanie's foot entering the frame. She didn't see him, she said. You were lying there alone. That picture convinced her."

Larrie let out a deep sigh. "So you know what happened. Jo was my genie. He was here. He's gone. End of story. You can have half the diamonds and emeralds. They're yours. Sorry you didn't find the Eye of the Snow Leopard."

Van glanced over at Aunt Lolly. "We've been talking about that, your aunt and I. We don't think it's coincidental that the fabled gem came from the guru's village, the same guru who enchanted your Jo."

"So? I don't see that it matters. It's connected. But how?"

Van looked at Aunt Lolly again. She nodded that he should continue. "I also understand that one of the conditions for breaking the spell was that Jo had to get you to believe in magic—in genies, to be precise."

Larrie sighed again. "That's right. I mean, how could I not believe by that point? I wasn't dreaming the whole thing. I was really there."

"So you absolutely do believe in magic?"

"Yes. Yes, I do."

"Okay, then I'll go on with my reasoning. You were taken into the past by magic. Jo performed all the things he did by magic. The old guru, Harkrishnan, had powers, tremendous powers like a sorcerer's, to perform magic. Are you still with me on this?"

"I really don't know what you're trying to say."

"Listen to me, Larrie. What is it that you really want at this point? Maybe that's too big a question to ask you so soon, but do you know?"

Larrie stared with stricken eyes toward the window, seeing but not caring about the blue sky outside it. She hugged Taco tightly. "Yes, I know. I want to go back to the past, to Jo, to the house in the village, and to the children. I have nothing important for me here except for Aunt Lolly, my dogs, and Kitty. I mean, I love my parents, but they have a good life and I'm a grown woman. They keep telling me I have to go on with my own destiny."

Larrie looked at her best friend. "And of course I care about you, Mel. But it's not the same as wanting to be where I'm needed"—she stopped and took a shaky breath—"and where I'm loved."

"If you go back, the animals and I could go with you. If you want us to, that is," Aunt Lolly said briskly, trying not to let the tremor in her voice be heard.

"Would you want to?"

Lolly's eyes sparkled. "If you'd take me, I wouldn't miss it for the world."

Larrie turned her attention back to Van. "So you're implying there's a good chance I can use magic to get me back to India."

"And back to Jo. He's key, I'm sure of it. But yes, that's exactly what I mean. Look, I searched for this treasure for a long time. There have been too many coincidences. Ms. Ydoboni calling me, and then saying she made a mistake doing it. Then calling you and having you show up when I was leaving. Then you discover she doesn't even seem to have existed—but the estate you bought is sitting down in the barn. Magic has been part of this all along. I have a gut feeling nothing about what's happened has been accidental."

Larrie couldn't help but think Van had a point. "It sounds fantastic, impossible, but everything that's already happened has been fantastical and impossible. What's your idea? How do I do it? I don't have a third wish now that Jo is gone."

Van's voice started to sound excited. "I think you have to go down to your shop and start looking through Josiah Ydoboni's things. Melanie suggested to me that the Eye of the Snow Leopard might be still hidden among them. I dismissed her suggestion. I should always listen to Melanie." His glance in her direction was filled with adoration. "But whatever is there, I wasn't supposed to find it. You are."

Doubt showed on Larrie's face. "I don't know. It sounds like wishful thinking. We don't have any good reason to think there is anything still hidden there."

Van started to laugh. "It *is* 'wishful' thinking. But seriously, Larrie, the guru has engineered this. He's had a plan all along. I cannot believe he meant for Jo to fall in love and then be made to suffer for it. It would undercut everything the guru was trying to teach him—to believe in love, to not be afraid to love, to love no matter what the consequences."

Larrie shook her head. Van's theory was starting to make sense, although she herself still couldn't make sense of what she found, or didn't find, in Centermoreland. But maybe there really was something else hidden in Josiah Ydoboni's estate, something she was supposed to find.

"Okay." Larrie stood up and put Taco on the floor. "Let's go to the barn."

The funny thing—which wasn't really funny ha-ha, but odd or unexpected, funny in a way that suggested the gods were laughing at a great big joke being played on her—the funny thing was that the minute Larrie stepped into the barn she knew. She saw it immediately. She had completely forgotten what was so blatant, so obvious.

But it sat there right in front of her: the tiger desk. She rushed over to it. She knew where to look for something she hadn't noticed the first time she inspected it. Carved in the skirt of the desk, the tiger's face was a ferocious snarl. She recognized it. After all, she had seen it in real life. And there on one of the desk's legs, which formed the legs of the tiger and ended at the floor in four tiger paws, was a beautifully detailed, perfectly carved, and quite large angry bee.

When she saw it, she sat right down on the floor because her legs had lost the strength to hold her up. She ran her fingers over the bee, and the buzzing of the swarm in the forest sounded in her head.

Van walked up. "See if it moves, Larrie. Wiggle it a little."

Larrie tried. It didn't budge. It wasn't attached to the wood, it was carved from it. Disappointment washed over her. Since her legs had regained their strength, she managed to stand. "I don't suppose it will do any good to open the desk drawer," she said. "Anything in it would have been found long ago."

Van wasn't really listening. He had gone down on his hands and knees, and he was looking carefully at the bee. "Mel?" he called out. "Do you still have that poem in your wallet?"

"Yes, why?"

"Read it again, will you. Let Larrie hear it."

Melanie took it out and read:

> Small places in big things
> You have to look for wings
> Near a rose in the middle
> Use the key to fiddle
> And the treasure you look for
> will spring

Larrie's heart started to race. "Van, the bee has wings. Do you see a rose anywhere?"

Van knew if there was a rose, it had to be near the wings. But nothing was near the bee except the tiger's foot at the bottom of the desk leg. He started to laugh. "Larrie, look at the tiger's toes!"

Larrie dropped down on her knees. The middle toe of the tiger's paw wasn't a toe at all. It was a rosebud. "Wriggle it, Larrie. You do it! The escutcheon on the armoire swung to the side."

"It moves! It really moves. Oh! There's a tiny key inside and a lock on the outside of a little compartment." She picked up the miniature key, put it in the lock, and turned. The compartment, which turned out to be a hollow inside the tiger's paw, swung open. Larrie reached in and found a small pouch. She brought it out.

Sitting cross-legged on the floor, her fingers shaking violently, she loosened the drawstring of the pouch and opened it. The most beautiful ruby she had ever seen lay inside. It was mounted in gold and encircled in diamonds.

Van stared. "You found the Eye of the Snow Leopard, Larrie. My God, it's extraordinary."

The ruby flashed and sparkled in the palm of Larrie's hand. "But it doesn't tell me anything. It doesn't tell me how to get back to Jo." She felt her hopes crashing down.

Van's voice was gentle. "Turn it over, Larrie. See if anything's inscribed on the back."

Larrie hadn't even thought to do that, and normally that's one of the first things any dealer would do, to look for a maker's mark or a date. She flipped the ruby over. She saw the words right away. She started to smile, and then she threw back her head and laughed.

"What's it say, Larrie? Come on, tell us!" Melanie couldn't wait any longer. She put her arm around Van's waist and hugged him.

Larrie looked up at her friend. "It says, 'Genies give three wishes. You do have one left. Make it.'"

*   *   *

Holding the Aladdin's lamp tightly in her arms, accompanied by Aunt Lolly, her three dogs, Kitty in a cat carrier, and the Eye of the Snow Leopard in her pocket, Larrie found herself standing in the wood-paneled colonial elegance of Jo's parlor.

It was a few days, in future time, after she and Van and Melanie found the fabulous gem in the tiger desk and the secret of returning to the past. Larrie, having learned from experience and Jo's example, resisted the impulse to leave the twenty-first century that very minute and spent ample time settling all her affairs before she made her wish.

She had signed the barn, along with the house and property, over to Melanie. Van had agreed to take over the antiques business—with the promise to keep Ticky as the handyman. The Sparrow's Nest would provide the fresh start he hoped for.

With Melanie's and Van's help, Larrie also dreamed up a cover story to tell to her parents. Larrie dropped in to see them and rattled on about meeting a young man at the research library, about taking a sabbatical in India, about being in touch with them but not knowing when she was coming home. And yes, she was taking Aunt Lolly along. She said good-bye to them with tears, but no regrets. She didn't feel as if she were leaving them. She felt as if she were going back to her real home.

Only after everything was ready, when every loose end she could think of had been addressed, did she hug Melanie and gather Aunt Lolly, the dogs carefully secured with leashes, and Kitty mewing in her carrier, next to her on the Persian rug.

Then she wished. A big wish. A life-altering wish. A wish she wanted with all her heart to make.

Now she was back in the Punjab. She had done it. She couldn't wait to see Jo. The dogs started to bark. Tara Singh ran into the room. "Memsahib, you're home!"

"Yes, Tara, I am. Where's Jo?"

Tara Singh's face changed from surprise to alarm. "Isn't Sahib Trelawny with you? He is not here."

Larrie's heart froze; her blood turned cold. Had she come back to the past only to find that Jo had not? Where was he? Was he even alive? She choked out the question, "Tara Singh, didn't Jo return?"

"Yes, yes! He came home yesterday. But memsahib, he was in a rage. He made me get his horse saddled. He wouldn't let me go with him. He said he was riding into the mountains, to Baltistan to find the old guru. He was going to make the old man tell him how to get back to Pennsylvania. Back to you."

For a long moment, Larrie stood there transfixed, panic threatening to overwhelm her. Then she lifted her chin and stopped her panic with a calm resolve. "Saddle me a horse, Tara. I'm going to get him."

"Yes, memsahib. But you know, do you not, that I am going too?"

Larrie understood. This wasn't a romantic dream. The mountains were far. This remote land would be dangerous for a woman riding alone, even one with short hair and trousers that made her look, to strangers' eyes, like a man.

It took two days of hard riding to reach Baltistan and find the village that wasn't far up a certain path, over a bridge, and sitting on a high plateau. Jo had a full day's head start on Larrie and Tara Singh. Larrie kept wishing with all her might that she wouldn't be too late. She pushed away the fear that before she could arrive, Jo would have convinced the old guru to send him to the twenty-first century.

The snows were gone from the village now that full summer was here. Blue columbine and orange daisies, yellow mountain primroses and white flowers like an edelweiss covered the steep mountainsides. Weary and travel-worn, Larrie and Tara Singh led their horses across a rope bridge and into a town which had houses made of granite blocks and narrow streets paved in stone.

Larrie saw Jo at once. He was sitting on a stone wall watching the bridge. A little boy sat at his side. Larrie dropped the horse's reins and ran into his open arms.

"Harkrishnan wouldn't send me to you," Jo said, holding Larrie against him and speaking with his cheek against her hair. "We nearly came to blows. But the townspeople grabbed me. They would have thrown me into the ravine, but Harkrishnan stopped them. Then he told me to wait here and get to know my son."

Larrie looked at the small boy who unmistakably resembled his father. "Will your son be coming home with us?"

Jo cupped his hand around the boy's cheek. "I wanted to take him there, but Harkrishnan says not yet. But yes, when he's older, he'll come. He's living with his grandparents now. Harkrishnan says they have lost a daughter, they cannot lose a grandchild. I told him I understand."

Larrie heard a thumping behind her as a staff hit the ground. She turned and saw the ancient guru standing there. "And so you have come," he said to Larrie. "You found my message then?"

Larrie couldn't help herself. She let go of Jo and grabbed the old man's hand. "How can I thank you, Harkrishnan?"

"Give me what you have brought me."

Larrie smiled, reached in her pocket, took out a pouch, and dropped the Eye of the Snow Leopard into the old man's hand.

"Now the circle has turned again. It is done," the old man said. Then he leaned on his staff and stretched his hand up into the air. A yellow butterfly left the petals of a nearby columbine and landed gracefully on his finger. It sat there for the space of a long breath, beating its wings, before flying off to feed at another flower.

"Yes, it is done," the old man said again.

Chapter 35

"Lady Larissa, Lady Larissa, wake up!" Amita Kaur stood next to Larrie's bed. Larrie opened her eyes. She felt so strange. There was something about this day. What was it that she should be remembering?

"You have much to do, Lady Larissa. It's your wedding day. You can sleep in tomorrow ... in Sahib Trelawny's arms." She giggled.

Larrie sat up. A wind scented with jasmine came through the window whose shutters opened out into the courtyard. She felt as if she had slept for a long time and had the strangest dream.

There was a tentative knock on the doorjamb. Bibi, the nanny, stood there holding Mayree's chubby brown hand. "You may go kiss Mama and give her a hug. But be quick about it."

Larrie opened her arms. The little girl ran across the room and flung herself into Larrie's embrace. Mayree's hair was black and shiny. Her skin was clear and her body no longer had a distended belly from malnutrition. She was a plump, healthy-looking five-year-old. Larrie kissed the child on both cheeks. She was growing so fast; all the orphans were.

Larrie couldn't quite remember how the children came to live here with her and Jo. So much seemed fuzzy about the past, but then there had been that gunshot at the ice-cream party. Mr. Gandhi hadn't been hurt. Ironically, only Larrie had been harmed, and not so terribly, it turned out. The bullet grazed her temple, the room went dark, and she remembered no more.

When she finally regained consciousness, Jo told her he'd never felt so scared in his life as when he saw she wasn't breathing. He also told her later, in whispers, that at that moment something broke loose deep inside him. He felt as if a lock had turned and opened his heart. It was when he thought he had lost her that he knew without a doubt that he loved her. So getting shot was a cloud with a silver lining after all.

But the bullet's impact against her temple had done terrible things to her memory. So much of it was scrambled or nonsensical or just plain gone. Poor Aunt Lolly had to keep filling Larrie in on the details she had forgotten—and Larrie suspected that Lolly was making up half of what she said. No doubt at eighty-three she couldn't remember everything either.

Larrie really didn't care what she had forgotten about the past. The present was so very delicious, and she was happy to live in the moment. She gave Mayree a hug and sent her off with Bibi to get dressed for the wedding. All the children were taking the train into Lahore. Jo and his friends insisted on riding their horses to the governor's mansion. Only the bride and Aunt Lolly were traveling in Sir Lancelot's Model N Ford, driven by Tara Singh in his new tuxedo.

Amita Kaur handed Larrie a cup of warm, sweet, milky tea. "Memsahib, you received another wedding present today."

"Another? Is it a chocolate pot and cups? We have already gotten three sets. They must be all the rage."

"No, memsahib. It's a very wonderful present. You must come see it. It's a desk carved like a snarling tiger.

It came on the train this morning, all the way from Baltistan."

At that moment a voice, a wonderful, familiar voice, came from the hall. An instant later, Jo appeared in the open doorway.

"How's my sleepy bride today? Head still hurt?" he asked, showing his white teeth in a jaunty grin.

"I feel fine," Larrie said. She did feel wonderful. "Is the groom going to meet me at the altar? We're scheduled for eleven and don't you dare be late. I think your friends in the Forty-first are taking bets about whether you'll appear, and if you manage to get there, whether you'll be able to utter the words 'I do.'"

Jo crossed the room and leaned over to kiss her. "I know. I've had your cousin Rollie place a rather large wager that I will appear—and say my vows. I intend to collect my winnings."

"It's just like you to bet on your own nuptials," Larrie said in a teasing voice and kissed him.

"I couldn't resist. The odds are twenty-to-one that I'll scarper. I stand to win a fortune. But I don't care about the odds. I've already won. I have you."

"You're a romantic fool, John Trelawny. But I love you."

"And I love you, Lady Larissa Smith. More than you will ever know."

Heather Lloyd's Snitz (Dried Apple) Pie

Ingredients

2 (8 oz) packages of Kauffman's Tart Apple Snitz*

1 quart of water (use bottled if tap is chlorinated)

1 orange

2 tablespoons of cinnamon

Generous pinch of salt

2 cups of cane sugar

Enough piecrust for an 8" pan and top crust

Directions

Preheat oven to 450 degrees.

Put the two packages of apples into a saucepan with the water.

Cook until the water and apples become a soft pulp.

Squeeze the orange and zest the rind.

Add the orange juice, zest, cinnamon, sugar, and salt to the pulp.

Mix well.

Pour the mixture into the bottom piecrust. Cover with top piecrust. Crimp the edges.

If you're artistic, use a fork and make holes in the form of a bird.

If not, just make a few holes.

Bake at 450 degrees for 10 minutes.

Reduce the heat to 350 degrees and bake for another 30 minutes.

Allow to cool before serving.

Will serve 6 to 8 people . . . or one genie and his girlfriend.

*Available from Kauffman's Fruit Farm,
3097 Old Philadelphia Pike,
Bird-in-Hand, PA 17505

Author's Note

Best Wishes Always is a work of pure imagination. People don't travel into the past on magic carpets and genies don't pop out of lamps—although I wish they could or would. As Samuel Taylor Coleridge wrote in the nineteenth century, reading poetry (or a novel, or watching a movie, or gazing at a TV crime show) requires "the willing suspension of disbelief." In other words, we know the author's creation isn't factual and never really happened, but for a short time we travel through his or her imaginary magical world and agree to believe in it while we are there.

My characters also exist only here, in this work of fiction, written for your entertainment—except for two real-life historical figures, Mahatma Gandhi and Annie Besant. I took the liberty of inviting them both to Larrie's engagement party in Lahore and they graciously accepted. In reality, Mahatma Gandhi was living in South Africa in 1906. In October of that year he traveled to England. I bent history by having him take a bit of a stopover in his home country on his way to London and, while there, narrowly escaping an assassination. Please know that there is no historical record of his ever having met my heroine or dodging a bullet in Lahore.

As for Larrie, I also admit to having made her a great

deal like myself. I too deal in "antiques and fabulous junque" at my shop, the Big Red Barn. All the vintage pieces I talk about, with the exception of Josiah Ydoboni's, are real and not the least bit rare. Most of them—a Metlox Teddy Bear cookie jar, old crackle glass, a 1960s head vase, or a Sadler teapot—can be found in almost any antiques shop you enter anywhere in the United States.

The information that I have Larrie or Van give about them is true too. For example, Meissen is indeed Europe's first porcelain maker, having begun in 1710. And you always should lift up a teacup or plate to check the maker's mark. But don't be fooled! Consult a reference such as *Kovel's Book of Marks*. You'll discover that Meissen's crossed swords logo has been copied by both Chinese and Japanese makers in order to fool the unsuspecting shopper. As Aunt Lolly would say, *Caveat emptor!* Let the buyer beware.

Yet even a little knowledge goes a long way when you browse through funky shops and sprawling flea markets, like Adamstown's famous one. If you choose to purchase something pretty, well-made, or interesting, you're sure to come out ahead. Besides, it's tremendous fun to begin collecting antiques. You can focus on the things that give you pleasure to look at, and the range of easy things to collect is vast, from McCoy pottery, depression glass, or TOC (turn-of-the-century) prints to Civil War weapons, banks and toys, or tin advertising signs.

But buying "old" is practical too. As I always tell a young couple starting out together, it's smart to furnish an apartment with affordable vintage furniture instead of purchasing on credit at the local chain store. If a table, chair, dresser, or bed was made before 1960, it's sure to be all wood (not pressed board). It's already lasted fifty or more years so it's not going to fall apart in a few months like today's shoddy imports. Plus, chances are it can be resold later, often at a profit. That kind of appreciation isn't true of most furniture made now, which ends up in the landfill within a few years.

One more tip I can't resist giving: Buy vintage silverware for a pittance at an auction, yard sale, or antiques shop, do the same for quality sets of china which are sold for ridiculously low prices (a Noritake or Mikasa dinner service for eight often brings less than a hundred dollars at auction), and even students can eat like royalty.

As you can tell, antiques are my passion. If you want to chat more, please stop by. I'd love to see you. The shop is open every weekend (as well as other times by appointment) from May to November, on the Old Highway which winds through the Pennsylvania countryside near silver ribbons of rivers and green rolling hills.

Lucy Finn at the Big Red Barn
280 Old Highway
Beaumont, Pennsylvania

Acknowledgments

Once upon a time, at a holiday party not so very long ago, my friend Maurisa Pieczynski told me a hilarious story about a chocolate fountain running amok at a bridal party. She then regaled me with a tale of her absentminded great-aunt who had just backed her car through a closed garage door. From such unexpected seeds, the idea for *Best Wishes Always* was planted.

With Maurisa's permission, and encouragement, I borrowed her out-of-control chocolate fountain to shake my heroine from the depths of grief and used my mental image of Maurisa's great-aunt to create Larrie's aunt Lolly. If Maurisa and Larrisa are similar names, hmmm, maybe that's a coincidence and maybe not. Therefore, let me give a big thank-you to Maurisa for her wonderful storytelling that fateful night and for her generosity in allowing me to transform her anecdotes into my own.

Thanks also to my good bud Hildy Morgan for reading this work in manuscript form.

Last, but certainly not least, thanks and a big hug to Brynda Huntley, president of Finn Fans, for her steadfast support and belief in me.

Also Available From
LUCY FINN

If Wishing Made it So

Sometimes love needs
a touch of magic...

Hildy Caldwell is lonely and loveless—so she
splurges on a summer rental on Long Beach
Island, where she hopes the wind might blow
a handsome man her way. Instead, she finds
an abandoned bottle—with a 2000-year-old
meddlesome genie inside. Magic and mayhem
follow, along with what Hildy's been wishing
for: a meeting with the man she has never
stopped loving...